HARD MAN

'Dark and splendid' *The Guardian*

'Guthrie writes with an urgency, energy, cynical realism and mastery of casual violence that is rarely encountered in British crime writing' *The Times*

'A witty and inventive stylist' *Washington Post*

'His prose is clinically efficient, his storytelling consummate, his dialogue sparkles and snaps on the page, and his blend of black humour and breathless action is impossible to put down' *The Herald*

'Guthrie's control of this dark material is sheer wizardry' *The Scotsman*

'A name to watch' *Waterstone's Quarterly Review*

'Easily the match for any of the modern American masters of the noir genre' *The Big Issue*

'A dark, perfectly placed journey through psychoses, surreality and the twilight world of noir that is Guthrie's twisted vision of Edinburgh' *Crime Scene Scotland*

'Damn good fiction' *The New Review*

'Guthrie has crafted a thoroughly engaging tale, complete with some twists that are so stealthily deployed they're pure genius . . . No tricks, no shortcuts, just brilliant storytelling.' *Spinetingler*

'Highly stylised and brutally realistic – the love-child of hardboiled fiction and crime reporting' *Behind The Black Mask*

'By turns hilarious and horrifying, Guthrie's original voice grabs the reader and doesn't let go' *Kirkus Reviews*

For JT Lindroos, Charles Ardai and Alison Rae

HARD MAN

Allan Guthrie

First published in Great Britain in 2007.
This edition published in Great Britain in 2008 by Polygon,
an imprint of Birlinn Ltd

West Newington House
10 Newington Road
Edinburgh
EH9 1QS
www.birlinn.co.uk

9 8 7 6 5 4 3 2

ISBN 10: 1 84697 022 9
ISBN 13: 978 1 84697 022 1

British Library Cataloguing-in-Publication Data
A catalogue record for this book is available
on request from the British Library

Typeset by Hewer Text UK Ltd, Edinburgh
Printed by Clays Ltd, St Ives plc

A HISTORY OF VIOLENCE

ANOTHER HOT DAY in July. That was four in a row. Pretty good for Scotland.

Not so good for the corpse in the boot.

Jacob Baxter put his hand over his nose to mask the smell, forgetting for a moment that his nose was broken. He gasped with pain. Time to take some more paracetamol, but he couldn't swallow the pills without a glass of water. He'd have to wait till he got back home. Why the doctor had refused to give him something stronger, he didn't know. But the doc just told Jacob to come back when the swelling had subsided and only then could he – how did he put it? – determine the extent of the damage. He assured Jacob that his nose wasn't broken, but Jacob wasn't convinced. He didn't have much faith in the medical profession.

He looked up from the corpse. His two sons kept their eyes on it, even when Jacob began to speak. 'We have to stop Wallace,' he said, 'before May gets hurt.'

'We'll try again,' Flash said.

Jacob said, 'Aye, right.'

Two nights ago, although it felt a lot longer, the three of them had gone down to Trinity where Wallace lived alone in the cramped split-level one-bedroom flat he'd shared with May for only a few months. Jacob noticed that Wallace had boarded up the basement windows recently and wondered if he'd heard they were coming. Might have been a wise safety precaution, since the windows were at street level, and easy to kick in, but it wasn't windows they wanted to smash. Anyway, there was no way Wallace could know they were coming. It wasn't as if they'd phoned ahead. No, chances were the windows had been broken already. Somebody else Wallace had provoked, or threatened, or beaten up. Plenty of candidates. Or maybe it was just a bunch of drunken louts at the weekend. This was a much sought-after area of the city, but it was only a stone's throw from Wardie, which wasn't.

Jacob had glanced at his sons, nodded, then rang the doorbell. He slapped a wrench against his open palm while he waited for an answer. Oh, aye. They were all tooled up, they'd handle Wallace no problem, reputation or not. He was only one man against three, and those three were Baxters. Admittedly Jacob wasn't a huge threat by himself, cause, well, he was sixty-six years old and not as fleet of foot as he once was. Flash, to be fair, was even less of a threat: skinny, small – not to be cruel to his younger son, but the word Jacob was looking for was 'weedy'. Rog was a different story. Hard to believe those two boys had the same parents. Rog was a big lad, weighed over twenty stone, gripped that hammer proudly in his massive fist, and Jacob felt pretty safe standing next to him. Rog was a bouncer. He was used to this kind of thing. And the suit Rog insisted on wearing all the time worked in his favour. Aye, Rog meant business in more ways than one.

Jacob was sure Wallace would cower in front of their combined might. So when Wallace opened the door, all baby-faced and clean-looking and innocent, Jacob confidently pointed his wrench at him and said, 'Stay away from May. Stay away from my family.'

Wallace took his glasses off, slipped them in his shirt pocket. He immediately looked more like his twenty-six years. 'She's my wife.'

True, but she was a poor wee misguided headstrong lass. Jacob said, 'She's only sixteen.'

'Fucks like a woman twice her age,' Wallace said. 'Must be all the practice she gets.'

There was no need for that. Blood pounded in Jacob's temples. There was no talking to this animal. Wallace only understood one thing. Jacob pulled back his wrist and swung the wrench.

And missed.

No, worse than missed. Missed and got caught. Wallace had grabbed Jacob's wrist, and was twisting it. Jacob couldn't hold on to the wrench any longer. He let it go with a howl, but had the presence of mind to punch Wallace with his free hand. Pick on an old man, would he? Jacob hit nothing but air. Again.

You'd hardly believe it, but Jacob was out of breath, felt his chest tighten.

What on earth were his sons doing? They should have jumped in by now. Knocked Wallace to the ground. Started kicking him.

Jacob turned, suddenly realising his wrist was free, saw Wallace standing in front of Rog. Wallace wouldn't be so brave now. Somebody nearer his own age. Somebody bigger than him. Aye, somebody who'd rip his limbs off, one by one. Somebody who'd teach him not to mess with the Baxters.

But, no. Jacob straightened up and saw that Wallace was smiling. Rog held his hammer aloft, not smiling back. Wallace held up the wrench he'd taken from Jacob. Still smiling, he dropped it. Deliberately. It clanged onto the path. Rog opened and closed his mouth, but no words came out.

'Come on, then,' Wallace said. 'Let's see what you've got, big guy.'

Rog looked at Flash. Mistake. Jacob saw it coming, and cried out too late. Before anybody could react, Wallace had whipped towards the big fella, smacked him at least twice in the stomach, brought him to his knees, swiped the hammer out of his hand, and gave his brother a blow in the gut with it.

Rog and Flash stared at each other, gasping for breath.

Jacob's gaze returned to Wallace. Had that just happened?

'I told you lot to mind your own business,' Wallace said, kicking Flash in the face and knocking him over. 'I wish you'd pay attention.' With the back of his hand, he punched Rog in the mouth and blood sprayed across the path. Rog didn't topple over, though. Kneeled there like a tree stump.

'Okay,' Jacob said. 'Enough.'

'I don't think so,' Wallace said, and Jacob's nose exploded with pain. 'Dad.'

Jacob's eyes streamed. Through his tears, he saw Wallace taking his mobile phone from his pocket.

Before he dialled, he grabbed Jacob by the hair and bent over. Despite the blood starting to trickle down his left nostril, Jacob could smell Wallace's sweat. Or maybe it was his own. Wallace said, 'I'm going to make your sick family wish it never existed.'

Sick? Jacob's family? Jacob would have laughed if his nose hadn't hurt so much.

Wallace let go of Jacob and spoke into his phone. 'Police. Yes. I'd like to report an assault. I've just been attacked. Huh? Outside my own house, would you believe.'

The three of them had spent a night in the cells. The indignity of it. The first time in Jacob's long life.

Rog had to have a couple of stitches in a cut just above his upper lip. They were being removed next week. Flash got away with body bruising and a sore chin.

Wallace hadn't broken sweat. All that ju-jitsu training May had warned them about. They should have listened, but when you're angry, you don't pay attention, do you?

Ah, well. Here they were, wondering what they should do now.

'He's *loco.*' Flash slammed the boot shut, cut off the stink. 'He's gone too far this time.'

Rog picked at some crap on his suit. 'What we going to do now?'

'I don't want to think about what this means,' Jacob said.

'We have to,' Flash said. 'This is a fucked-up situation.'

'I mean,' Jacob said, 'what'll he do next? He made threats against the family.'

'As long as May's safe,' Flash said, 'I don't care.'

'But is she?' Jacob said. 'How do we know this'll be an end to it? It's her he's riled at.'

'Speaking of May,' Rog said, running his finger over some grime on the boot, 'who's going to tell her that Louis's dead?'

PEARCE WONDERED WHY a hulking blue-suited figure with a stitched upper lip was framed in the sitting room doorway. *His* doorway. The fucker was in *his* fucking house and Pearce had just got out of the shower, only a towel wrapped round his waist. 'Who the —?' was all he managed to say before the stranger grabbed hold of his wrist, dragged him over the threshold and spun him towards the settee.

Pearce was really unimpressed with himself. Should have been quicker, sharper. As he was spinning he noticed a second guy, skinny, lurking in the corner. The second guy hadn't been invited either.

Pearce landed on his side and sank into the cushions. Braced himself to block a flying fist. He was alert now, prepared. But nothing happened. The big guy apparently wasn't about to trade punches. Pearce's towel had flown off, dropped to the floor. He relaxed. Well, as much as he could, given that he was bollock-naked in front of a pair of strange men. Young men. Who clearly weren't here to ask after his health. At least they weren't naked, too. That would have been really uncomfortable.

Pearce's dog, a three-legged Dandie Dinmont terrier, poked his nose round the doorframe, had a quick look, and hopped away. Little bastard was wise beyond its years. Pearce would have to have words with him later. Surely a warning bark wouldn't have been too much to ask for. Pearce ought to take him back to the Cat & Dog Home, see how he liked that.

Pearce levered himself upright and rested his arm on the back of the settee. Faced the big guy. The fat bastard was in deep shit, even if he did look capable of bench-pressing three hundred pounds without breaking sweat. He was lucky he'd caught Pearce off-guard. Another day, if Pearce hadn't been distracted, Fat Boy would have been in pieces all over the floor.

Fat Boy's tongue tracked over his stitched upper lip. He was holding a knife in his big paw.

Pearce was still damp under the scrotum, in the arse crack and between the toes. If he couldn't have a fucking shower and dry himself off in peace, he might as well still be in prison.

He didn't like being reminded of prison.

He glanced at the other guy. Slim was bony-faced, dressed like a prick. The arse of his jeans hung down to his knees, thick gold chain round his neck, trainers with the laces untied, trying to look cool as he scraped his chin stubble with his knife. Yeah, both of them had knives, the weapon of choice amongst Edinburgh lowlifes. Slim's was very nice. The serrated blade was seven, maybe eight, inches long. The hand holding the knife trembled slightly. Slim might be trying to look cool, but Pearce knew he shouldn't be here. Could tell he was out of his depth.

Zero threat.

Pearce ignored Slim and asked Fat Boy, 'What are you doing in my house?'

Suit, tie, gleaming shoes. Fat Boy even had a briefcase. Thug, or accountant? Bit of both? Definitely not the hard man he was pretending to be. Pearce wouldn't have been surprised if Fat Boy cut himself with his knife. Maybe that's how he got the sore lip.

Jesus. Pearce was pissed off with himself. If he'd been paying attention when he'd opened the door, he could have splattered Fat Boy all over the carpet. Now he'd have to wait and time this right. Pearce chewed the inside of his cheek. He'd slipped up. He was getting casual, and that would never do.

Fat Boy said, 'We believe you might be able to help us.'

Poncey language. Could be a lawyer, right enough. 'I doubt it,' Pearce told him.

'Well, we thought we might stay a while. Have a little chat.'

'I don't feel like talking.'

'Just listen, then.'

'I don't feel like listening either.'

'Now, that's really too bad. We were hoping you'd co-operate.'

'You finished?' Pearce asked him.

'Finished?' Fat Boy said. 'Haven't even started.' He turned to Slim. 'Flash?' he said.

Flash? What kind of name was that? Some kind of street name? Pearce should get one of those. What could he call himself? He couldn't think of anything. 'Pearce' would have to do.

Flash marked the end of his dry shave by tossing the hunting knife into the air. It landed point first, puncturing a floorboard. That was the kind of pansy-arsed showy bollocks that might have impressed a three-year-old. Probably been practising it for days, too. But if you wanted to create an impression, you didn't lob a knife in the air and watch it fall. No purpose in that. Flash watched the blade quiver for a bit, smirking. 'I've heard you're a pussy, Pearce,' he said. 'Went soft when your mummy died.'

How fucking stupid was this scrawny prick? Mother of Christ.

'Heard you got shot in the stomach,' Fat Boy took over. He was much bigger than his friend, but he certainly wasn't any smarter. 'Didn't have any appetite for violence after that.' He grinned, looked at Flash. 'Get it? Shot in the stomach. Lost his appetite.'

'Nice one,' Flash said. 'That's very funny. Don't you think so, Pussy?'

Pearce said nothing. He had no idea why they were trying to provoke him.

'I asked you a question,' Flash said.

Pearce stared at him and said, 'You're a dumb fuck.'

'Hear that?' Fat Boy said. 'Pussy's mad.'

'Better watch we don't get scratched, huh?'

The pair of buffoons were so busy laughing they didn't react when Pearce dived off the settee. At arms' stretch he clawed at Flash's knife, managed to grab the handle and pluck it out of the floorboard before Flash took a step towards him and said, 'Hey!' But by then it was too late.

Pearce brought the blade up between Flash's legs. Straight through the seam of his low-slung jeans, thrusting the blade through a good few inches. Almost hit home. It was close. Fuck, yeah, it was close. Pearce reckoned there'd been a fair chance of him screwing up. But life was all about taking chances, wasn't it?

'What was that about getting fucking scratched?' he said.

'Ah, shit.' Flash looked down between his legs, his face turning pale green.

Unusual, but Pearce had seen it once before. Happened in prison to an eighteen-year-old who'd wanted to show what a big man he was and ended up smoking more skunk than he could handle. His face may have turned green, but everyone called him Whitey after that.

Flash shouted, 'Dad?'

Crying for his daddy now, poor kid. Pearce wondered if he shouldn't just let go, get out of the way before Flash spewed all over him. Nah, fuck it. He'd take the chance, but there was no harm in issuing a warning. 'Puke over me,' he said, 'and I'll get really pissed off.' He applied a little more upwards pressure. 'You wouldn't like that.' Then just a bit more.

Flash yelped.

Touching skin now.

'Lose it,' Pearce said to Fat Boy.

Fat Boy looked at his hand in surprise as if the last thing he expected to see there was a knife. He glanced around, bemused. 'Where shall I put it?'

Jesus Christ. 'Over there,' Pearce said, indicating a safe area away from himself and his hostage.

Fat Boy tossed the knife. 'Let my brother go,' he said. 'Then we'll tell you why we're here.'

'Not interested,' Pearce said, wondering how these two could possibly be brothers.

Fat Boy said, 'Dad!'

Jesus, they were both at it. Pearce tensed his arm and Flash squeaked and Fat Boy shut up. 'I'll deal with you in a minute,' Pearce said to Fat Boy. Looked up at Flash, said, 'Ever wondered what it feels like to have your happy sack sliced in two, Flash?' He paused to give Flash a moment to think about it. 'Course, I might miss. Not get the middle of your ball-bag. End up cutting one of your nuts in half. That'd hurt, don't you think?'

Flash was making a mewling noise. Pearce was tempted to ask him who the pussy was now but he restrained himself.

Fat Boy's jaw had descended. Poor fucker looked like he'd been hit in the face with a stiff cat. Repeatedly.

Flash looked even more likely to throw up. And threats weren't going to stop him. Sod it. Pearce raised himself onto one knee and eased the knife out of Flash's trousers. A look of relief spread across Flash's face. His cheeks looked less green in no time. The transformation was short-lived, though.

Pearce balled his fist and slammed it into Flash's crotch.

Flash bent over, wobbled, toppled to the floor. After a second, he made a gagging sound and his cheeks puffed.

Pearce left him heaving while he strode over to Fat Boy.

Fat Boy hadn't moved an inch. Still wore that stunned look. Pearce placed Flash's knife on the floor, sure he no longer needed it, and smacked Fat Boy as hard as he could on the side of the head. Fat Boy rolled to the side, hovered on the edge of the settee, then hit the deck like the useless fucking fat sack of shit he was.

Pearce glanced at Flash, but he was no danger. Thumping a man in the gonads usually knocks the fight out of him. The skinny wee shite had dragged himself into the corner where he was curled up, moaning. He caught Pearce's eye and cried out for his daddy again.

Pearce picked up his dropped towel and draped it round his waist. He grabbed Fat Boy's briefcase and snapped it open. Inside was a picture. Nothing else. Full-length body shot of a blonde teenage girl: shades, cropped top, bit of a belly on her but that was okay, shorts, sandals, arms folded under ample breasts, pierced ears, nose, belly button and God alone knew where else. She wasn't Pearce's type, but he could see how Fat Boy might find her attractive. She was young, though. Probably no more than eighteen.

On the back of the photo was a phone number.

'Excuse me,' said a new voice. A man's voice, mature, local accent. 'Mr Pearce?'

Pearce smiled. There he was again. Not paying attention. He turned to look at the man who'd stepped into the sitting room. Did a double-take. This guy had a piece of raw meat where his nose should be. Which maybe wasn't quite so bad, since it drew attention away from the wrinkles crosshatching the corners of the old man's eyes, the grooves chiselled into his leathery cheeks and the lines running from the corners of his mouth to the point of his chin.

'Come in,' Pearce said. 'Open house today.'

'My name's Baxter.'

Pearce listened to Baxter breathing. Trace of a wheezy rattle. Sounded like he smoked too much. 'You got a surname?' Pearce asked.

'Baxter *is* my surname.'

'You got a first name, then?'

'Jacob.' He held out his hand. Pearce stared at it, but didn't move. 'I'm a bit late,' Baxter said, looking around. Fat Boy was still out cold. Flash was hugging himself, groaning more quietly now. Pearce gave Baxter no encouragement, but he went on, 'I was supposed to stop Rog and Flash getting hurt.'

Rog? Well, Fat Boy was full of surprises. Might as well call himself Pansy. Pearce said, 'You seem to have failed on that score.'

'I was outside.' Jacob pointed his thumb over his shoulder. 'My boys were supposed to call for me if things got hairy.'

Now Pearce knew who he was. Dad. *My boys.* A real family get-together. Pearce said, 'They did.'

Baxter tutted. 'I'm a bit slow, now and then,' he said. 'No fun getting old.' He pulled a packet of cigarettes out of his pocket and said, 'You mind?'

Pearce replied, 'As long as you don't mind me coming over to your house and pissing on your carpet.'

Baxter frowned, which wasn't a pretty sight, and, judging by the old guy's reaction, hurt his nose a bit. He tucked his fags back in his pocket.

Pearce put the photo back in the briefcase and slammed the lid shut. 'Baxter,' he said, 'I don't take kindly to people breaking into my home and threatening me.'

'I know. I'm sorry about that. Really, I am. If there was any other way . . .'

'Fat Boy and Slim here could have knocked first.'

'Didn't they? Look, I'm sorry . . .'

'No matter. I taught them some manners.'

Flash shouted, 'Cunt!'

Pearce looked at him, looked at the briefcase. Well made, sturdy. He stepped over to Flash, landed a swift blow with the edge of it to the rude little fucker's head. Flash moaned. Pearce hit him again and Flash stopped moaning.

'Mr Pearce,' Baxter said, grabbing his arm, 'please don't hurt them.'

'Bit late for that.'

'We need your help. That's all we want. Just some help with a little problem.'

'You could have asked.'

'We wanted to see if you could handle yourself first.'

'This some kind of test? These two? Don't make me laugh. They've never been in a fight in their lives, have they?'

'Not quite true.' Baxter was silent for a while, then when Pearce didn't prompt him, he said, 'Rog is a bouncer.'

'Yeah? Could have fooled me.'

'He's not used to people fighting back.'

'How long's he been a bouncer? A week?'

'He's very good at his job. Just got a pay rise. Look, they're game lads. Good lads, my boys.'

No way was Rog a bouncer, but Pearce let it pass. 'You shouldn't let them loose with knives. They might hurt themselves.'

Baxter said, 'Can we talk money?'

'We can always talk money.' Pearce wondered what was coming. 'How much?'

'Four grand.'

'What do you want me to do for four grand? Mow your lawn?'

'It's all we can raise.'

Pearce said, 'My heart bleeds.' Truth was, he could use the money. Four grand wasn't a fortune, but it would help. He had a mortgage and no job. 'What do you want me to do, Baxter?'

'Protect my grandchild.'

Pearce thought for a moment. Then said, 'From what?'

'Not "what". *Who.* From its father. You've seen the photo.' He inclined his head towards the briefcase.

'What about it?'

'The baby's my grandchild.'

Pearce opened the briefcase again, studied the picture. Shook his head. 'She's young,' he said, 'but she's no baby.'

PEARCE LISTENED WHILE Jacob Baxter explained the situation.

The girl in the photo was May, his daughter. She was sixteen, even younger than she looked, married to a man ten years older than her, and she was three months pregnant. Unfortunately, not with her husband's child. When Wallace, her husband, found out, he'd slapped her around and threw her out into the street. Fair enough, Baxter said, if only he'd left it at that. Baxter might have forgiven him for hitting her, maybe, under the circumstances. But subsequently, Wallace hadn't been able to leave her alone. Sending her threatening texts, leaving messages on her voicemail, turning up at her house, at school.

Pearce gave Baxter a hard stare. 'Married, pregnant, and at school? That's wrong.'

'Not her fault,' Baxter said. Then added, 'She's very bright.'

'What's she doing?'

'Looking for a summer job.'

Pearce nodded. 'You've told her husband to leave her alone?'

Baxter told him about the night they'd confronted him with hammers and wrenches, and how he'd given them all a pasting.

Didn't surprise Pearce in the least. He said, 'What do you think he wants?'

'What do you mean?'

'Does he want May back? Is that why he won't leave her alone?'

'He threw her out.'

'Pride?' Pearce suggested.

'He wouldn't take her back.'

'You sure?'

Jacob shrugged.

'So, what's his game plan?' Pearce asked.

'Revenge.'

'Against May?'

'Primarily. But he's after the rest of us, too. There was never any love lost between us anyway, but he really hates us now.'

'What about the baby's father? His biological one?'

'Done a runner. Not just from May, but disappeared completely.'

'Isn't that a bit extreme?'

'Not if he wants to stay alive. You don't know Wallace.'

'Very true,' Pearce said.

'Will you give us a hand?' Baxter said, looking towards his sons. He was doing a not-too-bad job of appearing calm and composed, not giving a shit. But he didn't fool Pearce. Maybe Baxter wasn't the type to bring flowers and grapes to a hospital bedside, but he wasn't hard. He had a face that was hard, but his mind was soft as a baby's bottom.

Of course, Pearce could be completely wrong.

Pearce helped Baxter prop Flash up against the wall and check that Rog hadn't swallowed his tongue or something. He put a cushion under the big guy's head.

'So what exactly do you want me to do?' Pearce said.

Baxter said, 'Just keep an eye on May.'

'You want a babysitter?'

They were standing in the middle of the sitting room now. Both men had their arms folded. Pearce let his eyes focus on Baxter's and wasn't at all surprised that Baxter couldn't hold his gaze.

Baxter said, 'I was thinking more of a bodyguard. Keep that sleekit Wallace away from her.'

'For how long?'

'As long as possible.'

'Four grand won't last long.'

'Till Wallace has calmed down. A month should do it.'

'What hours would I be working?'

'All the time.'

'Day, night, weekends?'

'Stay with us. We'll feed you, give you a bed.'

'I'm not very sociable.'

'We won't be paying you for your conversation.'

Pearce breathed out slowly. 'Where did you get my name?' he asked.

'Guy I know recommended you,' Baxter said.

'What guy?'

'My nephew. Cooper. Said you had what it takes. Said you'd do an honest day's work.'

Cooper, huh? Loan shark. At one point he'd been Pearce's boss. He was in the nick now. Eventually got what he deserved. 'That right?'

'To be exact, he said since you'd lost your sister and then your mother, he thought that maybe now you really didn't give a toss about anything.' Baxter unfolded his arms. His hand crept into the pocket where he kept his fags. Fiddled about in there for a second, then reappeared, empty. 'Do you?'

Pearce wondered if Cooper was right. Could be. 'If you're worried about her safety, why don't you contact the police?'

'After what just happened?' Baxter pointed to his nose. 'They'll think I'm setting Wallace up. Probably throw me in the cells again for harassment or what have you.'

Pearce nodded. 'Let me think about it, okay?'

Baxter looked hopeful. Then his brow ridged as Flash

stirred. He glanced at his son, then back at Pearce. 'Did you have to hit them so hard?'

'That wasn't hard,' Pearce told him.

Baxter shook his head, lips tight. 'I'm scared,' he said. 'I don't mind telling you. I'm scared for May.'

'I'm sure she'll be fine,' Pearce said. 'Guys like Wallace like to talk. But that's usually all they do.'

Flash spoke, a little breathlessly, 'Not in this case.'

'How's the head?' Pearce asked him.

'Like shit.'

'And the balls?'

'Fuck off.'

Had to give the scrawny fuck some credit. He was still game. But Pearce decided to use Flash's reply to get rid of them. He didn't want to get involved in this. He didn't think from what her dad had said that May was in serious danger. And Pearce didn't think he'd make much of a babysitter anyway. And he definitely didn't want to stay with this lot for a month. Not for twice the money.

Pearce prodded Rog, who moaned, snorted. Pearce poked him again. 'Hey, get up.'

'What's the matter?' Baxter said.

'I've thought about it. I'm not interested.'

'What?' Baxter said.

Pearce poked Rog again. 'I want you out of my house. The lot of you. Right now.'

Baxter said, 'When you meet Wallace, don't be fooled, Mr Pearce. He's older than he looks. Twenty-six, but looks not a day over eighteen. He's tough, though. Maybe even tougher than you. He's had training.'

Training, huh? Well, now. If Pearce was a bull, that was a red fucking rag.

Baxter said, 'Let's get my sons back on their feet. If you have a moment to spare, I'd like to show you something that might convince you the threat posed by Wallace is very serious indeed.'

'YOU A DOG lover, Mr Pearce?'

'Got a terrier.'

'I didn't notice.'

'He doesn't like strangers.'

'Well, brace yourself. Go on, Rog.'

The side of Rog's face was swollen. Looked like he'd had a fight with a lunatic dentist. He glanced around. The coast was clear so he popped the boot. Held it open a foot or so.

Pearce hunkered down and peered inside. A black mutt's body was crammed in there, looking ... dead. Certainly smelled like it was dead.

Yeah, Pearce liked dogs. But he preferred them alive. Dead dogs didn't have quite the same appeal.

Pearce stood up. 'Is that *yours*?' he asked.

Baxter nodded. 'Just look at the way his throat's been cut.'

Pearce didn't much want to look again. He said so.

'Go on,' Baxter said.

Pearce bent down again. Fido's head was hanging by a flap of skin, just a hair short of a beheading. Pearce said, 'Pretty nasty, I'll give you that. But I don't see what a dog with its throat cut has to do with May being in danger.'

Baxter looked around him. The car was parked down at the beach end of the street. Other cars were pulling in, driving off; couples strolled past arm in arm along the promenade in front of the car.

Pearce wondered if it was against the law to have a dead dog in your boot. Probably wasn't. Ought to be, though.

Baxter said, 'Too public here.'

Rog eased the boot shut.

Baxter got in the car. Flash hobbled into the back, hands hovering over his bruised groin, and Rog joined him. After a second or two, Pearce climbed into the passenger seat.

Pearce had closed the door before he realised how much the stench of dead dog had permeated the air inside the car. Felt as if he was sitting on top of the carcass. He breathed through his mouth.

Baxter reached into his pocket and took out his fags. He offered Flash one, and Flash shook his head. 'The dog was a message from Wallace,' Baxter said.

'And a warning,' Flash said, rubbing the back of his head.

'An omen,' Rog said.

Pearce said, 'Make your minds up, guys.'

'Found him there yesterday morning. Right there. In the boot.'

No wonder the fucking thing stank. 'What are you going to do with it?' Pearce asked.

'We'll bury him. When we're ready.'

'Better hurry. He's ripe.'

Baxter shrugged. 'We've been busy trying to console May.'

'Could have found a few minutes to dump it somewhere. Let it rot in peace.'

'We thought it would be good for you to see it firsthand,' Baxter said. 'Anyway, Louis is fine where he is. It's my car. My dog. My nose.'

And Pearce thought, yeah, enough of this shite. 'You can sit in this stink if you want,' he said. 'But I don't have to.' As he turned to get out of the car, he felt a hand on his arm.

'Please' – it was Rog – 'for May. Louis was her dog.'

Pearce looked at the fat fingers on his arm. He stared at

them until they moved away. He said, 'What makes you think I won't end up in your boot like poor Louis?'

'Maybe you will,' Baxter said. 'Wallace wouldn't think twice about killing you if he had to. And he's more than capable of doing it.'

For fuck's sake. You'd have thought the ugly bastard could have tried a bit of flattery. Did he want Pearce to accept this job or not? 'If that's what you think, why do you want to hire me?'

'We can't afford anyone else.'

Nice.

The smell was really getting to Pearce now. Dead dog and cigarette smoke. It had soaked into his skin. He wanted to scrub his cheeks till they shone. He opened his window. It made only a little difference, letting in the rumble of traffic and children's shouts and a trace of barbecue smoke which momentarily masked the other smells in the car. He looked to see if he could spot anyone having a barbecue. But whoever it was, they were further up the beach, out of sight.

Baxter picked at a fingernail. 'Mr Pearce,' he said, 'my daughter's husband is one nasty piece of work. You've seen what he did to my dog. We've told you what he did to us. You can see the evidence for yourself.' He indicated his nose. 'And he's already hit my pregnant daughter.'

'Wallace has a rep,' Flash told him. 'A serious rep. Ask around.'

Pearce looked away. Silence in the car for a while. He listened to the distant crash of waves, the beep of a reversing bus in the station away to his left. He stared out to sea. Gulls swooped for morsels at the water's edge. He had the strange feeling of timelessness. Like this could have been a hundred years ago. Then he heard the drone of a plane passing overhead. Shattered the illusion.

Just as well. He was turning into a bit of a fanny for a minute there.

'HE HIT MAY. He beat us up. He killed the dog. There's a progression there. That's worrying, man.' A muscle twitched in Rog's cheek. 'He's going to kill somebody.'

'You can't judge what he's going to do next on the basis of what he did to the dog,' Pearce said. 'Taking a human life is very different from killing a dog. Believe me. Fuck, you don't even know for definite it was *him* who killed the dog.'

Baxter said, 'Who else would have done such a thing?'

'Okay,' Pearce said. 'But why would he do this?'

Flash said, 'He's a sadistic fuck, has a history of violence. Forget what he did to us. That was nothing. When he was eighteen, Wallace kidnapped a guy off the street, complete stranger, flung him in his car, held him in his bedroom for a couple of days while he carved pretty patterns on his face, then sent him packing with a couple of his own severed fingers shoved up his arsehole.'

'Original. He do time?'

'Got away with it.'

'Guy was too scared, right?'

'Nope. Some kind of problem with the evidence being inadmissible. Everybody knew he'd done it, but he couldn't be tried for it.'

'And why did he do it?'

'He's crazy,' Flash said.

'Got a lot of company,' Pearce said. 'Okay, he's crazy. How do you think he really feels about May?'

'She's his wife. But the baby's not his. And he can't live with that idea.'

'So why doesn't he wash his hands of her?' Pearce asked.

'He doesn't want her,' Baxter said. 'But he doesn't want

anybody else to have her either. And he doesn't want her to have the baby.'

Pearce didn't doubt the truth of Baxter's statement for a minute. Wallace sounded like he'd wound these poor sad crazy bastards up pretty tight.

'You want the job?' Baxter asked.

'I'll think about it,' Pearce told him. The words were out of his mouth before he knew what he was saying. He really didn't want to think about it. The whole thing was pathetic. The crazy old fool and his slightly less crazy sons, the dead dog – and the smell wasn't getting any better – the teenage daughter, the unborn child, the vengeful dad. Family from hell. Did he want to get mixed up in that? He wasn't a social worker. Ah, shit, there wasn't a chance in a million anything seriously bad would happen. Just paranoia and craziness. 'But don't get your hopes up,' he said.

Pearce watched them drive away, Baxter at the wheel, Rog riding shotgun, Flash stretched out on the back seat and Louis the dog decomposing in the boot.

BACK AT HIS flat, Pearce found Hilda curled up in his basket. Yeah, the dog was called Hilda. He liked the idea of naming it after someone, a real person, and who better than his mother? True, the dog was male. But Pearce didn't think Hilda would mind. Either of them.

He told the dog that everything was fine now, the nasty men were gone. Hilda wagged his tail, hopped towards the door and stared at it.

Pearce shook his head. In Hilda's world, anything he didn't understand meant walkies. Fair enough. Pearce grabbed Hilda's lead off the cabinet in the hallway, fastened it. He could use some clean air after the stink in the Baxters' car. Live by the sea, you ought to take advantage of it as much as possible.

Hilda pulled all the way down the road towards the promenade. When they got there, Pearce unfastened his lead and Hilda skipped off into a patch of long grass at the edge of the beach where the local dogs were fond of relieving themselves. He hunted for the perfect spot before lifting his back leg. Never ceased to amaze Pearce how the wee bastard could piss on two legs without falling over.

From their very first walk along the beach, Hilda had proved himself to be a sniffer. Not too interested in chasing sticks. Which was fine. Poor bastard only had three legs, after all. In any case, Pearce would rather sniff than chase sticks, too.

Pearce headed east along the promenade, towards Joppa. Hilda would follow in his own time.

Okay. The Baxter family. Well, they were serious. There was no doubt they were scared of Wallace, genuinely believing him capable of hurting his wife badly enough to endanger her and, particularly, her unborn child.

But were they crazy fuckers, or did they have genuine reason to be worried?

Well, you'd have to be deranged beyond measure to harm your own family. That was something some other fuckbastard did. Wasn't Wallace's family, though. The kid wasn't his, but May was his wife . . . Ah, fuck. Shouldn't have started thinking about what people could do to your family.

Pearce leaned against the outside wall of an amusement arcade, breathing fast and shallow, the back of his neck cold with sweat. Memories leaked out of his head and burned acid paths down his throat and into his lungs. Holding his mum in his arms while blood pumped out of a stab wound in her neck – yeah, takes a lot of getting over. Maybe he'd never get over it. That was a possibility he'd have to face.

No point dwelling on it, though. He couldn't change what had happened. He pushed himself off the wall, carried on walking.

Just supposing for a moment that May was in danger.

Well, look at him. He wasn't in a position to protect anybody.

At least he was breathing normally again.

He looked behind him, checked that Hilda was still there. He was half-heartedly chasing another dog. Knew that with only three legs he'd never have a chance in hell, but it was fun trying.

The guilt was a killer. Not only did Pearce fail to save his mum, but he'd sold her flat. That really fucked him up and there wasn't anything he could do about it. The flat held too many reminders of her. You know, it was *hers*. Didn't feel he could buy new furniture, put up new pictures, strip the wallpaper. Any change he made was being disrespectful to her memory. Nothing he could do about it. It would never be his.

So he'd sold it. And maybe she'd haunt him forever as a result, but he thought she'd understand. She wouldn't haunt him. Christ, no, what was he saying? That was almost as mad a notion as the Baxter family's tale. Worse, even. At least Wallace was alive. But Pearce saw Mum all the time. Just glimpses. And sometimes he heard her speak. She'd ask how he was and he'd say he was fine. They'd talk about the weather. Banal snippets of dialogue. For a while, he did wonder about his sanity. And then he thought, fuck it. He was as sane as the next man. It was normal to miss your mother.

He'd bulldozed into action. Didn't bother to redecorate, put Mum's flat on the market as it was. Not surprisingly, he didn't get the best price for it, but what he did get was substantially more than he'd expected. Property prices were outrageous.

He went looking for a flat of his own. Something he'd never had. Had his own cell at Barlinnie, mind you. Only for two weeks, though, until that Irish guy, Seamus, moved in. Read all the time, like Pearce. But they didn't get on. Pearce resented him for ending his solitude. Not Seamus's fault. Anyway, having your own cell in Barlinnie didn't really count as having your own place.

Pearce wanted to stay in the east of the city. It was his old stomping ground and he preferred to live somewhere familiar. Anywhere else, he might as well move to England or America or Australia. He'd been checking the property pages for a couple of months, noticed that despite the generally ridiculous prices of flats in the capital, Portobello seemed just that bit cheaper than more central areas. Like Musselburgh used to be before everybody cottoned on to the fact. And Porty was okay. Bit of history, which didn't hurt. He hadn't got round to buying a car yet. Probably wouldn't. There was nowhere to park it. And he hadn't driven much recently. In fact, he hadn't driven much ever. Didn't own a car when he went inside, and, not surprisingly, didn't get much practice while he was locked up. Truth was, he wasn't entirely sure of himself behind a wheel. Fortunately, Portobello was a half-hour bus ride from town. And the number twenty-six ran every five minutes. No need for a car.

Portobello was Edinburgh's seaside (so claimed a road sign on the approach from either end of town) and once upon a time, before the dawn of the package holiday, people flocked to Portobello from all over Scotland to sun themselves and dip their toes in the sea. Must have been a sight. Like Southern California, but colder. And without the surfing. Or the bronzed babes. Used to have an outdoor swimming pool with a wave machine, so he'd heard from his neighbour, Mrs Hogg. It was highly popular, too.

These days, the vestiges of the old seaside resort remained. The amusements, fish and chip shop, ice-cream vendors. But most of the time it was a forlorn-looking place. Apart from the weekends. The weekends brought out the crowds. Pasty-skinned dads, pregnant mums with purple-veined white legs, screaming kids. Kids loved it. Sand and kids. When did that combination ever fail? Sitting on the beach building sand-castles and eating gritty ice cream as the haar rolled in.

Rest of the time, the beach was just for dog-walkers.

Pearce loved Portobello's faded glory. His kind of place. Made him nostalgic. Could you be nostalgic for something you'd never experienced? Yeah, fucking right you could.

And you know what? Mum would have loved living here.

He'd picked up a rare fixed-price property at the east end of town. A top-floor flat. Two bedrooms. One for him. The other, well, for the dog he'd promised himself he'd get once he'd moved in. Mainly for companionship. Not that he got lonely, as such, but he was aware that talking to his mother was a bit strange and having someone else to talk to might help. Of course, some people thought it was odd talking to a dog. Pearce didn't think there was anything wrong with that at all. So long as the dog wasn't dead.

He'd been amazed at how much haar there was round these parts. Atmospheric stuff. Out of his bedroom window, only a couple of days after he'd moved in, he'd watched it approach across the Forth from Fife. First it obliterated the little island with the lighthouse, then headed towards the coastline, rolled over the beach, and gradually consumed the bus station at the rear of his flat.

He'd opened the window, let the mist roll in. You could feel it. Like that stuff, ectoplasm. Felt like it had been in the fridge, chilling.

'Feel that, Mum?' he said.

BUT THERE WAS no mist today. Pearce sat down on a bench and gazed out to sea. It was clear and warm. A couple of tankers in anchorage in the distance looked like red toys in a big bath. You could see Kirkcaldy. Fine view. The finest you'd ever see of Kirkcaldy, cause the nearer you got, the worse it looked.

Shove those memories of Mum in your head and slam the lid on them.

Pearce should be concentrating on whether to accept Baxter's proposal or not.

The promenade wasn't too busy. The odd mother and child. A family enjoying a barbecue. A kid with a kite trailing behind him. A cyclist. A bunch of old folks squashed together on a bench. A lone tourist stomping past, lugging a rucksack.

Pearce couldn't sit still. He got to his feet, whistled on Hilda.

As he passed a couple of schemies sitting on the wall drinking Buckfast, one of them asked if he could spare any change.

'What do you think?' Pearce said.

Baxter. Mad fuck or caring parent?

On the beach, a guy was throwing sticks for a couple of dogs: a big lurcher-type, a sleek-looking creature with the body of a small greyhound; and a dumpy little mutt. Pearce paused to watch for a while. The mutt got to the stick first every time. Determined little fucker.

Pearce looked behind him for Hilda. There he was, sniffing some old dear's shopping bag.

Right, never mind the dog. He should be deciding whether to accept Baxter's proposal. He turned, carried on walking along the promenade.

Getting Hilda hadn't been a tough decision, even though he

knew dogs meant responsibility. You couldn't stay out all night, or go abroad. But Pearce never stayed out all night, or went abroad. And then you had to walk the fuckers at least twice a day. But he knew he'd take a walk every day, probably twice, in any case.

Then he got worried that if he got a dog, it would end up like everything else he'd ever loved. Like his sister. Like his mum.

Like Louis in Baxter's boot.

But he'd put that crap out of his head, thank fuck.

Anyway, Baxter. What was he going to do about him? Yeah, the money was undoubtedly attractive. Thing was, Pearce had sold his mum's flat, but ended up paying considerably more for his new one. He still couldn't get over how easy it was to get a mortgage. He'd imagined having a criminal record would have been held against him. Then again, his criminal record had nothing to do with fraud, so maybe that's why it had all been so straightforward.

He didn't even have to fabricate a job to secure the mortgage. Bottom line, his deposit of eighty grand was enough for the mortgage lender to be happy to lend him the remaining forty-five.

It was up to him how he met his monthly repayments.

He'd held onto a few grand to tide him over. But at some point he'd have to start looking for work. And that would be difficult.

What qualifications do you have for this job, Mr Pearce?

Stabbed a drug-dealer with a screwdriver so many times I lost count. He died. I went to prison. Got out ten years later only to watch my mother die. Got shot twice trying to nail the fucker who killed her. Qualifications? They belong to the real world. I don't think I do. Sorry to waste your time.

Pearce needed the money. Arsewipe. Maybe he should think about getting a proper job. Only thing he'd done since he got out of prison was debt collecting. And that wasn't an option now Cooper was inside. What else could he do?

Okay. Why should he help Baxter? He didn't know the ugly bastard. And Baxter was obviously overreacting to the situation. His daughter wasn't really in danger. Did Pearce want to take money from him for nothing? Well, it wouldn't be for nothing, precisely, cause he'd have to stay with the daft bastard and his family for a month. Jesus. Pearce didn't like that idea one little bit. What about the baby? Was it really in danger? Well, Wallace sounded fucked up, all right. Was it Pearce's responsibility? Could anybody else handle it? Wallace sounded like a dangerous guy.

And there was another topic for consideration. Wallace might well be the wrong person to mess with – if indeed he'd been responsible for killing the dog. On the other hand, maybe he was just a fuckwit. But was the risk worth four grand? Shit, yes. The guy might be able to beat up women and old men and boys who couldn't fight and kill dumb animals but Pearce was none of those.

That four grand *was* tempting. It was sad that he was even considering this, but there was no denying that on four grand he could live quite comfortably for three or four months. Maybe even get himself an IKEA table or replace his mum's settee with a large two-seater. Yeah, he'd sold her old flat but kept some of her furniture. Seemed wrong just to throw it out. When he curled up in the settee, sometimes it was like she was there beside him. He fell asleep on it once and he could have sworn he felt her hand on his brow.

For fuck's sake. What was he doing even considering the Baxter job?

What do you think, Mum?

You might get shot again, his mum said.

He didn't need reminding. He'd been shot twice. In the shoulder and in the gut.

PEARCE PUT HILDA on his lead, turned and retraced his steps. He perched on the edge of a bench and took out his phone. Then realised he didn't have Baxter's number. Damn, fuck and fuck.

Hands wedged in his pockets, he headed back home.

Was he a fool? Well, was he?

It seemed like the right decision, but what if he was wrong?

He kept his head down, didn't notice anything or anybody till he came to the corner at the bottom of his street. He started to climb the hill. By then, he'd made up his mind.

INTO THE KITCHEN, grabbed a bottle of Highland Spring from the fridge. Supposed to be for hangovers but he'd run out of beer and needed something cold. The bottle hissed when he opened it. He swigged a couple of mouthfuls, letting the fizz dance on his tongue. Went over the pros and cons one more time and reached the same conclusion.

In the sitting room, he picked up the photo of May, noticing her fingers spread over her stomach, and dialled the number on the back.

Baxter said, 'Mr Pearce?'

Recognised his number already, eh? 'I've decided,' Pearce said. He waited a while.

Baxter said, 'Well?'

'The answer's no.' Pearce hung up.

PEARCE WAS SURPRISED that Baxter left it a couple of days before calling him back. But he did.

'I've made my mind up,' Pearce told him. 'Don't bother trying to change it.'

'How about,' Baxter said, 'if I offer you double?'

Ah, the bastard. He was playing dirty now. Eight grand was a lot of cash. Well, two could play at that game. Pearce said, 'I'll think about it,' and hung up.

He slept well that night. Didn't get up next morning till ten. Hilda was bursting for a piss.

BAXTER CALLED, AS Pearce knew he would. It was only a matter of how long the poor bastard could hold out. His resolve caved in at two twenty-four, according to Pearce's watch.

Baxter's voice was full of tension. Sounded like someone was throttling him. 'You made your mind up yet?'

Pearce said, 'Ten.'

'Jesus Christ,' Baxter said. 'I'm retired.'

'Rog isn't. And you said he'd just got promoted.'

'Look, Jesus, hang on.'

Pearce hung on. He didn't imagine Baxter would go for it. But he came back to the phone and said, 'Okay.' Just went to show, it was always worth a try. Problem was, Pearce had no intention of taking the job. He'd made his mind up, and once he'd done that there was no changing it. If he had wanted the job, he'd have settled for four from the off.

'I'll need to get organised,' Baxter said. 'Get your room sorted out.'

Well, now. There was Baxter making a pretty big assumption. Pearce hadn't said he'd take the job. Hadn't even indicated that it might be a possibility, had he? Just said, 'Ten,' that was all.

Pearce was about to clear this up with Baxter when the old fool said, 'You'll need some background, I suppose. I'll get you the lowdown on Wallace's routine. That's no problem. Tends to work a bit later during the week so's he can get home early on a Friday. And you'll need to know where May goes and when. School holidays at the moment, so she goes all over the place, swimming and gym and shopping and stuff but mainly just lies about in the garden in the nice weather. And, well, I dunno. I just need to know when you're moving in. Pearce?'

Pearce didn't want to be cruel. Really, he didn't. He had to put the guy out of his misery. 'Baxter?'

'Yeah?'

'I can't do it.'

'What do you mean?' Baxter paused. 'You just said you would. Look, I'm good for the money, if that's what's worrying you.'

'I don't doubt it,' Pearce said. 'Why don't you buy something nice for May instead?'

JACOB HADN'T LONG hung up when Flash came round to the house and wandered into the kitchen where Jacob was nursing a cup of tea. Flash stood there moving his feet from side to side as if they'd gone to sleep and he was trying to stamp them awake. He was wearing trainers and the laces were undone. You'd have been excused for thinking he had foot problems of some sort, but Jacob knew this footwear was a fashion statement, not a health issue.

'How's the head?' Jacob asked. Sure, it was ages ago, but Pearce had really walloped Flash with the briefcase and you could never be too careful with head injuries.

Flash took a swig from a can of fizzy juice he'd brought with him. 'Fine,' he said, and scratched his scalp, as if to prove it no longer hurt. But maybe it did, cause he quickly moved on to scratch a scrawny arm just where his T-shirt stopped. 'How's the nose?'

'Fine,' Jacob said. It wasn't, but it was growing less tender by the day.

'So,' Flash said, 'did you call Pearce?'

Flash was painfully thin. Always had been. Really needed some home cooking to fatten him up. But that's not something Flash would get any time soon. Moved away from home when he was sixteen. These days he rented a room in a shared flat. Pretty good going, considering the boy's only job had been as a petrol station attendant, and that hadn't lasted very long before he was fired for pilfering. Natural born thief. Jacob didn't know where he got it from, but Flash had been nothing but trouble since he was old enough to put things that weren't his in his pocket. Lived on microwaved ready-made crap that contained very little nutrition. The boy needed a baked potato smothered in butter. A whole sack of them.

Thin or not, Flash had bottle, no question. Jacob didn't like to think about what he did to make a bob, definitely not, but he'd only been arrested twice, and had never done time, so he had to be good at it.

'Well?' Flash said, and Jacob remembered he'd been asked a question.

Jacob recapped his conversation with Pearce.

Once he'd finished, Flash said, 'May doesn't need "something nice". She needs protection.'

'Pearce doesn't have a daughter,' Jacob said. 'Doesn't know what it's like to be responsible for another human being.'

Flash took a long swallow of his juice. Then he said, 'Don't let it get to you, Dad.'

Jacob wondered what his son was talking about, then realised that he was right. Anger was surging through Jacob's muscles, his limbs tingling like they'd done after he'd spent an hour in the swimming baths with Norrie one Friday afternoon a few weeks back. Jacob said, 'Wallace would have torn him apart, anyway.'

Flash looked at him, lips slightly parted. He belched. 'I'm not so sure,' he said.

'Well,' Jacob said, 'we'll never know.' Truth was, Jacob thought Pearce was probably capable of doing the job. The glaikit lump wasn't that big, but he could undoubtedly handle himself. He'd taken Rog and Flash apart easily enough.

'What now?' Flash asked.

Jacob walked over to the drawer under the sink, took out the brochure, flipped it open to page eighty-three. Pointed to the property he'd circled.

Flash grabbed the brochure, pulled out a chair and sat at the table. 'Means dragging May away from school,' he said. 'Away from all her friends.' He burped again, crushed his can.

'But it'd get her away from that psycho husband of hers.' Pearce had left Jacob with his bum hanging out the window, naked as a baby's. May was vulnerable: he had no choice now. He'd have to put down a month's deposit on the villa. Wallace would never find them in a white mountain village in Andalusia. Looked nice in the brochure. Nice and quiet. Not too many people to ask awkward questions. Perfect, eh?

Spain, though. Made his stomach churn. Made his nose ache all the harder. Not so much Spain itself, he was sure it'd be fine, but the idea of leaving home after all this time. He didn't want to leave his familiar surroundings and learn a new language and live in constant heat, even if it was just for a year or two. Ah, he was being old and stupid again. Got to make sacrifices for your bairns or you were no kind of father. He couldn't risk staying, no doubt about that. Not with May in her condition. And anywhere else in Britain, Wallace would hunt them down. Jacob was sure of that. Distance. It was all about putting distance between Wallace and May.

Oh, it was bad. Pearce had let him down.

Wouldn't be quite as bad once the baby was born. Jacob wouldn't be so worried, and maybe they could come back then, but at the moment, he was terrified she'd lose it if they stayed.

That was that, then. Off to Andalusia.

The kitchen door swung open and Rog said, 'Seen my swimming goggles anywhere?'

Flash said, 'They so's you can stick your head underwater and grab an eyeful of young men in their bathing trunks?'

Rog ran over to him and punched him on the shoulder. 'How are your nuts?'

'*Maricon,*' Flash said, formed a fist and threatened Rog with it.

'Dad, help,' Rog said. 'He's using Spanish on me.'

Jacob couldn't take their schoolboy banter at the moment. He knew it didn't do any real harm, but it was driving him doolally. Having Rog around was fine, but having Flash and Rog around together was sometimes hard. He shouted, 'Will you two stop it?'

'Sorry, Dad,' Flash said.

Rog scurried out of the kitchen, grinning.

When Jacob first brought up the idea of leaving the country, Rog had offered to accompany May, but Jacob wouldn't let him. Rog had a life and a career here and Jacob didn't want to interrupt it. Jacob was retired, his wife had died nearly six years ago, and he only had one close friend, Norrie. He could leave the country tomorrow and hardly anybody would notice.

'Definitely got enough money for this?' Flash asked, indicating the brochure.

Jacob nodded. They had the money they were going to use to pay for a bodyguard. What with Jacob's savings, and a couple of grand that Flash had promised, the kitty stood at nearly fifteen thousand. It ought to be enough to rent the villa for as long as they needed. Didn't have a swimming pool, but May would just have to deal with that. Probably not safe anyway with a baby about. Didn't have to worry about their home in Edinburgh. Annie's death had paid off the mortgage, which was some small consolation for the fact that it wasn't right that a man's wife should die before him, not when she was younger by ten years. He missed her. He still missed her. When she died, it was as if his heart had been stolen, and he hadn't got it back yet.

Flash closed the brochure. 'There must be another way,' he said.

Jacob wished there was. He really didn't want to have to go to Spain.

If Pearce wasn't prepared to take on the job, maybe Jacob could look elsewhere. But he needed someone in place quickly. And how did you do that? Did bodyguards advertise? The sort he was looking for? Rog had proved that a bouncer was no use against a trained fighter. It was tricky. Anything to avoid Spain, though. Maybe he could try Cooper again, see if there wasn't someone else he could recommend.

A rap on the front door, and moments later a familiar face appeared in the kitchen doorway. Norrie nodded towards Flash. 'Cheers, boss,' he said to Jacob. 'You okay? Hard to tell with that nose of yours, but it looks to me like you've got your sad face on.'

Jacob was glad to see Norrie. 'Cup of tea, pal?'

ROG STOOD IN the kitchen doorway dangling his goggles on the end of his finger.

Jacob knew Flash was making obscene gestures under the table, but he said nothing.

'We're off, then,' May said, giving Jacob a peck on the cheek. 'Catch you later, Flash. Norrie.'

Norrie raised his mug of tea.

'Have fun,' Jacob said. She was still doing her best to come to terms with Louis's death and Jacob wished he could help her. Louis had been her dog. They'd buried him in the front garden last night. Hadn't let her see the body, just told her he'd been run over. No point alarming her.

She closed the door behind her.

Jacob worried every time she left the house. But he couldn't imprison her. And today she had Rog to chaperone her. Not great, but the best they could do under the circumstances. A public place, they'd be safe enough. If Wallace was going to try something, he'd do it where there weren't any witnesses. He was mad, but he was also canny.

Anyway, now May was gone, Jacob, Flash and Norrie could talk freely. Norrie was a rock. He'd come out of his accident stronger than ever. A bit distracted maybe sometimes, but not so you'd noticed if you weren't looking or didn't know what had happened.

Flash said, 'So if it's definitely Spain, I'll need to give you a crash course in *español.*'

Big family joke. When Flash was about ten years old, he'd claimed to be a fluent Spanish speaker. And he was serious. He'd picked up about half a dozen words, and thought he'd mastered the language. He was odd that way. Jacob remembered when Flash was a toddler, about three years old, sitting in the back of the car, saying, 'Daddy. I know everything.' What he meant, Jacob realised afterwards, was that he could name everything he could see. It was as if his imagination was constricted. He couldn't see beyond what he knew. These days, Flash still thought he knew everything. He could say *no problemo*, so he was *muy fluente*.

'I'd appreciate that,' Jacob said.

'You can't go to Spain,' Norrie said. 'It's not right. That . . . swine can't dic . . . tate where you should live your life.'

'Been thinking that, too,' Jacob said. 'But I don't see an alternative.'

'There's only one thing to do, Jacob,' Norrie said. 'You know that. Flash knows that. Even Rog knows that.'

Flash got to his feet, walked a few steps, then bent over and started to play with the lace on his right shoe. He tied a bow, then untied the whole thing and straightened up. He wedged his hands into the pockets of his baggy pants and looked at Norrie, the shadows under his eyes darker than usual. 'You mean what I think you mean?' he said.

'It's the only way to be sure.'

'If we can't find a bodyguard for May,' Flash said, rubbing his shoulder, 'how are we going to persuade somebody to kill Wallace?' He looked at his father.

Well, now, that was a good question. Jacob had considered asking Cooper if he could talk to his friend, Park. Park was a hit man. Well, not officially, but it was an open secret. He was in prison at the moment, got sent down with Cooper, but he might know someone else in the same line of work. Dunno, did hit men socialise together? Jacob had considered doing the dirty deed himself. But taking Wallace out, pleasure though it may be, was not as easy as it might seem. Might be possible to get close enough. But getting away with it was a different story.

Flash was clearly thinking the same thing. 'Be pretty obvious we were responsible.'

Norrie looked at him. 'Wallace has a million enemies.'

Jacob said, 'Tell that to the police, Norrie.' He still couldn't believe they'd spent the night in jail. Wallace threatens them, they defend themselves against him, and they're the ones who're punished. Is that justice?

No wonder Wallace was grinning all over his baby face.

Maybe Norrie had the right idea. Consign Plan A to the dustbin. Implement Plan B. They'd reached the end of the line.

Just a matter of finding someone to do the job. Wasn't it always?

Flash said, 'Maybe we could offer Wallace the money on condition he fucks off for good.'

Jacob said, 'You'd trust him to uphold his side of the deal?'

'I suppose not.'

There was more. Jacob could tell that Flash wasn't finished. He sat back in his seat, folded his arms and waited.

After a bit of lip-chewing and a quick pull on his gold earring, Flash said, 'Maybe we can persuade Pearce. Maybe . . .' He paused while Jacob indicated with a brief shake of the head that he should continue. '. . . we should apply a bit more pressure.'

Same thing had occurred to Jacob. Question was, how? Pearce was as tough as, maybe tougher than, Wallace. Which is why Jacob had dismissed the idea. 'Threatening Pearce won't do any good.'

'Depends,' Flash said, 'on the threat.'

Jacob looked at Norrie. 'What do you think?'

Norrie said, 'Nah.'

'I agree with Norrie,' Jacob said. 'It's kill Wallace or nothing.'

REVOLVER

JACOB WATCHED MAY through the window. Her hair was still damp from swimming. She was talking to the dog, or rather to the mound of earth under which Louis was dead and buried. She hadn't cried once, which worried Jacob. Norrie was standing next to her, head down.

Jacob turned to face his sons and said, 'I'll do it.'

'Even if we agree to this,' Flash said, '*you* can't kill him'. Flash had taken Rog aside and briefed him on what he'd missed while he was out with May. Rog had agreed that killing Wallace was a good idea.

Jacob said, 'Why not?'

'Dad, you know why not. You'll get caught, sent to prison.'

'And you think that's too high a price to pay? How can you say that, Flash? How can you put a price on the life of May's unborn child?'

Flash lowered his gaze. Jacob knew there was no answer. So did his son. Well, both his sons knew.

Rog said, 'You think you could do it, Dad? Really think you could pull the trigger?'

Jacob looked at his hands. Old man's hands. Knobbly and thick-veined, with a constant little shake to them. Could he? Once upon a time, aye. But now? The truth was he didn't know. 'There's only one way to find out.'

'Dad,' Flash said. 'I'll do it.'

JACOB PAID COOPER a prison visit. He was surprised that the visiting room was open-planned. He'd expected partitions, having to speak to Cooper on the phone. But they were sitting at a desk. They could touch if they wanted to. Only two guards in the room, although there were lots of cameras and probably other guards watching the video.

Cooper had a yellowing bruise on his chin, a cut over his left eye.

Jacob said, 'You're looking well.'

'Like you can speak, Jake.'

Jacob's hand went to his nose, hovered there without touching it, then dropped back to the table. 'Still the hard man, eh? That's what I like to see.'

Cooper said, 'Okay, I look a right bloody mess and I know it. It's no fucking picnic in here, whatever the papers might have you believe.' He flexed his fingers. The index finger was nicotine-stained. 'You should see the other guy.' He smiled. Couldn't hold it. His lips began twitching.

'Only one?' Jacob asked him.

Cooper dropped the smile and pursed his lips. His voice was quiet. 'Four,' he said. 'There were four of them.'

Sounded like Cooper could use some counselling. Jacob was going to suggest it, but decided that counselling probably wasn't Cooper's bag.

After a while, Cooper sniffed hard, said, 'No luck with Pearce, then?'

Jacob shook his head.

'Didn't offer him enough money?' Cooper asked.

'Just the job. He didn't much fancy it. I don't think I managed to convince him of the seriousness of the situation. He thought I was overreacting.'

Cooper scratched his earlobe. 'What you going to do, then?'

Jacob glanced around, then whispered, 'Kill him.'

'Kill Pearce? That's harsh.'

'Cut it out, Cooper. You know who I mean.'

'If you weren't my uncle I'd plant you for telling me what to do.'

Jacob stared at him. Cooper was such a big-mouthed fathead. Even as a kid, he annoyed the crap out of everybody with his cockiness. His dad should have skelped his bahookie more often. His dad, Jacob's brother-in-law, had been a real waste of space, though. Quietly drank himself to death over the years while nobody was looking.

'Yeah,' Cooper said, the muscles in his cheeks taut. 'But lucky for you, you are.'

'Come on, Cooper. Drop the macho crap, will you?'

'Drop the fucking macho crap in here you'll have some queer up your arse first time you bend down to tie your laces.'

Jacob couldn't help feeling sorry for his nephew, even if he was a complete animal. Blood was thicker than disgust. Mind you, where Cooper was concerned, it was a close-run thing.

'So,' Cooper continued, his voice breaking, 'you looking to take out a contract on Wallace?'

'I was thinking of doing it myself,' Jacob said.

Cooper put his hand over his mouth. He cleared his throat. Jacob could see that Cooper was grinning behind his fingers. And on this occasion he wasn't having any trouble holding his smile.

'What do you have to smirk about?' Jacob said. Couldn't help himself.

Cooper shook his head, still grinning. He let his fingers slip from his mouth.

Jacob leaned forward, his stomach pitching and rolling, a buzzing in his temples, and said, 'Maybe one of your boy-friends might fancy the job? Want to ask for me?'

Cooper stood up, fists balled.

Jacob thought, here we go. Lights out. Jesus, he'd made a big mistake. Cooper would go crazy, tear him into strips. Jacob's stomach was somersaulting. But he got to his feet, too, and realised they were attracting unwanted attention. 'You're a disgrace to your family,' he said in a whisper. If Cooper had been . . . you know . . . by those four, well, that was a kind of justice. Maybe not justice enough for what he'd done to end up in prison – beaten a poor woman to death with a baseball bat – but it was something. 'Now sit down and compose yourself,' Jacob said, 'or you'll have a . . . guard over here.' He'd been about to say 'screw' but caught himself at the last minute.

Cooper clenched his teeth. His eyes swept the room. Slowly, he sat down. He shifted in his chair, staring at Jacob, the heat gradually leaving his face.

'Hate me all you like,' Jacob said. 'I don't give a tinker's curse. Just tell me where I can get a gun.'

Cooper said, 'Why should I?'

Jacob shrugged. 'Rumours, Cooper,' he told him. 'They can hurt a man. Damage his reputation.'

Cooper eyeballed him. Jesus, he looked mad. Maybe Jacob had gone too far. How the hell had this happened? Something to do with the fact that he'd been pleased when he realised what had happened to Cooper. Couldn't keep it a secret. Didn't want to keep it a secret. That was it. He wanted Cooper to know what he thought of him.

Aye, screw him. The guy was blood, but he was bad blood.

Cooper was looking down at his hands. After a while, he looked up and told Jacob where he could get a gun. Then he told him where he could shove it.

TWENTY-FOUR HOURS later, Jacob and Norrie were sitting opposite a heavy man with a Mohican haircut, who was holding a gun that looked like it was last used during the American Civil War.

'You claiming that thing works?' Norrie asked.

'Trust me.' Joe-Bob pulled a face. Presumably it was

supposed to convey innocence, but it was the kind of face you'd pull if you were lying through your teeth.

Anyway, how could you trust someone called Joe-Bob?

'He doesn't want it,' Norrie said. 'Eh, boss?'

Jacob nodded.

Joe-Bob said, 'Well, that's all I've got.'

Norrie nudged Jacob. Jacob said, 'Then I'll take my business elsewhere.'

'Best of luck.'

'Thanks, but I won't need it.'

'Yeah?' Joe-Bob said. 'Think it's easy to find someone to sell you a gun?'

'I found you. I can find someone else.' Jacob paused. 'Worst case scenario, I'll go through to Glasgow.' He waited a minute. 'Go to any pub in Govan.' He grinned to show he wasn't being serious. 'Isn't that how it works?'

Joe-Bob ran his tongue over his lips. 'I like your style, Mr Smith.' He took the gun from the table, held it. 'And Mr Jones isn't wrong about this,' he said, turning towards Norrie. 'It's a real piece of shit.'

FLASH SAID, 'YOU can't do it, Dad.'

'What alternative is there?'

'I told you. *I'll* do it.' Flash was serious, poor kid.

'Who are you trying to fool?' Jacob asked him. 'Pearce beat the crap out of you. What chance would you have against Wallace?'

'I didn't have a gun before.'

'That's right. Just a knife.' Jacob paused. He'd hurt Flash with that comment and he hadn't meant to. 'Look,' he said, 'maybe I can find someone else to do it.'

'We can't afford it.'

Jacob was silent. Flash was probably right.

'Anyway,' Flash said, 'we'd be throwing our money away. I'll do it for free.'

'You won't,' Jacob said. 'There's no point gaining a grandson only to lose a son. I don't want you spending the rest of your life in prison.' He thought of Cooper. *There were four of them.* 'You never know what might happen to you inside.'

PEARCE FINISHED READING an article in the newspaper about yet another rape. The police suspected it was the fourth by the same guy. Offered lifts to his victims, then drove them to a secluded spot, like an industrial estate or a churchyard. Yeah, two were abused in God's shadow. Fucking God by proxy, Pearce figured. Guy was clearly a religious nut. Probably couldn't hack it as a priest. Too friendly with his parishioners. Got ex-communicated and was paying God back in his own special way. If Pearce was God he'd get a baseball bat and fuck the bastard with it, then pound the shit out of his balls until they burst. Give him a full-length circumcision with a pair of scissors to round things off. Wouldn't be so keen to use his cock after that.

Underneath the piece on the rapist, there was an article about a guy who'd had his jaw relocated to his back. Well, to his side. There was a picture, posed by a model, from the neck down, with arrows indicating where this guy's new jaw had been positioned. On the right-hand side, just under his armpit. Unfortunately, you couldn't make out very much, even with the helpful arrows. It was fascinating, but what Pearce really wanted to see was the real guy's face. You couldn't help wonder why he'd had to have his jaw repositioned in the first place. The article didn't say. Apparently, the poor bastard hadn't eaten properly in four years. But now he was munching away. Right there, just under his armpit. Didn't have any teeth, though.

Still, can't have everything.

ROG WAS SWEATING, despite all the car windows being open. What was wrong with the weather this year? Where was all the fucking rain? You got to rely on it and you missed it when it wasn't there. This heat was making him sweat and the sweat was making his stitches itch. He licked his lip and tasted salt. Man. And there was also that frigging stink, even with the windows open. He'd already poured the best part of a bottle of disinfectant all over the boot. End result, instead of smelling like dead dog, the car smelled like clean dead dog. An improvement, yeah, but a stink was a stink, even if it was a clean stink. And now the inside of the boot was sopping wet.

They'd stopped the car to talk.

Rog said to Flash, 'Park's the only man who might have done it and he's in prison.' He dipped his head out the window and breathed in some fresh air. Only, it wasn't so fresh. The traffic fumes were pretty bad, as you might expect at one o'clock on the Glasgow Road. What was he doing here anyway? Flash wanted to talk in private, reckoned May was safe enough at home with Dad now he had a gun. For a while, anyway. Once they were in the car, Flash asked if he'd help with another burglary, cash was tight, but Rog didn't have the stomach for it. He'd been on four with Flash already, and they'd all been successful – in the sense that they'd got a few quid and some electronic equipment and a stack of jewellery and, most importantly, got away with it – but Rog hadn't managed to get used to the whole experience, not one little bit. In fact, each successive occasion was worse than the last. So he'd cried off, saying, 'Now isn't the right time.' And credit to Flash, he'd shut up about it. Asked him instead if he fancied helping him get a tyre collection service established, and explained how there was money to be made in taking away old tyres from garages and disposing of them in an environmentally friendly manner, according to the law passed in Scotland in 2003. He knew a guy who knew a guy who owned several garages who apparently paid seventy grand a year to have all his used tyres taken away. Lot of money in tyre disposal. Rog thought it sounded like an interesting proposition, but he said no when Flash explained he was planning on illegally dumping the tyres in the countryside cause you had to save on costs somehow.

Rog tucked his head back inside the car. He should think about getting a bite to eat, man. But he wasn't hungry. Hadn't had much of an appetite for a while. And he couldn't remember that ever happening before. 'We can't let Dad do it,' he said. God, Dad would kill him if he knew how he'd really been making money recently. He hated lying to Dad about being a bouncer, but it made the old guy happy and what was the harm in that? Truth was, Rog had worked behind the bar in a Grassmarket pub for a while, but he was let go for being too slow.

'*Muchacha* alert,' Flash said. 'Would you look at that arse?' He turned in the passenger seat so he could carry on watching the *muchacha*. Or rather, the *muchacha*'s arse. '*Muy* nice.'

It *was* nice. Rog couldn't argue with that. A J Lo arse. Something to get your teeth into and chomp on.

Flash continued, 'Wouldn't you just love to take a plank of wood to it?'

The thought hadn't crossed Rog's mind. But now that Flash mentioned it, he couldn't get the image out of his head. He gripped the steering wheel, squeezing it as if he were somehow able to squeeze the image from his brain. No joy. The picture stayed where it was. If anything, it was lodged even tighter and was in sharper focus. There she was, the *muchacha*, bare-arsed, oh yeah, bent over the back of a low chair, Rog about to give her a whack with a plank. Why, he had no fucking idea. But there he was, all planked up. He wasn't thinking straight at all. Having all sorts of strange notions. Hallucinating, practically, like he was tripping, but he hadn't indulged for at least six months now and he'd never been a heavy user, so it wasn't a flashback. He felt fucking odd, though. 'Why would I want to do that?' he asked Flash.

'Just, you know, cause it would . . . fuck, I dunno, do I?'

'You're a perv, Flash.' Which was true. He was. Rog needed to get his mind off the babe. He was being too easily distracted. And he knew why. He didn't want to think about what he was going to have to do. But there was no way out. He'd have to concentrate. He said to Flash, 'Pay attention, huh?'

'I'm listening.'

'Look at me.'

Flash turned, reluctantly. 'I'm looking. Prefer the *muchacha*, though.'

Rog didn't return Flash's smile. He squeezed the steering wheel harder. 'We can't let Dad do it,' he said.

Flash snatched another look at the *muchacha*. 'Rusty nails,' he said.

'What the fuck are you on about now?'

'Rusty nails in the plank of wood.'

Rog pictured it. Jesus. His brother was sick. 'You're sick,' he told Flash.

'Maybe.'

'Anyway,' Rog said, 'she'd eat you for breakfast.'

'Let's hope so.'

Flash had a good laugh at his own joke. Rog wasn't in a mood for Flash's jocularity today. Somehow, he didn't think he'd be in the mood for it tomorrow, either. If he ever saw tomorrow. After a while he said, 'I've made my mind up.'

Flash said, 'What about?'

Rog didn't bother replying.

Flash said, 'You're not thinking what I think you're thinking, are you?'

Rog had his attention now. 'I don't know.' String it out. It's what Flash deserved. 'What do you think I'm thinking?'

'Jesus. You can't. If anyone's doing it, it's *me*.'

'I'm not asking for your permission.'

'Rog, you can't.'

'Why not, Flash? Why the fuck not?' And that's what he wanted to know. It wasn't a rhetorical question. Apart from the law, what was there to stop him? Fuck, you know, he wasn't thick. Scored pretty well in tests at school and could have gone to college if he'd wanted. But he didn't need a degree to know about personal responsibility. Anyone could do anything they wanted if they were prepared to take the consequences. That's why suicide bombers were so hard to defend against.

'You have the rest of your life to think about,' Flash said.

'And you don't?'

'Well, I decided first.'

'And I'm your big brother and I'm undeciding you.'

'Christ.' Flash ran his hand over his face. 'This isn't fair.'

'Tell you the truth,' Rog said. 'I think you'd fuck it up, man.'

'Rog, *compadre*, that's bullshit and you know it.'

Rog screwed his eyes together as sunlight glinted off the windscreen of a double-decker bus pulling into a bus stop up ahead. The doors opened and a couple of passengers got out. Rog watched in a daze. It was as if this mundane action, the doors swinging open, passengers getting out, were a riveting scene in a film he'd spent his whole life watching. The bus pulled away. As it passed, an advertising band along the side advised Rog to keep the zing in his thing. He had no idea what it was advertising. Or which thing he was supposed to keep his zing in. It saddened him that he might never find out.

Flash prodded him. 'I'm talking to you.'

Rog was suddenly angry. He didn't appreciate being poked in the ribs, but under normal circumstances he'd have let Flash off with it. Shit, he was stressing out. He said, 'Fucking don't do that, will you?' An overreaction. But he couldn't help himself. Saw that gorgeous arse again. The plank of wood. A rusty nail. Holy crap, his mind was rotten.

'Well, you fucking pay attention, then, *verga*. You tell me off for *muchacha*-watching, then five minutes later you're away with the fairies yourself. Did you hear a word I was saying?'

'Watch who you're calling a fairy.' There it was. He couldn't resist the banter. When things get serious, take the piss out of the situation. Use humour to crack the tension. The way they'd always been, the way they'd grown up. All they knew. Which made this whole process so much harder.

'You know what?' Flash said. 'I think you're full of shit.'

Rog punched him on the arm.

Flash said, 'Ow,' and punched him back.

Rog was going to miss him. 'I've got bigger *cojones* than you,' he said.

'Impressive,' Flash said. '*Cojones*. Very good.'

Rog was aware that he could spend some time devising a foolproof plan to get away with what Dad referred to as Plan B. But what was the point? He'd get caught eventually. There was no point postponing the inevitable. If he was going to kill his brother-in-law, he'd get banged up. For a long time. End of story.

Unless he shot himself afterwards.

He only had twenty-four hours to think about it, cause he was going to do it tomorrow.

TOMORROW, AND A slight breeze tickled the back of Rog's neck. He pressed the buzzer of Wallace's flat, the gun tucked down the back of his trousers digging into the base of his spine. He wanted to run away. Like some kid. Scared of what was to come. *Don't be fucking pathetic.* He ought to be thoroughly ashamed of himself.

He told Flash he'd wait a while. Think it over. Now Rog wished that was the truth.

Wallace answered the door, looking bigger than he had when Rog last saw him. Looked older, too. Less of the baby face about him. More of a pinched look. 'You shouldn't be here,' Wallace said. 'Unless you're planning on dying.'

He knew. Somehow the fucker knew.

Wallace's eyes, magnified by the lenses of his glasses, were dull. No joy in them. No sparkle, not a trace of humour. As if something had sucked the shine out of them. For the briefest moment, Rog wanted to hug him. Tell him what he was going to do, apologise, but explain that it was necessary. And he wanted to apologise for his sister. How fucked up was that? But, you know, she'd slept with somebody else and she was married to Wallace and Rog had spoken to her about it pretty sternly. Not like he'd be going behind her back. But he couldn't apologise to Wallace before he shot him, now, could he? That was ridiculous and he was nervous which was why he wasn't thinking straight.

He'd seen Wallace arrive home in his Range Rover ten minutes ago. Watched him park outside, lock the car, open his front door. His usual routine, in other words. It was a Friday, and he liked to leave work early. May's departure hadn't changed that.

'What do you want?'

Rog felt a knot in his throat. Shit, shit, shit. He had to go through with it. Fuck, he'd nicked the gun easily enough. He hadn't thought to ask for it. He knew Dad wouldn't let him, any more than he'd let Flash. Didn't rate their expertise on the old assassination front. But Dad wasn't expecting Rog to be the one who might try to steal his nice new weapon. Dad was keeping an eye on Flash, so it was easy for Rog to go to the bedroom, lift the mattress, rescue the gun. Living in the same house had its benefits.

Dad would notice it had gone soon enough, though.

But not for a while. He was out with Norrie this afternoon, off for a quiet pint or two, try to take his mind off things. Nice that Dad had a good friend. All you needed, one good friend. And Norrie was a good friend, otherwise he wouldn't have decided to take two weeks off work at the factory to help out the family.

Rog took a breath, then another, and another. Shook his hands by his side like a dog shaking water off its coat.

'You going to leave or do I have to kick the crap out of you again?' Wallace asked.

Rog nodded, which probably confused Wallace.

'Fine, I'll call the police,' Wallace said, turned and started to move away, his cream-coloured shirt untucked at the back. Rog shoved the door hard and barged into the hall.

'GET OUT OF my house, Roger,' Wallace said.

So bloody young and innocent. About five ten, medium build, no threat at all to look at.

Rog wanted to speak, say something cool like, 'Eat lead, motherfucker.' But his throat was tight and he knew he had no chance of saying anything at all. Or if he did, it would sound squeaky. Which wouldn't be the least bit cool. Come to think of it, fuck being cool.

Shit. Get a grip. *You're bigger than him.*

His size was usually an advantage. Not with Wallace. Wallace wasn't intimidated in the slightest.

Rog brushed sweat off his forehead with his wrist.

You have a fucking gun.

He took the gun out of his waistband. Held it. Pointed it at Wallace.

Now the wanker would be intimidated.

Wallace stared. Didn't flinch. His eyes never wavered for a second.

Fuck, you had to hand it to him. Rog was about to piss himself and he was the one with the gun. Could he do this?

Yes. He cocked the gun. Held it with both hands. One trying to steady the other. Both shaking. His palms were sweaty. His finger tightened on the trigger.

'What's this shit?' Wallace said, his voice perfectly even.

'You're dead,' Rog said, his voice trembling.

'Why don't you put the gun down, Roger? We can talk about this.'

'We can't.'

'Sure we can.'

When Wallace moved, Rog yelped and pulled the trigger.

THE RECOIL THREW Rog backwards. He hadn't expected that. The gun jumped out of his greasy fingers and clattered to the floor.

'I'll take this,' Wallace said, picking up the gun. He wiped the butt on his trousers. 'Before somebody gets hurt.'

Rog tried to sit up, pains in his chest when he tried to breathe. What a fuck-up. He deserved what was coming to him. He just hoped it was quick.

Wallace bent over him. Rog's heartbeat speeded up. He had no idea his heart was capable of beating this fast. Holy shit.

Wallace looked around. 'Lucky all you did was damage a bit of the ceiling there.' He indicated the hole in the roof at the top of the stairs leading to the basement. 'Bit of a mess, eh?' A chunk of plaster had fallen onto the staircase and kicked up a cloud of dust. He patted Rog on the leg. 'I'll send you the bill.'

Rog struggled to take a breath and finally managed to say, 'What're you going to do?'

'Get a plasterer in.'

Rog wheezed. His breath wasn't coming at all now. His chest felt tighter than ever. 'To me,' he gasped. 'What're you going to do to me?'

'You look pale. You need a doctor?'

Rog shook his head.

'Drink of water?'

Rog nodded.

'Well, that's a shame,' Wallace said. 'Now let's be serious, huh?'

Rog wasn't entirely sure what hyperventilating felt like. But he suspected that's what he was doing. His chest had a steel band round it. His heart – fuck, was he having a heart attack? His arms, legs, mouth were all tingling. Wallace was going to shoot him. He knew. Christ, who wouldn't hyperventilate? Who wouldn't have a fucking heart attack? Maybe he was having both? For fuck's sake, why didn't the bastard just get it over with?

'Shoot me,' Rog said. 'You fucker.'

'Okay,' Wallace said.

WALLACE PLACED THE gun against Rog's forehead.

'Ow,' Rog said, pulling his head back. The muzzle was red hot. Well, it felt like it was.

Wallace looked at him, not making the connection between Rog's pain and the gun. Then when Rog put his hand to his forehead to touch the spot where the gun had burned his skin, Wallace wrapped his fingers round the barrel, testing it suspiciously, and sharply pulled them away again. 'Never realised,' he said. 'That is very fucking hot.'

Then he stuck the gun against Rog's lip. Right against the stitches.

Rog's head snapped back once more, but this time Wallace leaned in, forcing the gun against Rog's mouth. The back of Rog's head was mashed into the wall and couldn't go back any further.

The gun wasn't red hot. Not like a branding iron. But it still hurt like a bastard. And blood was dripping onto Rog's tongue. Rog reached up, grabbed Wallace's arm.

'Nope,' Wallace said.

'What do you mean?' Rog said, the pain making his eyes water. He could smell the gun smoke, and it made him feel sick.

'Put your hand back down or I'll pull the trigger,' Wallace said.

Rog stared him in the eye. He was serious. Rog let his hand flop back down to his side. His lip was burning, but he was so cold inside that he started shaking.

Cause this was bad. Worse than if Wallace had turned the gun on him and shot him point blank. Because Wallace was doing this shit, and he'd probably still turn the gun on him and shoot him anyway once he'd had his fun.

Rog hardly dared breathe, yet the pain was going to make him scream.

Or maybe it wasn't the pain. Maybe it was just the situation. Having a pissed-off madman with a gun standing over him, pressing the muzzle against his damaged mouth. That was probably enough to make him scream.

And if he screamed, the sudden noise might make Wallace pull the trigger. Without meaning to.

Or he might pull the trigger anyway. Intentionally. Scream or no scream.

So Rog might as well scream.

Unless Wallace wasn't planning on shooting him. But that wasn't very likely.

But it was possible.

And possibilities were worth exploring when you were on the point of getting shot.

Rog said, breathlessly, 'Are you going to shoot me?'

Wallace pulled a face and pressed the gun hard against Rog's stitches. And twisted.

Rog said, muffled, 'Ah, fuck, ah,' 'cause the pain of the muzzle digging into his skin far outweighed the burning.

Wallace pulled the gun back an inch from Rog's face and said, 'Maybe.'

'Look,' Rog said, spreading his fingers, 'this is all a big misunderstanding.'

'Yeah?' Wallace said. 'I find that hard to believe.'

'I just wanted to scare you,' Rog said. 'Warn you off.'

Wallace said, 'I should shoot you for telling lies. You pointed this gun at me.' Wallace jabbed his gun arm forward and Rog thought the gun was going to go straight through his cheek and knock his teeth out.

Wallace said, 'You told me I was dead.'

Rog said, 'I didn't mean it.'

'No?'

'I'd never have killed you.'

'No?'

'No.' All over his body, Rog's muscles were loose. Felt like they weren't attached to anything, just lumps of fat and sinew floating inside big flaps of skin. 'A misunderstanding,' he repeated in a wet whisper, his tongue slack in his bleeding mouth.

'Yeah?'

'Honest.'

'Oh, well,' Wallace said. 'In that case . . .' He lowered his arm.

Rog started to breathe again, but he was suspicious that this was a bluff, that Wallace was just being sadistic, giving Rog hope and any minute he'd whisk his arm back up again and fire a bullet clean through Rog's skull. Clean through. At this distance most of Rog's brain would spurt out the back of his head. Oh, shit. The fucker was going to do it. Rog knew it, for sure.

Any second now.

His trigger finger. Little pink tip, whitening with the slight pressure he was putting on it. Short, chewed fingernail.

Rog didn't want to die on account of that finger.

Irrational. He knew he was being irrational. But he didn't want to. Not that. God, no, anything but that. But what difference did it make whether Wallace's fingernail was chewed or not?

Calm down, calm the fuck down.

Hold out till the police got here. Neighbours would have heard the shot, called the cops, they'd be here soon.

But this was Friday afternoon in Edinburgh, could have been anything. Fireworks City. Loud bangs were an everyday everywhere occurrence.

Everyday everywhere. Did that make sense? Rog felt light-headed. Words were like bubbles and he didn't want to burst them.

God, he was cold and itchy and couldn't breathe and he was hot and his mouth was wet with blood and it was cold and his teeth hurt and his lip hurt and his bowels were not good, not good at all but he couldn't let go, just couldn't allow himself to get into that state where he didn't know if he was hot or cold or anything much of anything else anyway. Had to pull himself together and face this. Come on. What was the worst that could happen? Wallace would kill him. So face it. Brace himself for the worst case scenario. And if he got through that, he'd be okay, cause everything else would be an improvement.

Wallace was going to kill him. And it was okay. Right?

Wallace was sitting on his hookers, eyeing Rog.

His trigger finger relaxed and so did Rog.

For all of the time it took Wallace to swing the gun back up, and place the muzzle on Rog's left knee. 'How much do you think that would hurt?' he asked.

Rog shook his head. Shit. He could feel the warmth of the gun through his trousers. He was sweating like he'd never sweated before. Pools of moisture were running down his back. He was going to lose consciousness, have a heart attack, both, something.

'You don't know? Fuck, well, let's find out, shall we?'

'No,' Rog screamed. 'Don't do that. It would hurt. A lot.'

'Is that all?' Wallace said. 'Just "a lot"?'

'Fuck, it would hurt like the sorest fucking thing I can fucking imagine.'

'I can imagine something sorer,' Wallace said. 'Want to know what it is?'

Rog shook his head. He didn't want to know. His worst case scenario wasn't the worst case scenario at all. He'd rather die than have his kneecap blown off. He closed his eyes.

It didn't help. Wallace told him anyway. 'Imagine I pop a cap in your knee, here, like this.' He made a 'bang' sound.

Rog's eyes snapped open and he about crapped himself. No kidding. He knew now what people meant when they said they had loose bowels. 'And you're screaming in agony,' Wallace continued. 'Then imagine I pop a cap in your other knee.' He moved the gun to Rog's other leg, pressed the muzzle hard into his kneecap. 'Bang. You with me?'

Rog nodded. He was with him alright. He could feel the pain just as if Wallace had really shot him. And he had a pain in his chest as if he'd been shot there too.

Wallace said, 'Now, would both kneecaps be twice as sore as the single kneecap, do you think?'

'I really don't know,' Rog said.

'But what do you think?'

'Probably, yes.'

'Want to try it?'

Oh, fuck. Here it was. The fucking end. *The* fucking end. The police weren't coming. Neighbours hadn't called it in. Car backfiring. Firework. None of their business.

Rog said, 'Just fucking shoot me if you're going to.'

'Okay,' Wallace said. He stood up.

Rog refused to pray. Didn't care how close to death he was, he wasn't going to start with that shit. Even though, somehow, it was the only thing he could think of that might save him.

'You better go,' Wallace said.

Rog looked at him. Another bluff? What a bastard.

'Go,' Wallace said again. 'I might change my mind.'

What was the sadistic fucker's plan now? Would he wait till Rog had got to his feet, then shoot him? Would he wait till Rog's back was turned? Would he wait till Rog was halfway out the door?

Or would he shoot him right this minute, despite what he was saying?

Well, Rog didn't have much of a choice. He had to go.

He got to his feet, unsteady, wishing he could ask Wallace to let him lean on his shoulder. Legs were feeble, like the bones had turned to mush. He dragged himself to the door. Opened it. All the time, feeling a massive itch in his back where Wallace was pointing the gun.

But Rog got out the door without being shot. Down the path. And he broke into a run.

Wallace shouted, 'Bang!'

Tears welled in Rog's eyes.

He rounded the corner and relief coursed through him. He was safe. Spat blood out of his mouth. Got into the car. Sat behind the wheel and realised he couldn't drive with his hands shaking like this. Got out and climbed in the back. Amazed he was still alive. But still terrified. He lay down on the back seat. He'd be safe there till he composed himself.

A wave of exhilaration swept through him. He couldn't believe his luck. He ought to be dead. Yet here he was, as alive as he'd ever been. More so. He felt like singing. But he didn't know any songs.

He lay in the back for ages, a tight fit but he didn't care. Snug meant safe. He'd have locked himself in the boot if it didn't stink of Louis. He wasn't sure how long he lay there, but eventually he snapped awake, got a grip of himself. Realised with a horrible clarity that it was entirely possible that Wallace could storm out of his house any minute and shoot Rog where he lay. He wasn't safe in the least. He was doing that ostrich thing of sticking his head in the sand and thinking that because he couldn't see anyone else, then no one else could see him.

He jumped out of the car, got in the front, started the engine and accelerated away. Screamed round the first corner, straight on, flew over a speed bump, slammed down with a stomach-jarring thump, then slowed to a crawl. Still wasn't ready to drive. He pulled over.

Got out his phone. Called Flash. Then opened the door and spewed.

When he looked up, a teenage girl was leading her parents' Labrador across the road. He nodded at her as she passed. She called him a minging cunt.

After that, he felt almost normal again.

'WISH YOU'D TOLD me you were going to do it today,' Flash whispered, later, in the garden. Rog was lying down, shades on, lip throbbing, drinking a beer. May was lying on her front, reading, next to the spot where they'd buried Louis. 'I'd have told you you weren't ready,' Flash said. 'I'd have done it instead.'

Rog knew it was just words, but he nearly burst into tears. He wasn't right yet. He was still shaken up by the whole experience. He knew he wasn't going to sleep a wink and his emotions were all over the place.

He was happy to be alive, yet terrified by his near death encounter. Simultaneously.

He hadn't told Dad what had happened. Not yet. That little treat was going to come later. And Dad wouldn't be happy, cause Wallace now had the gun, so he was even more of a danger to May than he'd been before.

'What're you pair whispering about?' May looked up from her book.

'Nothing,' Flash said.

She flicked her hair out behind her, gave Rog a stare. 'Your lip's not healing.'

'It's fine,' he said. 'Just a bit swollen from the stitches.'

'Aha?' she said, then turned back to her book.

Which was just as well. Rog couldn't trust himself to speak.

He could have sorted out Wallace once and for all. Rog had had the opportunity and he'd blown it. If he wasn't such a fuck-up, his wee sister would be safe.

He felt his eyelashes moisten.

God, if May saw him crying she'd be onto it. Bad enough lying about what happened to Louis, but having to lie again was more than Rog was ready for.

Thank God for the sunglasses.

'I'm going to get another glass of Coke,' she said, getting to her feet. 'You lying bastards want anything?'

'Cut the language,' Flash said. 'Dad'll hear you.'

'Away and shite,' May told him. 'You want anything or what?'

Flash and Rog both shook their heads.

Dad hadn't noticed the gun was missing. At least, Rog didn't think so. Dad hadn't said anything. But maybe he wouldn't. When they'd got back, Dad had been in the kitchen chatting to Norrie about Andalusia and Rog hadn't wanted to disturb him.

Actually, Rog didn't want Dad knowing what a fuck-up his son was.

May was in her room.

Flash went in to speak to her and after a minute they strolled back out and invited Rog to join them in the garden. Soak in what was left of the sun. He couldn't speak.

He'd fetched his shades, got a drink.

Right. Feel better after a beer. And he had. A little, anyway.

'Maybe I should just go ahead and tell Dad now,' he said to Flash, lifting his glasses to wipe his eyes. Look, it had been a fucking difficult time, all right? And big men cried, occasionally. There was no shame in it. He felt like such a tosser, though. Shame or no shame. His lip really hadn't been hurt too badly. It wasn't *that* he was crying about.

'I think you should,' Flash said.

Rog waited till May came back with her long glass of Coke,

then he went inside and locked himself in the toilet. He sobbed his heart out for a good ten minutes.

Then he went to the kitchen, asked Dad if he could speak to him in private, but Dad said he didn't have secrets from Norrie. So Rog told them what he'd done.

If Dad still had his gun, he'd have shot Rog there and then.

NEXT MORNING AND fortunately Rog hadn't burst into tears once since he'd got up, but he hadn't been able to sleep a wink all night. Telling Dad had been hard. You'd think there'd be some truth in the saying about a problem shared and all that. But there wasn't. Crock of shite, it was. Dad and Norrie wanted details, so he gave them details. Told them about Wallace threatening to blow his kneecaps off, about how he hid in the back seat of the car.

Dad told him he was a fool. He was lucky to be alive.

All night Rog kept replaying the events of that day in his head. The more he went over it, the more he realised that Dad was right. If Rog had been a betting man, he'd have wagered a shitload of money that Wallace would never have let him go.

It wasn't right, man. Wallace wasn't the sort of person to behave like Gandhi. Okay, so that wasn't exactly how he'd behaved, but by his standards, that was as near as dammit.

Rog thought about how composed Wallace had been. Someone strolls into your house and fires a couple of bullets at you, you don't stop to think how you're going to respond, do you? You kick the shit out of the bastard. At the very least. Well, that's how a normal person would respond. Wallace was very far from being normal. From the outset, he messed with Rog's head. And he was continuing to do so. And doing a fuck of a good job of it, too.

THE NEXT NIGHT, around two o'clock in the morning, Rog was in bed listening to the welcome patter of rain on his window – this heat didn't help when you were having trouble sleeping – when he heard a noise, like chair legs scraping, that sounded as if it came from the kitchen. Wasn't May. She slept like a horse. Could be Dad, his busted nose keeping him awake. Or a bit peckish, making himself a sandwich or grabbing a biscuit. But what if it wasn't Dad?

Rog got out of bed, quietly, reached under it for the black wood Louisville Slugger baseball bat he'd kept for protection since May had moved in.

He crept along the corridor. Poked his head into the sitting room.

Nothing.

Carried on along the corridor. Braced himself. Firm grip on the bat. Poked his head round the kitchen door.

Nothing.

He switched on the light, just to make sure. Nothing. Nobody. He breathed out hard. Went over to the sink, poured himself a glass of water, drank it, switched off the light again. Wished he could calm his nerves.

Wallace wasn't stupid. He wouldn't come here. If he was carrying a grudge, he'd play it out on his own patch. He wouldn't —

Wham! The side of Rog's head exploded. He staggered, tried not to go down. Tried to keep hold of the baseball bat, but his grip had slackened with the blow to his head. He felt dizzy. Wham! A second blow dropped him to his knees. Lights flashed in front of his eyes. The baseball bat slipped out of his fingers. They had no strength in them at all.

'Wallace?' he said, then asked the craziest question: 'Did you just shoot me?'

A third blow, across the bridge of his nose, knocked him backwards. His face filled with pain.

Then he felt a hand on his leg. 'Wallace?' he said again.

And an explosion. He knew what it was, what it meant. He had his answer. The first three blows weren't shots. This was. For a second, he was left with only his imagination. And during that time, his imagination tried to prepare him for the ensuing pain by conjuring up what it thought was a suitable agony. But it fell way short. When the pain came, it was like nothing he'd ever experienced. At the same instant, a hundred mallets slammed into his kneecap. Pulverised it. The pain overloaded his senses. He couldn't believe this much pain was possible. But it was. He roared, told himself the pain wasn't so bad. Roared again at the lie. Choked on the blood from his smashed nose.

He didn't notice what Wallace was doing. Not that he could have stopped him.

The second explosion followed quickly. The same blinding pain. This time, the other knee. Through the pain, the thought that he'd never walk again. Not caring, if he could only stop the pain.

He heard the outside door slam.

A split second later, he passed out.

PEARCE HEARD ABOUT it first on the radio. It was in the newspapers, too, and on the TV news.

Somebody'd done both knees at close range with a handgun. Pearce recognised the big guy's name. Wondered what Rog Baxter had done to piss Wallace off.

None of his business, though, was it?

GHOST DOG

GUAPA WAS FLASH'S favourite word, so much so that he kept it to himself, and used *muchacha* instead when he was messing around with Rog. A *guapa* was a babe, and *guapas* were always wanting to know why he was called Flash.

Well, he could hardly own up to the real source of his nickname, could he, you know? It wouldn't be right to say to some lovely lady he'd just met, 'Hello, darlin'. They call me Flash cause I nick things. Quick as a flash.' He knew some people who'd have done just that but no, Flash had a bit of style and when he took a girl out on a date, he didn't take her to Burger King, no chance, mate, no. He wined and dined his women at Pizza Hut or somewhere classy like that, maybe even Pizza Express if the lady was really special, and threw in a bit of *español* which usually did the trick maybe because, who knows, it sounded a bit dirty.

For a while, he'd taken to telling all the *guapas* he met that his name was Gordon and that he was known by the nickname Flash and after a minute they'd get it and go: *A-ha. King of the universe.*

Never failed. Well, sometimes it did but you win some and anyway the point is he was pissed off when he found out Pearce's first name was Gordon because it was as if the fucker had stolen his monicker, even though Flash's parents had saddled him with the name Fraser, not Gordon.

Gordon Pearce. The bastard was called Gordon. That's what Dad told him.

Anyway, he was supposed to be doing something here, *pronto*. Flash was ready to rumble, even though his mouth was dry, but as Dad had kept saying, there was no danger and he was right, of course. No danger at all, just a phone call, so what was he so frigging jumpy about? Flash blew his cheeks out, tapped his foot, made a fist and thumped his knuckles into the palm of his other hand. Yeah, bring on a barrel load of radges, he was ready, man, fucking primed.

Not that he had to beat anybody up, not this time, no, all he had to do was make this shagging phone call.

He could use a fag right now but he'd given up, hoping to prove to Dad how easy it was, just a matter of willpower and that was the same as being stubborn and Dad was stubborn all right, so no problem.

And it wasn't as if he was going to be face to face with Wallace, so there was nothing to get all steamed up about, but the truth was he was friggin' terrified of what the fucker was going to do next.

Flash couldn't quite get his head round what had happened to Rog. Never heard of anything so fucking cowardly in his life, apart from hitting May and what the jizzwad did to Louis, maybe, but the point was that it was pretty fucking low to shoot somebody like that in the fucking knees when they weren't looking and had no means of defending themselves, apart from the baseball bat, but that wasn't likely to be much good against a gun, was it, so didn't amount to much, almost nothing, which was the point, right, as he said.

Wallace really deserved what he was going to get. No doubt about that, and Flash would dearly love to give it to him, but as if Wallace wasn't a tough enough proposition in the first place, he now had a fucking gun to contend with, which was an absolute pisser of a situation.

Which is why Pearce was the man for the job. So he'd turned it down already and Dad had given up on him, but Flash reckoned he could still be persuaded. And he wasn't afraid of guns. Been shot already, hadn't he, and survived.

Flash picked up the phone and dialled.

HILDA STARED AT the phone, tail wagging. Looked like he was about to attack the handset. Pearce picked it up and said, 'Speak.'

'Seen what happened?' a voice he vaguely recognised said.

Pearce waited but he couldn't place the voice and it didn't say anything else so he hung up.

Seconds later, the phone rang again. 'The fuck you hang up for, *amigo?*' the same voice said. 'That's Pearce, isn't it?'

Baxter's son. The one who was still walking. The one Pearce had threatened to castrate. Pearce said, 'I said no.'

He hung up again. Bent down, scooped up Hilda, tucked him under his arm. He went through to the bedroom, stood by the window, looked out across the Firth stroking Hilda's head. Another hot clear day. Too hot to be bothered with this kind of hassle.

Wallace. Devil Daddy. The Baxters' nemesis. Shot Big Rog's knees full of lead. The fuck was wrong with the mad fucker? What did Rog do to upset him? The big guy would be in hospital for a while and, according to the newspapers, when he did get out, it'd be in a wheelchair. Probably wouldn't ever walk again.

But was it Wallace? Highly possible that Rog could have pissed off somebody else. Somebody with that kind of sadistic temper, though? Somebody harbouring sufficient rage to break into your home and fire a couple of bullets into you? Pearce could think of one or two candidates. Suitably provoked,

Cooper would do that without blinking. But then, he was in prison. And Seamus, Pearce's old cellmate, wouldn't have batted an eyelid. Mind you, handguns weren't his weapon of choice. People he didn't like, he used to slice chunks of their torsos off with a machete. While they were alive.

After lockdown, Pearce sometimes had trouble sleeping knowing Seamus was in the same room, machete or no.

PEARCE HELD OUT till evening. Then he gave in. He'd slotted the photo of May in a drawer in the kitchen once he'd decided Baxter's offer wasn't for him. Hadn't been able to toss the photo in the bin, though he wasn't sure why. He dug it out now, smoothing out the slight crease in the top right-hand corner.

He flipped it over, dialled the number on the back.

A girl answered.

Pearce said, 'Who's this?'

'May.' She sounded pissed off. 'Hurry up. I'm on my way out.'

'Can I speak to Baxter?'

'Who do you want? Flash or Dad?'

'I'll have Dad, please.'

When Baxter came to the phone, Pearce said, 'I need to talk to you.'

'What about?'

'Wallace,' Pearce said.

'You changed your mind?'

'I didn't say that. I just want to talk to you.'

'You want to come over?'

'Nope.'

After a minute, Baxter said, 'Oh, I get it. I'm on my way.'

THE BAXTERS HAD had fish for dinner. Pearce smelled it on them the minute they walked in the door. So did Hilda. He appeared from the sitting room, had a quick look round, wagging his tail like a demented rattlesnake, and then went back to his basket.

'Weird dog,' Flash said. 'What sort is it?'

Pearce told him. Flash had never heard of a Dandie Dinmont. He was slouching so hard with his hands in his pockets he looked like he was going to collapse into his own stomach.

The dad offered Pearce his hand. He, at least, had some semblance of politeness. His face reminded Pearce of a car thief he'd shared a cell with for a month. Guy called Rocky. You could have cut off his nose and sewn it back on upside down and it would have been an improvement. Rocky didn't have those dark bruises under his eyes, though.

'Wasn't expecting the pair of you,' Pearce said.

'Flash is as concerned about May as I am,' Baxter said.

'Where is she now?'

'Visiting our brother in hospital,' Flash said. 'Where Wallace put him.'

'Is she safe?'

'Course she is,' Baxter said. 'Public place. She's with a friend of mine. And we're picking them up after we leave here.'

Pearce asked, 'The baby okay?'

'May's upset,' Baxter said. 'We all are. But on this occasion the damage to May has been psychological. Physically, she's fine.'

'Good,' Pearce said. He asked Flash, 'Got a knife with you this time, hard man?'

Flash's hand moved in front of his crotch. He said nothing.

Pearce turned, led the way into the sitting room. The Baxters carried the smell of fish with them as they followed. And Pearce realised why he'd been thinking about Rocky. You see, Rocky had claimed that a skate was the perfect sexual substitute for a woman. He swore by it. Just like the real thing, apparently. Advised Pearce to go to Deep Sea World at North Queensferry just to see if he wasn't telling the truth. 'It's cool there,' Rocky said. 'Scores of flatfish swimming over your head in these glass-ceilinged tunnels. Honest, pal, they have re-markably fanny-looking fannies. And if you want to touch and not just look, I know a good fishmonger in Slateford.'

Pearce couldn't help but wonder if the Baxters had been diddling a skate.

'What's funny?' Jacob Baxter said, arms folded, standing in front of Pearce.

Pearce shook his head. 'Take a seat,' he said. Then, to distract him, 'How's the wife?'

Baxter glared at him. 'She's dead,' he said.

'Oh,' Pearce said. 'I'm sorry to hear that.'

'Happened a while ago,' Baxter told him. 'I'm over the worst of it.'

Pearce folded his arms. 'And Rog?'

Baxter shrugged. 'Won't be walking again any time soon.' He breathed out heavily. 'But he's alive. Mind if I smoke?'

'As long as you don't mind me coming over to your house and pissing all over your carpet,' Pearce told him.

'I forgot,' Baxter said. 'What did you want to speak to us about?'

'I know what happened,' Pearce said. 'I read the newspapers. What I'd like you to do is tell me why.'

Baxter stood for a while longer, then finally decided to plonk his arse down on Pearce's mum's settee. He wiped the cushion first, as if there were crumbs or dog hairs on it. There weren't dog hairs on it, cause Pearce didn't let Hilda up on the settee. They had an understanding. The wee bastard had his own basket over by the window and Pearce never tried to get into it.

Although Flash might. He was walking over there now. Bending over, muttering to Hilda. Hilda opened his mouth, let his tongue loll out. Flash stared at him, fascinated by the missing leg. Hilda's tail was going again. When the dog wasn't a coward, it was a whore.

Pearce focused on Baxter again. Baxter sniffed, stuck his hand in his jacket pocket, withdrew it, empty. He ran the palm of his hand across his brow.

'Nobody going to say anything?' Pearce said.

Flash straightened, shifted his weight, what little there was of it, from one foot to the other, but didn't look like opening his mouth any time soon.

'Does it matter?' Baxter said.

'Tell me. Then I'll decide.'

'Christ's sake, Pearce, you saw what he did to the dog.'

Pearce, huh? What happened to the 'mister'? 'I did,' Pearce said. 'But I wasn't asking about the dog.'

Baxter's lips were pursed, deep wrinkles running down his jaw. 'And Rog? What was that? A forgivable fit of temper?'

'How do you know Wallace was responsible?'

'You serious?'

'Perfectly.'

Baxter leaned back in the settee, stretched. Then he sat forward suddenly. 'This goes no further than us,' he said.

After Pearce nodded, Baxter proceeded to tell him about Rog trying to kill Wallace. About Rog failing. About Wallace getting hold of the gun. About Wallace threatening to shoot Rog in the kneecaps.

Pearce said, 'So, let me get this straight. Rog intended killing Wallace?'

Flash approached Pearce, hands thrust in his pockets. 'Too fucking right.'

'And he fucked up?'

Flash nodded.

'And Wallace taught him a lesson by pumping a couple of slugs in him?'

'Well, that's not how I'd look at it, Mr Pearce.'

'But that's how Wallace would look at it.'

Silence for a while. Then Baxter said, 'The important question is, how do *you* look at it?'

Pearce smacked his lips, then said, 'Rog was asking for it.'

TEN O'CLOCK, PEARCE took Hilda out for a bedtime stroll. Walked down to the end of the street, passed a tiny old lady all dolled up, hair in a high coiffure, teetering from one side of the pavement to the other. Whether the poor balance was a result of alcohol or her high heels was anybody's guess. She looked happy, though.

He let Hilda off the lead at the steps down to the beach. Looked over to his left, saw a guy in a pink suit, maybe red, hard to tell under the outside light from the pub on the corner. The guy was hefting a suitcase and looked like a freak.

Pearce didn't want any hassle. Hoped the freak didn't follow him down to the beach.

Hilda bounced off into the distance, sniffing at the sand, snorting. Any minute he'd start barking at the slow-winking light from the lighthouse on the island over to the west.

Pearce followed, heading towards the sea, crossing over the loose-packed sand towards the firmer footing further out. A flock of birds took off on his left, too far away to be able to tell what kind they were, glided over the water and out of sight. The waves slapped and splashed and made a sound like rustling paper.

Overhead, the drone of a plane. He resisted the temptation to look up.

'Hilda,' he said, not loudly. He meant the dog, but he started thinking of his mother. She'd lived in Edinburgh all her life, but he never remembered her taking him to the beach.

'All that sand.'

'Yeah, Mum.'

'Gets in your shoes.'

'Yeah. Take them off.'

'Yuck. All that grit between your toes.'

'Yeah. I know.'

'In your hair. In everything.'

'I know.' She'd have loved it, though.

Waves rolled towards him. Each one a birth and a death. He stared into the distance. Getting melancholic. A birth and a death? Fuck that. They were fucking waves. He should get back home. Hilda had had long enough to take a piss. Where was the little fucker? 'Hilda,' he said, in a mock-serious tone.

He turned, looked behind him. Footprints in the sand. The streetlamps along the promenade created a weird orange glow all around. He peered through slitted eyes, which made no difference, and shouted on the dog again. Next he knew, Hilda was ten feet away and closing, big grin on his face, bouncing on his two back legs, hopping on the front one.

'Jump,' Pearce said, when Hilda was close enough.

Hilda gave a little yap, leapt into the air.

Pearce caught him, got a faceful of dog tongue, wet sand all over his arm. Not bad. The little guy had potential. That hadn't taken him too long to learn. Not long at all. And he hardly ever fell over now.

FLASH SPOKE TO Dad in the car and told him his plan but Dad wasn't listening, he'd been to see the doctor about his nose, got it taped up now, so Flash had to tell it to him again and said, you know, that it was probably the craziest plan Dad had ever heard, but Dad said he'd heard crazier and that it was worth a try cause they had nothing to lose and they didn't have enough spare cash to interest anyone in killing Wallace, so why not?

'You mean it?' Flash felt good, felt like he was doing something at last.

Dad nodded and Flash felt even better. By the time they got to the hospital, Flash was feeling guilty about feeling so good. Wished he could share his plan with Rog, but it wasn't appropriate under the circumstances.

It had been tough, not just for Rog but for everybody. Flash's first reaction had been to go straight over to Wallace's and kill the jizzwad, and he'd asked Dad if he could get another gun and let him have a go but Dad had said no, he wasn't risking having another son crippled or worse, cause he felt bad enough about Rog as it was.

So not being able to take direct action against Wallace was pretty shitty, but what made it worse was that there was the police to deal with. Now those fuckers didn't believe a word of their claim that Wallace was responsible for the shooting, said it was all hearsay and that there was absolutely no evidence to suppose that Wallace had anything to do with it and of course Flash couldn't say anything to the police about Rog having intended whacking Wallace because then he'd get banged up for attempted murder or something, which nobody wanted, so they had to keep their mouths shut on Wallace's real motivation and try to persuade the police that he was pissed off from their earlier visit, which the police had a record of. But since it was Wallace who'd filed the complaint on the previous occasion, and since it was Flash, Rog and Dad who'd ended up in jail, the police saw Wallace as the innocent victim in all this, and it didn't help their case that his wife had left him on account of getting pregnant with somebody else's baby. Or that he'd been threatened.

It was clear that the bastard police didn't have any other suspects, but Flash had pointed all this out anyway. They wouldn't be swayed.

'A burglar, most likely,' the detective had said to him. Window had been left open, which was careless, really fucking careless, and Flash had complained to Dad about it and Dad had said, 'You saying Rog brought this on himself?' and Flash had shut up because if Rog had been responsible for leaving the window open then that's exactly what he was saying and it was a pretty fucking horrible thing to say.

Anyway, the police weren't going to find anybody, cause it was Wallace and he was the one person they wouldn't look for. Who else had a gun and was fucked up enough to shoot somebody in the kneecaps? A fucking burglar? Give the boys in blue a slow handclap. Fact was, Wallace had been waiting for an opportunity and when it came his way, he'd seized it. Fucker was no doubt laughing his balls off, planning his next move.

THEY ARRIVED AT the hospital a little early. Dad wanted to go in, see Rog again instead of waiting for May and Norrie outside as they'd agreed and Flash said he'd stay in the car cause seeing his *hermano* in such a bad way was upsetting, but Dad persuaded him to accompany him cause Rog would be more upset if Flash wasn't there than Flash would be if he was.

Flash wasn't sure if Dad was right, though, cause just seeing Flash was enough to trigger Rog's waterworks and that wasn't going to do anybody any favours, was it? Big brother had had five operations already and was pumped full of morphine and God knows what else – a nurse was busy right now doing stuff with a tube and a syringe – and there were more operations and more drugs to come, lots more, and the doctors still couldn't predict the lasting damage although they'd predicted that it would be lasting. Sort of.

Flash grabbed hold of Rog's hand, thinking that once upon a time he'd have found the fact that Dad and Rog both had their noses taped up really funny, but it didn't seem funny in the least right now. Once the nurse had finished her flusterings, Flash followed her out of the room and asked her the question none of the doctors were prepared to answer. 'Will he be able to walk again?'

'I'm not a doctor,' she said.

'I know,' Flash said. 'That's the reason I'm asking.'

She put her hand to her forehead, peered at Flash as if she was weighing him up, and finally said, 'It's possible that he might be able to get around, slowly, with a couple of canes after a long, long time, assuming there isn't too much muscle damage.'

See, both Rog's kneecaps were shattered beyond repair. Didn't bear thinking about. Flash imagined being struck on the kneecap by a hammer. Then he imagined being struck hard enough to break the bone. Then he imagined being struck hard enough to shatter the patella (couldn't forget that word, it sounded Spanish) so badly that the surgeon had to pick dozens of pieces of bone fragments out of the surrounding tissue.

The nurse said, 'But he's not going to be winning any marathons.'

If she'd been male, Flash would have thumped her.

She disappeared before Flash could change his mind about the male thing and he returned to Rog's room in time to hear Norrie ask, 'We going to get moving?'

Flash would have liked to stay, now that Rog was dry-eyed if not bushy-tailed, sit next to Rog and chat to him for a while, tell him everything was going to be fine, that he had the situation under control. But May was just that bit more vulnerable if Flash wasn't with her – she'd lost one of her protectors now with Rog in hospital. Although Flash reckoned that if Wallace were to try anything, he'd do the same as he'd done with Rog and strike in a quiet spot, when they least expected it and in any case Flash reckoned that Wallace was still enjoying what had happened to Rog too much to deflect attention from it. Anyway, Flash wasn't going to stay behind again, cause last night Rog hadn't felt like speaking, said it hurt him to talk and at first Flash didn't understand how that could be because although Rog's nose had taken a serious crunching, his mouth was okay – apart from the stitches, but they were just above his lip and the wound seemed to be on the mend again after Wallace had messed with it – but then he realised that Rog had meant it hurt him emotionally and that there was no physical pain from speaking as such but that the very act of moving his lips, shaping words, deciding what to say – those were what hurt, because they reminded him of what had happened, reminded him of the other pain, the pain of being shot and the pain of putting his shattered legs back together again.

So Flash wasn't going to remind him and, you know, there were other things Flash had to focus on now. 'Yeah,' he said. 'We should be going.'

Rog looked relieved.

The sooner Flash got his plan in motion, the better.

Outside, he grabbed Norrie by the arm and whispered, 'We need to talk.'

NORRIE WAS STILL on holiday from the factory, so he offered to spend some of his free time watching Pearce so Flash and Dad could do the bodyguarding job on May, who was well freaked out by what had happened to Rog. Flash had asked Norrie to get a handle on Pearce's routine, which Norrie did for the next two days. Strange guy, Pearce, it seemed. Didn't have any emotional ties, very much a loner, didn't visit anybody, nobody came to visit him. In fact, it was almost like he didn't know anybody. Flash knew Pearce had a phone cause he'd called it, but he wondered why Pearce bothered cause he couldn't imagine Pearce talking to anyone on it, not for a chat. Maybe he did have some friends, but even then, he wasn't the talkative sort, probably just grunted hello and grunted good-bye and hung up. Probably his friends were guys he met in prison, anyway. He didn't have a job, just had the stupid yappy three-legged dog that, according to Norrie, he took on regular walks down to the beach.

Which was fine. Flash had a fair idea of how he was going to play this.

Third day, Flash changed places with Norrie, which was a relief, cause as much as Flash trusted him, he knew that Norrie wasn't completely reliable on account of the accident. Lost it sometimes, you'd be talking to him and you knew he was somewhere else.

Anyway, it seemed Pearce had changed his routine. He'd gone out, visited the library. God knows what he was up to in there, cause obviously Flash hadn't wanted to follow him inside because he didn't want Pearce to notice him, did he? Flash took a seat on a bench round the corner, where he could keep an eye on the library entrance. Problem was, the bench was across the street and along a bit from the police station and Flash felt exposed. Still, not a lot he could do other than try to avoid looking at the uniforms going in and out of the station. He tried to spot *guapas* instead.

Spotted one straight away, but she was a *guapa* in police uniform, so she didn't count. Spotted a few after that, a lot more than he'd expected. It was still warm, even though the air was much cooler now than it was this morning, you could feel it, and the warm weather always brought them out, although he couldn't explain his attraction to the policewoman, which was worrying. Never thought he'd find a cop attractive, not in uniform anyway with those clumpy shoes and the daft hat. It'd be different if she was bare-arsed, wearing just a Kevlar vest and maybe toting some of the hardware accessories, cause they kind of had an S&M appeal, handcuffs and baton and the like, yeah, he could definitely find a use for them.

He looked towards the library again, saw the dog still tied up, no sign of Pearce.

The bench jostled under him and he turned to see a large wheezy woman waggling her buttocks into a comfortable position. He instinctively moved over even though she had plenty of room. She took out a packet of fags and offered him one and he said no, so she lit up and told him her name was Virginia but that her husband had always called her Vagina and his name was Rick so guess what she called him?

Flash said nothing but she asked him again, so he told him to shut up and she said aye and asked him his name and he told her and she said aye, but what was his real name, and he got fucked off and stood up.

She said something else to him but he didn't catch it cause Pearce came out of the library, couple of books tucked under his arm, bent over, untied the mutt from the railing. He looked up and frowned as he stared towards the bench Flash had just vacated.

Flash turned, thinking he was a bit obvious stood here like a prune right enough, knew he should sit down, keep his back to Pearce, pick up his conversation with Vagina where they'd left off, but he couldn't bear it. He knew what he was going to do and had a fair idea of when, so, hoping to Christ Pearce hadn't clocked him, he stuck his hands in his pockets, started to walk away, feeling Pearce's eyes on his back. Shit. Had the fucker seen him? Flash started walking quicker and quicker, and by the time he'd reached the crossroads, he'd broken into a jog.

FLASH HEADED TOWARDS the beach at a slow jog, then he looked around for a good five minutes but saw no sign of Pearce. So Pearce hadn't been following him, most likely hadn't spotted him back at the library. Flash found a shop selling ice cream and got a double scoop and sat on the beach wall, plucked his phone out of his pocket and called Dad.

They needed to act sooner rather than later, cause every day they did nothing was another day Wallace might carry out his threat, although the jizzwad was unlikely to do anything else so soon after fucking up Rog, but still. Wallace was tough to predict. Anyway, Flash knew what he was going to do and he didn't need his old man's advice, not really, but sometimes it was good to get some feedback, just to confirm that you were doing the right thing. Dad answered, agreed wholeheartedly.

It was on.

Of course, Flash wanted to discuss it with Rog, too, but Rog couldn't know about all this, it'd upset him too much, so even if Rog had wanted in on the plan, Flash couldn't have said a word, which was a pity, any way you looked at it, you know, cause Rog could use some cheering up and this would have done the business, no doubt. The situation with Rog was confusing him no end. Thing about hospitals was they made you depressed, even if you were perfectly healthy, which was a bit like churches if you can imagine being locked up in a church for weeks on end with all that morbid music wailing through the speakers. Anyway, hospitals were fucking grim enough places even as a visitor so God knows what they felt like when your knees had been shot to fuck and the more you thought about it the less surprising it was Rog hadn't smiled since Wallace had shot him and it was really not surprising in the least that it hurt Rog to talk, was it?

Flash took a good long lick of his ice cream. That was a narrow escape from Pearce back at the library and he couldn't afford to be seen again, so there was nothing for it now other than to get prepared, get the few bits and bobs he needed, scout out the territory for a good hiding place and make his move tonight.

Yeah. Tonight was the night, definitely, and a bonus factor, the fog starting to roll in, cause it wouldn't get properly dark till well after ten.

Bring it on.

Flash knew the plan was unlikely to persuade Pearce to help protect May, but what he hoped was that it would make Pearce keen to beat the shit out of Wallace and that was a second prize Flash was more than happy to take.

So much more than happy, in fact, that he almost dropped his ice cream.

A CHILL TOUCHED Pearce's cheeks and made him smile. He could taste the haar in his mouth. And with it, this time, a much-needed cooling off. When the temperature dropped, Scotland was more like it ought to be. If you wanted heat, you'd move to sunnier shores. You wouldn't stay in Scotland. Not unless you were one of those arseholes who just loved to complain.

'An end to the good weather, eh?'

Like this guy jerking towards him, straining to control a weird bastard of a mutt – head like a Bull Terrier and a body like a Great Dane – at the end of a short lead. The dog had stumpy legs and a tail that looked capable of taking your head clean off with a single swipe. Its mouth hung open, tongue practically dragging along the sand.

Its owner was the only other person on the beach, at least that Pearce could see. Mind you, he couldn't see very far. The mist was pretty thick.

Pearce said, 'You don't like it, then fuck off and live somewhere else.'

The miserable tosser glanced at him, maybe considering having a go. But he decided against it. Not brave enough, even with the ugly dog as backup, and once he'd made up his mind that tonight wasn't the night to commit sudden acts of violence, he seemed happy to let the dog pull him away at a trot.

Having said all that, about complaining about the weather, Pearce himself had a definite complaint. This year was pretty bad. He couldn't take much heat. Even in winter he'd go around without a jacket, often without a jumper. Didn't feel the cold like other people. The heat had been causing him the odd sleepless night lately. Last night he'd resorted to a single sheet, nothing else, but even then he had to cast it aside after a while. And lying on the bed naked was no way to encourage sleep, not when he got the occasional nocturnal visit from Hilda sneaking through from the spare room. Last thing Pearce wanted was to wake up to find Hilda licking his balls. Jesus.

Pearce had suffered from insomnia all his life. Didn't sleep particularly well in prison. Other people in the room capable of killing you while you slept, definitely didn't promote deep slumber. But even as a kid he'd lie there awake, night after night. He used to have this thing about moths. Funnily enough, it didn't apply to other flying insects. Just moths. And it was based on nothing at all. At least, he couldn't remember ever having swallowed a moth or anything like that. But he was utterly convinced that if he went to sleep, a moth would fly into his open mouth and choke him. He was the only kid he knew who went to school not having slept at all the night before. Which meant his concentration wasn't always too good. Which meant that adults thought he was a bit slow.

He was happy with that. He didn't much care what they thought. For the most part, it meant they either left him alone or indulged him. And as a kid, that was a pretty good deal.

But he did care what Mum thought. She used to go on at him about making friends. But he could never understand why. What would he do with a friend that he couldn't have much more fun doing on his own? Eventually she realised he was perfectly happy and gave up. Told her cronies he was 'solitary'. Which wasn't true, cause he did spend a lot of time with Muriel.

But fuck it, what was he dragging all that up for? The two people he'd ever loved, both dead. His sister had junked up, fucked up and got fucked. The latter, literally. After she'd

OD'ed. His mum got it in the neck. Literally. Trying to stop a post office robbery.

He was there. He could have prevented it.

Yeah, yeah, yeah, yeah. He wasn't going to beat himself up about it. It was done. Nothing he could do to change anything now.

This was the kind of introspective shit that crept up on you when you owned a dog. All these walks kind of forced you to think, and thinking really sucked.

Introspection was for cissies and lags. Time to get the dog, go home, watch some mindless crap on TV. Or read his library books. He'd picked up a couple of American crime novels, having developed a taste for them while he was in prison. Anything to pass the time. Anything to forget about the past. *Just get the fucking dog.* Okay. Where was the little bastard?

He'd run off when the Bull Terrier-Great Dane cross had appeared. Last Pearce had seen of him, he was scurrying about among some rocks off to the left. Playing with dead crabs probably (he liked to toss them in the air, then run after them, grab them, shake them to bits). Fooling himself into thinking he was some remarkable killing machine. Or maybe he was chasing ghosts in the mist. Pearce was too far away to tell what he was up to.

The Fife coastline was gone. The island, Inchsomething, was gone. Pearce looked behind him. Orange glow through the mist all that was left of the town. 'Hilda?' he said.

Pearce might get some sleep tonight. Cool enough that he might even drag the quilt out of the cupboard. Ah, to sleep with something weighing down on him. And he didn't mean another body. Or bad thoughts.

THE BIRD WAS standing at the water's edge. Black and white, stretched-out-of-shape little body complete with beer-gut. Looked like a tiny penguin. It wasn't moving. For a second, Pearce thought someone had placed a statue in the sand. But the bird gave a tiny jerk of its head as Pearce approached. He kept expecting it to flap its wings and take off. But it sat there, as if it were stuck. Had it been facing the other way, it might have been engrossed in the task of watching for fish. But it was facing the deserted promenade. Looking towards the station, where there was nothing to catch other than a bus. In any case, the station was shrouded in mist and if you didn't know it was there, you'd be unable to tell. Tonight, even an eagle wouldn't have seen shit.

He walked right up to the bird. It gave him a sideways glance. Then ignored him. He bent down, still expecting it to take off, and picked it up. It gave a half-arsed squawk, beat its wings a couple of times, kicked its legs. Then played dead again.

So it hadn't been stuck in the wet sand. Hadn't sunk in there under its own pot-bellied weight. Hadn't dug its heels in. Hadn't been rammed in feet-first by a sadistic dog-walker.

Eleven o'clock, dark, the mist filtering out most of the moonlight. He used the light from his mobile phone to check that the bird wasn't injured. Its wings looked okay. Its legs seemed fine. Looked perfectly healthy, as far as he could tell. Like a bird ought to look. So why was it sitting there like a right sorry fuck?

He put it back down. It stared towards the promenade, motionless. For all the world it appeared to have given up on life. Was it old? Was it sitting here waiting for the end, was that it? How did you tell how old a bird was? Was it tired? Just taking a rest? Nah, it would have summoned some energy from somewhere. Was it crazy? Did you get insane birds? He crouched down and spoke to it. Asked it the questions he'd just asked himself. After a while he realised that what he imagined was comforting to the poor creature was probably distressing the fuck out of it. And if it was already suicidal, maybe that wasn't the best thing for it. Should he go, just leave it alone? It was waiting for something to kill it. Birds probably found it hard to kill themselves. Can't very well pick up a gun, shove it in the old beak and pull the trigger. Should he help? Wring its neck? Smash its skull between a couple of big stones? Was that the right thing to do?

Pearce turned, walked away from the bird. He didn't feel like killing anything today.

What had he been doing? Oh, yeah. Acting on his plan for what was left of the evening. Fetch Hilda, go home, watch TV. Maybe drag the quilt out of the cupboard, hopefully get a good night's sleep. Where *was* the bloody dog? He hadn't seen Hilda for ages now. He called his name.

'Are you sure you're doing the right thing?' his mum asked him. 'Leaving that poor bird?'

'You're dead, Mum,' he said. 'Give it a rest, huh?'

PIECE OF PISS. The buzz was pretty close to the buzz Flash got from a successful burglary because, okay, you always imagined you'd get away with it, otherwise you wouldn't take the chance in the first place, but there was usually a moment when you knew you'd pulled it off and this was it.

Everything was cool and Dad would be pleased and Rog, when he told Rog, when Rog was ready to hear about it, maybe he'd break into that long-overdue smile.

Flash pressed down against the dog's head with one hand and started to pull the zip up with the other. His fingers were numb and he swore because he should have brought gloves, but who'd have thought that the mist would make it so friggin' cold? The dog licked his wrist, oblivious to the shrinking world over its head and the funny thing was it wasn't wriggling, wasn't kicking as much as a single one of its three legs and in fact seemed to be enjoying the novelty of being stuffed in a large sports bag, fucking freakshow of a creature.

Flash left a small gap so the wee fucktard could breathe and he spoke to it continuously, just in case it decided to start barking and warned its owner of its whereabouts, although it seemed nice and relaxed, scarcely moving inside the bag, probably thinking it was bedtime or some similar kind of stupid dog thought, but then what did you expect, because something that small can't have much of a brain even though horses were pretty big and only had brains the size of a pea but were quite bright, so Flash had heard. Oh, well, that was one for the scientists.

Flash got to his feet and peeked out from behind the mound of boulders where he'd been hiding for the past couple of hours and where if it hadn't been for the mist he'd have been just fine but, Christ, his balls were just about frozen solid and his legs were stiff and his back hurt when he stood up and he couldn't help but think that this is what it must feel like to be as old as Dad. Flash hoped somebody would shoot him before he ended up in a permanent state like this because quality of life, *amigo*, that's what it was all about and if you lost that, you might as well lose everything, like his Uncle Cam who went into hospital with a small lump on his shoulder and died within a couple of days. Cancer. No clue, other than a week or so before he'd had a strange experience when he lost all feeling in his mouth. Cam had been a mountain climber and everybody agreed it was as well he'd gone so quickly otherwise the misery in store for him if it had been drawn out, well, it didn't bear thinking about, did it, because if you're going to go, go quickly and don't hang around cause there's no point.

Fifty yards behind Flash, waves crashed against the sea wall. There didn't seem to be any beach back there, but he didn't understand why that was, just that the sea slapped against the wall. There was more beach here, where he'd been hiding, maybe because the coastline curved inwards. Another one for the scientists.

The bag tipped, the weight moving from one end to the other as the dog finally started to get jumpy, damn the little fucker, but as long as it didn't start making a noise everything would be okay. But it might start making a noise any minute, so Flash got a move on.

The sand gave way under each of his footsteps and the dog was lurching from one end of the bag to the other but still didn't yap. Well-behaved little pooch.

Not much further.

Flash crept towards the steps and started up them and it occurred to him that once he got onto the promenade, instead of taking the dog back to the car with him, he could head back to where the water was lapping against the sea wall and, well, drop the bag over the railing.

Hang on, it wasn't something he'd actually do cause no, he wasn't a great dog lover, but there were limits, obviously, and it just occurred to him momentarily as being an easier option cause if he got rid of the mutt now, he wouldn't have to take it to Dad's and ask him to take care of it and all that shit cause Dad would probably tell him it was his responsibility and Flash wasn't looking forward to walking it and feeding it, and, anyway, he couldn't keep it in his flat cause his flatmates would object, so fuck that for fun.

Just walk along a bit and – *whee* – over the railing, like that. Simple and effective.

On the other hand, Pearce shouldn't really have to pay for what Wallace had done and Flash didn't want to get those two thugs mixed up even if Pearce had given him a pasting. Getting hit in the balls was bad enough, and being smacked on the head with the edge of a briefcase hurt a lot more than you'd imagine, but it was the sound of that knife tearing through his trousers that made Flash squirm. Even now, he broke out in a sweat just thinking about it. So he wouldn't think about it, not if he could help it. Anyway, he needed Pearce. Now, if it was Wallace's dog, Flash might have to rethink his plan, especially after what Wallace did to Louis, but as it was, Flash dismissed the idea of dumping the dog in the sea and headed for the car.

It was unlikely Pearce would be able to see him, you know, with the thick-rolled blanket of mist, but if he did, all he'd be able to make out would be a distant figure carrying a sports bag and think it was somebody heading for the five-a-side practice pitches up the road cause you wouldn't imagine anyone would have your dog in their bag, now, would you?

AN HOUR LATER, it had started to rain. Pearce didn't give a shit about the weather. He knew he'd lost the three-legged bastard. He'd hunted everywhere he could think of. No sign. He'd whistled repeatedly, shouted till he was hoarse. Nothing. He retraced his footsteps. Nope. Finally he decided to go home. Figured that Hilda might have thought the same thing, that he'd be waiting outside the door looking sheepish. Or, more accurately given his size, lambish.

Once Pearce had left the beach, he walked home in the

middle of the road. All the way worrying that maybe Hilda had been run over. Couldn't help but glance to the side, lower his head to look under parked cars.

Nothing.

He sat at home for thirty minutes. But he couldn't sit still. He got up and went out to look some more.

It was pissing down now. He got soaked and Hilda's whereabouts remained a mystery.

Back home again he removed his wet clothes, ran a bath and tried to relax. But there was a tightness in his gut that wouldn't go away.

Pearce didn't get any sleep that night after all. Kept imagining Hilda outside the door, tail wagging, stirring a puddle.

Twice Pearce got up to see if he'd come home.

Of course he hadn't.

As soon as daylight broke, Pearce went back out. He was prepared for the worst. Finding Hilda's mashed remains by the side of the road. Or finding his bloated, matted body washed up on the beach.

Not even a dead cat lay sprawled out by the roadside, although half a dozen dead birds were washed up on the beach (the fat little penguin wasn't one of them – Pearce liked to think he'd survived).

Of Hilda, there was no trace.

THROUGH THE SITTING room window at Dad's, Flash watched May playing with the dog in the garden and he was impressed that the pooch could run – in fact it could run pretty fast, considering its physical limitations.

He hadn't thought about how May would respond to

Pearce's dog, how she'd lost Louis, how she'd be delighted to have another mutt round the house. It was great to see her happy again.

When he returned to Dad's last night, May had oohed and aahed as he removed the dog from the bag and once she'd noticed its missing leg, Flash had exchanged glances with Dad and Norrie and they all knew they were going to have trouble prising the dog out of her grasp when the time came to return it.

'Where did you get him?' she said.

'Found him,' he said. 'Abandoned.'

'Oh, what a cutey-pie.'

Flash assumed she didn't mean him and certainly the dog knew who she meant cause it started dancing on its three legs, tail wagging, a wind-up toy, licking her hand like it was covered in ice cream.

And since then, it hadn't left her side.

Flash looked away from the window and dialled Pearce's number.

'This is Flash Baxter,' Flash told him when he picked up. 'Got a message from Wallace this morning. He wanted to know how your dog's doing.'

PEARCE'S INITIAL REACTION was relief. All thoughts of Hilda's demise were nothing more than wild fantasies.

The wee bastard was safe. Wallace had nabbed him.

But Pearce didn't know Wallace. Wallace didn't know him. 'What's Wallace want with Hilda?' he asked Flash.

'Somebody must have seen you talking to us,' Flash said. 'Wallace wanted to warn you off.'

More likely one of the Baxters had told him Pearce was helping them, thinking it'd scare him off. Stupid fucks.

And then Pearce's thoughts twisted in another direction as he recalled his only glimpse of the Baxters' dog. In their car boot, throat slit from ear to ear. 'What's the fucker done to Hilda?' he asked Flash.

Flash said, 'I don't know how to tell you this.'

Pearce said nothing.

After a while, Flash said, 'He said the dog dropped like a stone when it hit the water. Probably on account of the boulder he put in the bag to keep it company.'

TRUE ROMANCE

SCENARIO ONE. THAT'S what Norrie decided on today. Close his eyes. Oh, yeah. And open, open wide, yeah. There it was. As real as real could be.

The gasps from the back seat of his car told Norrie that his old friend was having fun. Good. All he wanted was for Jacob to be happy. Really, that was it, it, it. Nothing more. Nah, no way. That was all. Made it worthwhile Norrie taking the time off work. Happy Jacob made for a happy Norrie. Life was simple. Well, it should be, no need to complicate it, eh?

Norrie was a couple of years younger than Jacob. Younger men were supposed to have an advantage, but from the floppy state of Norrie's wee boaby, you'd never have guessed.

Norrie was thinking too much. Sexy stuff and thinking didn't go together. He was never going to enjoy it after all he'd been through recently. This was for Jacob, not for himself. His mind was racing – *whiz* – he didn't know what it was racing, but it refused to slow down. It had been this way since . . . ah, Jeez. If he was going to have as much fun as Jacob, he'd have to concentrate. Join in. *Be* here in the warmth of his car, not in some cold dark place in his mind. Life had never been this hard. He'd certainly never had such a tough choice to make. And he still wondered if it had been the right one.

Yes, yep, yipee. No two ways about it. It had to be the right decision. Andalusia had been a great idea, but Norrie couldn't let Jacob go. No way, boss. Getting rid of Wallace and staying in Edinburgh was a much better idea. Wasn't it? Even though . . .

Well, these moments of self . . . self-doubt were only natural. Of course they were. You couldn't know what he now knew and carry on as if nothing had happened, although that's how it appeared. Oh, yeah. It was done. Over. Finished. Term . . . inated. No use beating himself up about it. There was nothing he could do now. You couldn't rewrite history, right? That's what they said, and he wasn't going to argue with them. You could write the future, though, so that's what he was going to concentrate on. The present, too, if he was able – fuck the past. Oops. Jacob wouldn't like that. Swearing was bad, terrible, awful. Money in the swear box. Okay, boss.

Flash's plan was full of holes, full of danger. If Pearce found out who'd really taken the dog, they'd all be in serious trouble. Norrie wondered sometimes if he was just being an old fool. Being too protective. Maybe, possibly, probably. But he'd started now and he had to keep going. Jacob had to be protected. Obviously May had to be protected, too, but Jacob was his first concern. Bottom line, Norrie wanted Wallace out of the way whatever the cost.

The bastard – oops – the bad man had been tearing Jacob apart for too long. And it wasn't going to end unless somebody put a stop to it. Every day Wallace failed to act was another day Jacob suffered. There was nothing for it but to do what had to be done. Now that Flash had put the next part of the plan into action, Norrie knew that Jacob was beginning to tense up all over again, worrying about it all.

God, he could feel himself shaking and it wasn't because of what the girl was doing to his wee boaby. No, that was more annoying than enjoyable now, even if he was as stiff as a fossilised jobby.

Move on to scenario two. Hmmm? Nah, this was the best, if only he could continue to concentrate.

Sometimes Norrie couldn't believe what he'd seen.

Sometimes in his memory what had happened was too strange to be credible, and he beat himself up for imagining things. But then it hit him full on, lu . . . cid as a nightmare. He wished it could have remained airy and cottonwoolly. Dream-like. Continued to have a kind of unreality about it. That would have been something. That notion he could try to hold onto; he wasn't really there; it must have been somebody else. Yep, yippee, sure, boss. Somebody else. Not me.

Norrie had sat down and cried for hours afterwards, and he wasn't the sort to cry. That night had been the worst night of his miserable old life, worse than the accident, and he did feel old right now, even though he was younger than Jacob by those two whole years and ought to have no trouble getting his pecker up. Things had had to change. Pearce wouldn't play along with the original plan. It was Pearce's fault. Okay, not the dog, but the dog was supposed to bring Pearce into the picture. Supposed to get him to help. Bastard. Oops. Already had a second chance. Fifty pence in the swear box, Jacob. All the time, Jacob was under the worst kind of pressure.

See, Norrie knew what Jacob had kept from his children. Jacob had a bad heart. He really didn't need this hassle.

Anyway, what had happened to Rog gave Jacob a way out. A way he could save May and the baby without having to leave the country. Or at least, that was the idea. Norrie had thought it would be obvious to the police that Wallace was the culprit. And with Wallace locked up for a good few years, May wouldn't be at risk. And who knows, he might have calmed down by the time he got out. Point was, that didn't matter. By that time, anything could have happened. Fucking stupid bastard pigs, though. Another fifty pee. No, two fifty pees. Completely failed to see what was glaringly obvious. No evidence that it was Wallace, they said. Which meant it was just as well Flash had embarked on the insurance policy option. That's where Pearce came in, again. If this worked out right, Pearce would take Wallace out of the picture for good. And if not, if Wallace killed Pearce, he'd be banged up for long enough, which is all Norrie ever wanted in the first place. That way, May would be safe and her kid would be born safely and, most importantly, most hugely importantly of all, right, Jacob would be safe. And with any luck, the prosecution would convict Wallace of shooting Rog, too. The only wrong outcome would be if the pair of them decided not to kill one another. But given their violent natures, that kind of conc . . . lusion was extremely unlikely.

Well, it was a good plan, then.

Ah, boy, it was hard seeing Rog lying there pumped full of bullets. Hard, hugely hard, tough. But Norrie had come through it. Just. Although he wasn't enjoying this here frolic one little bit. But he had to persevere as best he could. Didn't want Jacob to guess. Had to carry on as usual. Do what they did every Friday. Pretend everything was okay.

Norrie looked after Jacob. That's how their relationship worked. At first, Jacob hadn't been too keen. Felt it was wrong to be doing this. After Annie died, Jacob hadn't felt like meeting any other woman, but he did get urges now and then, as he'd admitted to Norrie.

Norrie told him what he did about those urges and suggested Jacob do the same. But Jacob didn't do anything. One day Norrie sorted him out with a pretty lass who could satisfy those urges. And Jacob had broken down in front of him. Told him he'd never thought he'd do it again, hadn't even known he could still get his boaby up. Well, there was little doubt about that, as Norrie could see in the rear-view mirror. Okay, that was scenario two. In fact, the scenarios were getting a bit mixed up.

They'd both been to the hospital this morning (true). Norrie thought it might be difficult being in the same room as Rog. Guilt, guilt, guilt. Guilt could be a heavy coat weighing on his shoulders if he let it. Could make him sweat badly and get short of breath. But he was fine. Just remembered how it was.

It had happened so quickly. Bam, in the face with the rolling pin, then bang, bang, the knees were done.

And he was out of there before anyone got to the kitchen.

No problem getting the gun, you know. Knew where to go, didn't he? The Mohican guy, tried to sell him that antique again until he remembered he'd tried it before.

'Ouch.' Norrie opened his fist. His palm was tacky with blood where he'd gouged a hole with his car keys.

'Sorry.'

'Not you.' He stroked the girl's hair with his uninjured hand. Her hair felt rough, not soft and smooth like you'd imagine it to feel. Of course, this one was a junkie. Lived rough since she left school. Three years ago, she'd said. Didn't have much opportunity to pamper herself. Probably just as well. She was heavy, despite her ill health and poor diet. You wouldn't think it, you know, a fat junkie. But Norrie had seen a few fat vegetarians, so anything was possible. Anyway, above her scabby knee, he saw her thigh, creamy white, thick. If she'd stayed on at school, become a secretary, she'd have become a fat secretary. 'You're doing just fine.' He tugged gently on her ear lobe as her lips slid up and down his shaft.

In the back seat Jacob's grunts were louder now. The problem with cars: if you couldn't get the seats down, there was no room for anything other than a good old toot on the horn. But that wasn't too much of a problem, really, when you thought about it. At their age, having your horn blown was about the only kind of sexual act that worked, so there was never any need to put the seats down.

Norrie wasn't going to feel guilty. No, shag that. What he'd done was he'd shown the family, and he'd shown Pearce too, that there was no doubt Wallace was a man capable of anything. All this wasn't just Jacob's del . . . uded whimsy. Or worse, paranoia.

Cause that's about how it was until Norrie cut the dog's throat.

'Oh, Norrie,' Norrie heard from the back seat. 'I'm gonna —'

'Boss.'

Jacob thrust out his hand and Norrie grasped it.

Norrie turned his head to face Jacob. Jacob opened his eyes, smiled. '— come,' he said, his hips bucking.

Norrie squeezed his hand. Jacob squeezed back. And Norrie felt himself reach the point of no return.

Love was always much more effective than sex.

Five minutes later, cleaned up, the girl said to Norrie: 'Who's the guy you pretend's in the back, the one you call Boss?'

Norrie gave her a slap and told her to mind her own fucking business. She disappeared like that, like that, see, like snapping fingers, snap, *pfff*, bye-bye. And, no, fuck the swear box, Jacob had gone.

Norrie tucked himself away, got up off his settee, went through to the kitchen to make a brew.

One of the side effects of the accident was that he could see things that weren't really there. He could imagine he was watching a TV programme, make up the images in his head, and his brain would respond just the way it would if he was watching the real thing. As far as he was concerned, it was the real thing. Like vivid dreaming, but while he was awake. Could be good fun, sometimes. He'd learned to control it for certain occasions, like these special afternoons with Jacob.

He lifted the gun off the mug hook. Smith & Wesson .38. Bang, bang, bang. Smokin'. Didn't know if he should still be holding on to it, but he needed it for protection. He put it back, watched it rock to and fro while the water boiled in the kettle.

Anyway, seeing things wasn't the worst leg . . . acy of the

accident. Some words he had to scrabble around for, sure, getting stuck in the middle, but the worst thing was that he kept thinking straight and he wasn't sure that other people did. You know, he'd work something out, the obvious thing to do, and it'd surprise him when other people came up with a different obvious thing. It was hard to explain. Maybe it was like the terminator in those sci-fi films. The obvious thing to do to people who were in your way was to shoot them. Well, that's how Norrie felt. And he had to keep quiet about it, cause he knew nobody else thought the same. Not everybody with a brain injury was stupid, you know.

THE TALL GUY bumped into Pearce – or maybe it was the other way round – and said, 'Hey, man. Be cool, huh?' He was about fifty. His eyes were wide, muscles around his mouth twitching. A wonder his nose wasn't twitching, the amount of aftershave he was wearing. The guy was wired. Still, no excuse for being rude.

The fucker grinned.

Another day, Pearce might have let it go. But after finding out that Hilda was dead he was none too rational and none too forgiving. After he'd finished speaking to Flash, he'd dashed straight out of the house before he did something he regretted, jogged down to the beach, and was now heading along the promenade at a furious walking pace. No destination in mind. Just had to keep moving or he'd explode.

This junkie had fucked Pearce's momentum and that fucking grin was – Jesus, Pearce couldn't even take a deep breath to calm himself down because of the reek of aftershave – totally out of order. Fuck, he could taste the pillock's aftershave on the roof of his mouth.

They'd collided at the point on the whitewashed wall surrounding the indoor funfair where a graffiti artist had scrawled: WALL, HUH, WHAT IS IT GOOD FOR?

Once before, Pearce had owned a dog. When he was a kid. It had been run over and he'd seen the result. Poor bastard, still alive, crouched under a car. It crawled towards him, whimpering, dragging a fleshy mess that used to be one of its legs.

Fucking funny, eh? Look at that junkie cunt laugh.

Life was one big fucking joke, eh? Everything you grew attached to ended up dying. Split your sides at that, junkie fuck.

Your sister ODs.

You kill her dealer.

You go to prison for ten years.

Is that funny? Is it? Laugh. That's right.

You're back on the outside for a few months and some fuckhead stabs your mother.

You get over that.

You get a dog.

Some fucker kills your dog.

Ha bloody ha.

Try to shed some of the rage and some arsehole junkie Happy Harry Fuckbastard bumps into you. And he's stinking of cheap aftershave. And he's laughing.

Pearce hated junkies but he particularly hated old junkies. They should fucking know better.

He slung a fist in the fucker's gut and that wiped the grin off him.

Happy Harry doubled over, one arm stretched out for balance.

Pearce wanted to hit the fucker again, but stopped himself. He was aware that people were watching now, but that wasn't the reason he held back. He didn't particularly care if he made a spectacle of himself. A young couple, hand in hand, were giving Pearce dirty looks. Especially the bloke. Showing off to his girlfriend. But, no, the reason Pearce didn't hit the junkie again was because he wasn't sure he'd be able to stop. Maybe just plant a quick forehead on his nose. But, no. It was really Wallace he wanted to nut and he shouldn't accept this sad bundle of counterfeit joyous shit as a substitute, even if it would make him feel infinitely better to kick the crap out of him.

Pearce composed himself as best he could and said, loudly, 'This man's a known paedophile. Shouldn't be allowed near a beach,' and, fuck, did those watching faces change. If Pearce wasn't so torn up inside, he might have found something to laugh at, finally. For a second or two, he thought they were going to lynch poor old Harry. But Harry righted himself, no trace of a smile now, and legged it, clutching his stomach. Maybe he *was* a paedo. Otherwise, wouldn't he have hung around a while to defend his honour? Mind you, that's the kind of allegation that's hard to shake off. The guy was probably right to scarper.

'Hey,' the girl said to Pearce, pointing. She had at least one ring on every finger. 'You can't just go around assaulting people.'

'Why not?' Pearce asked her. He was genuinely interested in her answer. At the moment, he couldn't think of a single good reason why he shouldn't 'assault' Wallace and he was hoping she might persuade him there was an alternative. Because he couldn't fucking see one, no matter how hard he looked.

And God knows, assault was a serious thing.

And God knows he didn't want to do any more time.

But she didn't reply, just turned up her studded nose and urged her boyfriend to get moving.

Interesting that she hadn't asked Pearce where he got his information. Call someone a paedophile, that's what they are. Nothing sticks like shit.

Pearce had hoped going outside for a walk might have calmed him down. And it might have done, were it not for this little incident. But he was just as keen to fuck Wallace up as he'd been when Flash gave him the news about Hilda. And that was pretty keen. But at least he hadn't smashed the TV or kicked the shit out of the mirror in the hall or broken all the crockery or snapped all his mum's CDs in half. Although he did have to go back home. There was something he had to pick up.

He dialled Baxter's number on the way. The old man answered quickly. 'Wallace's address,' Pearce said. 'I need it now.'

'PERFECT TIMING.'

Jacob was taking the baking tray out of the oven just as Flash and May arrived back with the dog. The mutt was getting spoiled, more exercise already than Louis got his whole short life. But May and Flash were torn-faced of late, and Jacob had thought some home-made scones – with jam and cream, of course – would cheer them up. When Flash was a bairn, he used to love helping his old dad bake. Rog was different. Didn't like getting his hands messy.

May said she wasn't hungry. 'Can I go outside in the garden with Cutey-pie?'

'As long as you stay where we can see you,' Jacob said.

She went to her room, came back with a handbag. Spoke to Pearce's dog and they went outside.

'Keep an eye on her, Flash, eh?' Jacob set the baking tray down on the worktop.

'Ow,' Flash said. 'I hate seeing you do that.'

Jacob grinned. Working in the bakery in the factory all those years had desensitized his fingertips. You get burnt repeatedly, eventually your skin toughens up. He never used oven gloves to take things out of the oven. He felt the heat, aye, but for a few seconds – which is all it took – the pain was perfectly tolerable.

Flash dragged a chair out from the table, sat down. Could use a shave. He looked like he was about to say something. Glanced at Jacob, but said nothing. Passed a hand through his hair and sighed.

'They'll need five minutes to cool down,' Jacob said.

Flash cleared his throat. 'Smell great.'

They did. Hot sweet smell that reminded Jacob of family weekends when the kids were still young enough to be innocent and Annie and him were still young enough not to care what age they were.

Jacob stuck his hands under the cold tap. Well, after a while the heat penetrated the toughened skin and his fingers did begin to burn. Took a long time, though. And, if he was honest, there was an element of showing off. Impressing Flash with his party piece, even if Flash had seen it a hundred times over the years. Like Granny Spence. The old woman could drink vinegar straight out of the bottle. And not just a sip but the whole bottle. He turned off the tap, shook the water off his hands, then grabbed a dish towel and dried his hands on it.

'Some mess,' Flash said.

Jacob did a quick scan. Flour everywhere. Bits of dough stuck to the worktop. Mixing bowl, rolling pin, butter wrapper, empty milk carton. He always made a bit of a mess. At the bakery, he had an assistant to clean up after him. Not so at home. 'You can clean up, if you like,' he said to Flash.

'I don't mind the mess,' Flash said. 'Just commenting on it. Not complaining.'

Jacob sat opposite his son, wondered if he should say anything or if he should wait till Flash was ready to bring up the subject, whatever it was. Christ, though, Jacob wasn't sure he could stand that girning face much longer. No, he definitely couldn't. 'What's on your mind?' he said.

Flash's neck shrank a couple of inches. Well, that's what it looked like. As if someone had clubbed him on the top of the head. 'What do you mean?' Took after his mother. That sinking into himself. Then, he was always so much more like her than Rog was. Even as a baby. Not just mannerisms. Character, too.

'Spit it out,' Jacob said. 'Can't be that hard.'

Flash got up, opened the fridge door, rummaged around until he found the carton of cream Jacob had bought earlier. 'Jam in here?' he asked.

'In the cupboard. I fancy the strawberry.'

Flash placed the cream next to the scones, walked over to the cupboard, turned before he opened the cupboard door. 'Something *is* on my mind.'

Jacob waited. And waited.

'Rog,' Flash said. Paused. Then: 'I was wondering . . .' He opened the cupboard door, plucked a jar of jam from the middle shelf. He went red in the face as he tried to open the lid. 'What if Pearce was right?' he said, puffing his cheeks out and trying again. 'What if it wasn't Wallace?'

'How can you ask that?' Jacob said. 'You've heard what Rog has to say.'

'Come on, Dad. He couldn't be sure. He *thinks* it was Wallace. Couldn't see him, though. It was dark. Rog was taken by surprise.'

'Course it was Wallace. Who else could it have been?'

'That's what I've been wondering.' Flash passed the jar to Jacob.

Jacob twisted the lid and it popped open. Amazing he'd managed to do that without allowing his hands to shake. Out of sight, his leg was trembling under the table. He handed the jam back to Flash. 'You worried that the wrong guy might get hurt?'

'If Pearce kills Wallace I'll be as happy as the next man. It's not that. It's just that if Wallace wasn't responsible for shooting Rog, then what happened to Rog is going to go unpunished.' Flash opened the cupboard above his head and removed a couple of side plates. He turned, one plate in each hand. 'Doesn't that worry you?'

Jacob had to be canny. That was a difficult question. He cowped over his fag packet, picked up one of the two fags that fell out. Offered it to Flash.

'I'm just about to eat, Dad.'

'Have a fag first. Let the scones cool a bit.'

'Given up.'

'Again?'

'For good. Anyway, that's your last.'

'There's two.'

'I don't want one.'

'Being fiky cause it's not a Silk Cut?'

'If I wanted to cadge a fag, I'd ask. I've given up.'

'Okay.' Jacob put the cigarette back in the packet. He added the other one. 'I'll not have one either.' He drummed his fingers on the table. Couldn't help wondering how Pearce was getting on. 'Screw it,' he said. 'Pass us a scone.'

BAXTER HAD ADVISED Pearce he should wait until Wallace got home. Wouldn't be too long, he'd said. It was now ten past four.

No chance.

Pearce had said, 'Give me his work address.'

'Too public.'

'Too public for what?'

'Look, you can't go there.'

'What's stopping me?'

'It's not a good idea, Mr Pearce.'

Ah, back to mister, now. Pearce let his voice get louder. 'If you don't tell me, I'll find out for myself.'

'He'll have colleagues there. At home, he's all alone. If you wait —'

'Only Wallace will get hurt.'

'How do you know? He has a gun.'

'He'll have got rid of it if he has any sense,' Pearce said. 'Give me his fucking work address.'

Baxter gave him Wallace's work address.

After Pearce hung up, he ransacked the kitchen cupboards for the knives he'd confiscated from the Baxter brothers. Found them under some of his mum's tea towels. Opted for Flash's, cause it was bigger and sharper.

He could have got a gun. He knew a guy who sold them. Knew how to get hold of him. But a gun was no good to Pearce. He'd fired one once. Missed by a mile.

He didn't think he'd miss with a knife.

EI8HT

WALLACE WORKED FOR an advertising agency. Never have thought he was an office boy, but that's how deceiving reputations can be. The office was tucked away off the road in a side street down in Leith.

Pearce had taken a taxi. Told the driver to drop him off at the bottom of the Walk, though. Didn't want the driver remembering the fare he'd had on the day of the murder.

Only when a blonde girl with glasses and a strawberry birthmark on her chin opened the office door did Pearce realise that he wasn't going to be able to kill Wallace here. Too many witnesses. Voices carried from inside. To the right, off the corridor. Not just one witness, but several. Baxter had been right. Pearce was going to have to wait until Wallace got home.

'Wallace around?' Pearce said.

'Sure. You want to come in?'

'Nah.'

She looked nonplussed. 'You don't want to come in? Since you're here? Or I can fetch him for you.'

'It's okay.'

'Well, if you're sure . . .'

'Yeah, I'm off now.'

'Well, I . . .'

'Thanks.'

'Can I ask who called?'

'I'll come back later.' And Pearce left, amazed at how pushy some people can be.

PEARCE HAD TWO options. He could take Wallace here, outside his office. Relatively secluded, in that it was off from the main road. But there were his colleagues to consider. Innocent bystanders were a real pain in the arse. The second option was to go to Wallace's house and wait for him there.

Pearce called Baxter. Asked what time Wallace finished work. Baxter told him to hang on, he'd ask May.

Couple of minutes later he came back on the line. 'It varies,' he said.

PEARCE FELT AS if somebody had punched a hole in his chest and left their hand inside. Not a good feeling. Last time he'd felt like this was at his mother's funeral. Took a couple of days before he'd felt the hand retreat. And even then, it left a big messy hole.

A cab appeared and the front door of number six opened shortly afterwards. After strapping her kid into a child seat, a woman got into the taxi. She looked flustered and tired.

Wallace lived next door, number eight, a main-door flat. Alone. The windows were boarded up at street level, which suggested that the lower floor was unoccupied. Either that, or Wallace really liked it dark. Or his windows had been broken and he hadn't got round to fixing them.

With the house now empty, there was nothing stopping Pearce from barging on in and making himself at home. Give Wallace a nice little surprise when he opened the front door. Tempting.

Of course, when he thought more about it, he realised there was one thing stopping him. He had no idea how to break in. At least, not with any subtlety. He could kick the door in, but somebody might see him. And anyway, if he caused any visible damage, Wallace would know there was someone waiting for him inside.

He'd just have to keep his distance for now. Sit on the wall opposite, pretend he was talking to somebody on his mobile so as not to look too suspicious. Then take Wallace as he was entering the house.

Yep. That smacked of military precision.

Ah.

Was that the best time to ambush him?

Maybe better to let him settle, relax a bit. Then Pearce could do what he did all those years ago with Priestley. Ring the bell and when the fucker answered, catch him in his slippers with a drink in his hand. A man in his slippers is an easy target.

Although Wallace was unlikely to be quite the pushover the drug dealer was.

This piece of shit had a rep. Well, a rep of some kind.

And maybe he wouldn't be all that relaxed. After all, Pearce had called at his office, and no doubt that visit had been commented on by the pushy blonde.

Well, fuck it. Pearce felt the knife inside his coat pocket. He wanted to get this over with. There was fuck all he could do about Wallace's state of preparedness. There was only so much you could do to stop justice running its course. No matter how prepared you were.

He knew there'd be people who'd condemn him for what he was about to do. People who'd no doubt sympathise if he told them what had happened to his nearest and dearest, and his resulting violent reactions. But because

Hilda was a dog, they'd think he was unjustified in doing the same thing.

Just a dog.

Well, fuck them. Hilda wasn't just a dog. Hilda was *his* dog.

'WALLACE IS THE best suspect we've got,' Jacob said to Flash for the umpteenth time.

'We need to get a confession out of him,' Flash said. 'That's the only way to be sure.' He scooped a dollop of cream onto a fourth scone.

'I doubt Pearce'll be up for that.'

'After what Wallace did to his dog?'

'Wallace is going to deny he touched it.'

'But Pearce is hardly likely to believe him, is he?' Flash took a bite of his scone, chewed for a while, then said, 'Look, I'm sure Pearce won't object to a few minutes of torture. Probably quite like the idea.'

'You'll need to call him, then. He might have other plans.'

The doorbell rang. Flash got to his feet.

'That'll be Norrie,' Jacob said. 'Door's open. He'll let himself in. You call Pearce.'

PEARCE WAS PRETENDING to have a conversation on his mobile when it rang. He pressed the green button and said, 'Speak.'

Flash Baxter. Again. He wanted a favour. He asked Pearce if he'd torture Wallace.

'You want me to do what?' Pearce said.

'Get a confession out of him.'

'You're off your fucking trolley.'

'Hang on a minute. Let me ex—'

Pearce hung up. He preferred talking to himself.

JACOB COULD TELL, even before Flash said, 'I think that was a no.'

'Never mind,' Jacob said. 'It was a long shot.'

Flash grabbed another scone.

Norrie took one too, said, 'Jacob, boss, these are good, great, brilliant.' Then he bit into it.

Flash said, 'That dog's got fleas.'

Jacob gave him a look.

'Swear to God.' Flash plopped his bitten, half-moon-shaped scone on the table, rolled back his sleeve and exposed the pale underside of his skinny arm.

'What are we looking at?' Norrie asked.

Flash was a skinny runt. Ate as many scones as he could stuff down his throat, yet stayed pencil-slim.

Flash said, 'Spots.'

'You see spots, Jacob?'

Jacob shrugged.

'Look.' Flash pointed to a small blemish on his wrist. 'There's one.' He moved his finger down a couple of milli-metres. Jacob couldn't see anything. He did, however, notice that there was dirt under Flash's fingernail. 'And there's another.'

'Oh, aye,' Jacob said.

'Hundreds of them.'

'Right enough. And they're flea bites, are they?'

Flash reeled back in his seat as if Jacob had bad breath. 'What else?'

Norrie said, 'So Pearce told you to fuck off' – he looked at Jacob, said 'Fifty pee, boss,' and continued – 'about what?'

Flash told him.

Norrie said, 'You were going to torture a con . . . fession out of him?'

Jacob said, 'Medieval, eh?'

Norrie nodded. 'Why do you need a confession, lads?'

'Flash thinks there may be some doubt as to who shot his brother.'

'You're joking, right? Wallace had motive and opportunity and a fucking – excuse my language, Jacob – gun.'

'Looks damning, right enough,' Jacob said.

'Next you'll be telling me somebody else cut Louis's throat.'

Flash said, 'I hadn't considered that.'

'You think there's only so far Wallace will go?' Norrie said. He was getting animated, waving his hands about, scattering crumbs. 'Slits dogs' throats, alright, but draws the line at kneecapping? Get your head in gear, Flash. This is Wallace we're talking about.'

'Pearce might kill him,' Flash said. 'Just wanted to be a hundred per cent sure.'

Norrie said, 'I'm a hundred per cent sure. How about you, boss?'

Jacob said, 'Hundred and ten.'

Norrie looked at Flash and shrugged. 'So what exactly is Pearce doing at the moment?'

Jacob said, 'Waiting for Wallace to get home.'

'And then he's going to do what?'

'He thinks Wallace killed his dog,' Jacob said. 'When Pearce's sister died from a heroin overdose, Pearce stabbed her dealer twenty-six times with a screwdriver. When Pearce's mother was knifed in a post office robbery, Pearce made sure the guy who did it took a dive from a high building with a bullet wound to his crotch.'

'But Wallace has a gun,' Norrie said.

Flash said, 'Maybe Pearce has a bulletproof vest.'

Jacob said, 'Pearce thinks Wallace will have chucked the gun.'

'Let's hope so,' Flash said.

'And how is the dog?' Norrie asked.

Flash picked up another scone, started to cut it in half.

Jacob shook his head.

Flash said, 'What? I can't have three?'

'Eat up. And answer Norrie.'

'May's fallen in love with it,' Flash said. 'She's soft like that. Anything with fur, her mental age takes a nosedive. Sinks about ten years.'

'The dog's safe with a six-year-old?'

Flash gave him a look as if they were in a minister's house and Norrie's pecker was poking out of his flies. Then he gave a little nod and said, 'Funny'. Jacob felt his eyes water, and thought it strange that of all things, this was making him feel sad. God, could be anything. He saw someone being hit on TV, and he knew it was only a soap opera, and he started blubbing. He had to be tough. All front. Didn't matter that behind the front was mush. No spine, that was Jacob's problem. He hadn't been prepared to take on Wallace. But Rog had. Jacob missed the big lug.

'All right if I have another scone?' Norrie asked.

'Catch up on Flash,' Jacob said, getting to his feet. 'And teach him how to count while you're at it. I'll be right back.'

PEARCE'S ARSE HAD gone numb sitting on the wall. He'd had to jump off it and stride up and down the pavement for a while, working the stiffness out of his legs. They were fine now, as was his arse, but he had a rhythm going that he didn't want to interrupt. Head lowered, scuffing the heels of his boots as he plodded along trying not to step on the cracks in the pavement. Got dull after a while so he added a variation: every second time he passed it, he kicked an empty milk carton.

Waiting was no fun. Pearce wanted to get this over with. *Come on, Wallace, you fucker.*

Traffic rumbled steadily past. He was getting good at picking out the different vehicle sounds without looking up. Motorbike. Transit van. Ah, this was a difficult one. Bus, maybe a lorry? He glanced up to see which it was. Right first time. Single-decker. And it was jammed full. A kid near the back, four or five, with a shaved head, gave him a smile.

The milk carton. Was that once or twice he'd passed it? If in doubt . . . he belted it. It hit the front bumper of a parked car and shot high into the air. Smacked down on the bonnet. He held his breath, expecting the car alarm to go off and draw attention to him.

It didn't.

He picked the carton off the bonnet, dropped it on the ground and nudged it with his foot. Everything returned to normal.

Although it wasn't normal.

Killing someone wasn't normal.

He should have smiled back at the kid on the bus. Too late now.

That milk carton. What was he thinking? Could have spoiled things there.

Concentrate on Wallace.

Put the carton in a rubbish bin.

Wallace. You couldn't help make the comparison, could you? Well, Pearce couldn't. When he thought of Wallace, he thought of William Wallace. Braveheart.

If Wallace looked like Mel Gibson, Pearce was in for an easy evening.

Couldn't see a bin.

No time anyway, because at that point he heard what he'd been listening out for. A car was approaching, slowing all the way. Pearce moved back from the kerb and watched the Range Rover pull into a space alongside number eight.

Guy got out. Medium build. Suit. Slip-on shoes. Glasses. Looked like he wouldn't harm a fly. Or a baby. Or a wife. Or a dog. Didn't look like Mel Gibson, though.

Already undoing his tie. Other hand in his pocket, scrabbling around. Took out his keys.

In a few minutes, Pearce would see how brave he was.

Let him get inside first. Didn't want to fight on the street. Somebody'd phone the police and ruin everything.

Wallace disappeared inside. Pearce could hear a faint click as the door closed.

Pearce watched the minute hand on his watch. He'd give Wallace two minutes exactly. Enough time for him to get into his returning-home routine, and not enough time to complete it.

Enough time for Pearce to get to the bin at the end of the street.

The journey there and back took one minute and thirty-seven seconds.

When it was at last time to make his move, Pearce discovered that the knife had caught in the lining of his pocket and the only way he could get it out was to tear the fabric. Lucky he'd decided to get it out now. Had he been planning on impressing Wallace with a quick draw, he'd have looked pretty damn stupid. He placed the knife in his left hand, flush against his palm, handle towards his elbow. Gripped the point of the blade with his fingertips. That way it stayed hidden from passers-by. And wouldn't snag on anything. Other than his fingers. But he was going to be careful. He wasn't planning on cutting himself.

He crossed the street. Strolled up to the door. Rang the bell.

He was calm. Slight speeding up of his heartbeat, but that was only to be expected. And, yes, a light sweat. But what the fuck, this was more dangerous than a fucking job interview, and people sweated at those.

Wallace answered the door, a piece of paper in his hand, probably a bill, judging by the torn brown envelope on the floor by his feet.

Pearce gauged the situation instantly, grabbed the frame of the door and shoved.

Cracked against Wallace's forehead. Knocked his glasses at an angle. Almost comical, but nobody was laughing.

Pearce pushed the door again.

Wallace managed to scamper out of the way before he was hit a second time. Just as well. Had to be a good joke to be funny twice.

Pearce stepped inside, switching the knife into his right hand.

One side of the tiny hall was lined with shoe racks. Three-deep. Wallace liked his footwear. A leafy plant with a solid rope-like stalk stood in the opposite corner, leaves bendy with thirst. Couple of plant pots on the window ledge contained flimsy herb-like things that had seen better days. There was a faint smell of drains.

Wallace stood at the far end of the hall, a flight of stairs to his right, a door to his left. A tiny cut had opened on his forehead above his right eye and a thin trickle of blood ran towards his eyebrow. 'Haven't a fucking clue who you are,' he said, straightening his glasses. 'But I'm going to cut your balls off and make you eat them.'

Pearce closed the door. 'You'll need a knife.'

'I'll use yours.'

Pearce couldn't help but admire this guy, despite what he'd done to Hilda. He had no weapon, but listen to him. A bit of a gamble, maybe, but Pearce hadn't expected Wallace to answer the door with a gun in his hand. Pearce was banking on Wallace having got rid of it, now it had been used on Rog Baxter. Anyway, even if Wallace was tooled up, he'd be second favourite – not that he was to know that, of course. Yet to hear him now, you'd think he was toting a machine gun.

Pearce checked Wallace's hands, just to make sure he wasn't.

The guy had unbelievable confidence. Made Pearce look bad. Made him feel less confident than normal. Couldn't let that happen. Had to redress the balance.

He flipped his knife over and took a step towards Wallace. Wallace leaned back. Not scared. Just protective. Pearce held out the knife, handle-first. 'Go on, then.'

Wallace said, 'Yeah, right.'

'Take it.'

Wallace looked at the knife. Looked at Pearce. Back at the knife.

Pearce sighed. 'Don't trust me?'

'Who the fuck *are* you?'

'The knife's yours. Take it.'

'Go fuck yourself.'

'Okay,' Pearce said. 'Step back.'

Wallace didn't move.

'Just take one step back. What harm can that do?'

Wallace didn't move for a few seconds. Then he took a step back.

Not taking his eyes off Wallace's, Pearce bent down and placed the knife on the floor. He stepped away from the knife until it was the same distance from both of them.

'You going to tell me who you are?' Wallace said.

'Skip the mind games, Wallace.'

Before Pearce had finished his sentence, Wallace dived for the knife.

Pearce's timing was slightly off. His boot connected with Wallace's shoulder instead of his chin and sent them both spinning. Wallace bounced off the near wall, knocking a couple of shoes onto the floor, and launched himself at the knife again.

This time, Pearce's fist caught him a blow on the jaw before his hand reached the handle. Wallace's head jerked back. A spot of blood popped from his lip almost immediately. He wiped it off with the back of his hand.

Pearce flung his fist at him again, but Wallace blocked the punch. Pearce kicked the knife away from Wallace's scrabbling hand and waited. Let his knuckles cool down. Felt like his pinkie might have gone.

The knife nestled against the skirting board.

Wallace stood up. 'I don't need a knife,' he said. 'I'll skin you with my bare hands.' He reached up, removed his glasses. Opened the door behind him and disappeared inside.

Pearce glanced at the knife. Did he have time to pick it up? Nah. Had to move now. Follow Wallace inside. Because by the time Pearce got the knife, Wallace would have legged it to wherever he kept his gun. Cause there was always the possibility, however slim, that he hadn't chucked the gun after kneecapping Rog. Fuck.

Move.

Why the fuck had Wallace turned his back on him, though? And left the door open? It was downright fucking arrogant.

This guy was something else.

Pearce launched himself through the doorway. He didn't see the punch coming. It knocked him off his feet. Jolted his spine when he landed hard on his arse. He felt dazed and instantly knew he was in trouble. He grabbed hold of the doorframe, tried to pull himself up.

Wallace stood a couple of feet in front of him. 'I don't like fighting in a cramped space,' he said. He placed his glasses on a sideboard. His lip was beginning to swell. And his eyebrow was red where the blood from his cut forehead had matted. 'Get up. Been a while since I've had any competition.' He stepped further back into his sitting room.

Pearce hauled himself to his feet. The punch had hit him on the cheek. Could have been worse. But it had been a solid blow. He hadn't taken too many that had floored him like that. The inside of his mouth was bleeding. At least, it tasted like blood.

Wallace was standing in front of his settee. Nice white leather job. Very seventies. Pile of blankets on the floor by its side. Behind it, the kitchen.

Wallace liked his shoes. Bet he liked his furniture, too.

Pearce sucked his cheek and launched a gob of red spittle at the settee. Watched the fucker's composure disintegrate.

Fuck, he was fast. Pearce managed to block the punch, but the kick caught him on the shin. Bastard had been aiming for his knee. And if the sole of his foot had landed the way he was hoping, Pearce's knee would have snapped. As it was, his shin was on fire.

Wallace said, 'Am I doing okay for a blind man?'

Pearce moved in with a punch and kick combo of his own. Wallace blocked the punch, sidestepped the kick. Pearce tried again. Same result. Third time lucky? Pearce didn't think so.

Neither did Wallace, apparently, for he said, 'I suggest you try something else.'

'Your turn,' Pearce said.

Wallace shrugged, nodded, and hit Pearce three times in the ribs.

Pearce landed on the floor again. Banged his shoulder against the sideboard. When he tried to get up, he felt a bolt of pain in his side. Wallace had busted something. Fuck. Pearce was wishing he'd kept the knife. He'd underestimated Wallace. Or overestimated himself. Came to the same thing. He had to buy himself some recovery time. 'Why did you do it, Wallace?'

'Tell me what I'm supposed to have done and I might be able to give you an answer.'

His refusal to tell Pearce was enraging. Fuck recovery time. His anger helped Pearce scramble to his feet. His leg wasn't quite so bad, but his side was going to be something of a hindrance. Every time he took a deep breath, it was like somebody was sticking a knife in him. Luckily, it was his left side. He'd still be able to swing with his right. And if it hurt, so fucking what?

'I have no idea who you are,' Wallace said. 'I answer my door and next thing I know you're slamming it in my face and thrusting a knife at me.'

'You know fucking why.'

'I've never seen you before.'

'Course you fucking have.'

'Well, pretend for a minute that I haven't.'

'Fuck you.'

'Okay. As you wish. Give me your best shot, hard man.'

Pearce steadied himself. If he didn't get it right this time, and Wallace retaliated with another few blows of his own with the same class as before, Pearce would be out of it. He needed to get in close. Wallace had had some kind of training, Pearce remembered. Cheating bastard.

Pearce feigned a punch with his right, then another, then brought his foot down as hard as he could on Wallace's toe. Wallace yelled. Pearce imagined Wallace's face was a football and headed it.

Wallace slammed back into the settee.

As he bounced forward again, Pearce thumped him in the nose. Yep. Pearce's pinkie was definitely broken now. He cradled his hand in his other one as Wallace moaned.

Fuck it. He couldn't punch again with that hand and his ribs were hurting too much to punch with the other. His forehead was smarting too. Maybe he could kick the bastard to death.

Whatever he was going to do, he needed to do it quickly and finish this before Wallace had the chance to recover. He leaned across, trying to keep his pinkie out of the way, and grabbed the back of Wallace's neck. Pearce brought his knee up at the same time as he yanked Wallace's head down. The two collided hard.

Wallace snorted, then made gasping sounds.

Pearce had gunk all over his jeans now.

Wallace's nose was a bloody mess, his mouth was hanging open, red threads dangling from his lower lip. He looked up at Pearce. His eyes weren't focusing. You could tell he didn't know what time of day it was.

Pearce tilted Wallace's head back and nutted him again.

Then Pearce turned round, walked out of the sitting room and into the hall, picked up the knife from where it had landed against the skirting board. Was he going to kill him? He wasn't sure yet. But if he didn't, Wallace would come back to haunt him. No way would a man like Wallace take this lying down. Course, Pearce could cut off his hands or something. Disable him. He returned to the sitting room and noticed that Wallace —

Straight into another punch he didn't see coming.

Fuck, that was a punch and a half.

No, it wasn't a punch. He'd collided with the butt of a gun.

Pearce crumpled to the floor. Tried to keep hold of the knife but his fingers wouldn't respond. Kind of funny. He'd taken a fuck of a crack on his forehead, but what he felt most was the throbbing of his pinkie. He tried to stay conscious but his brain wanted to shut down. And it was hard to resist.

Didn't help when the fucker hit him on the head again with the gun. Right on the crown this time.

One last attempt to get up. Nah. Fuck it. He wasn't going anywhere.

PITCH BLACK

WHEN PEARCE WOKE up he wished he hadn't. Pain in his head, his cheek, his side, the knuckle of his little finger. He didn't know which was worst. He tried not to focus, let them all blend together so that he just sort of hurt all over. Much better that way. For seconds at a time, it got so that he hardly noticed.

He tried to sit up, but couldn't. A belt or a rope was stretched across his chest, pinning him down. His wrists were clamped to whatever he was lying on. And when he tried to move his legs, straps across his shins and thighs prevented him.

He didn't like this. Bondage. Always thought of it as a picnic in hell.

To make matters worse, it was pitch black. He squeezed his eyes shut and opened them again. Speckles of random-coloured lights zipped around in the darkness.

Okay, so he couldn't move and he couldn't see. And he was in considerable pain in several parts of his anatomy. Couldn't get any worse, right? Well, there was one other thing. An unholy stink. From the moment he'd woken up he'd been vaguely aware of something vile crawling up his nose. Now the stench had lodged in his nostrils like a couple of small decomposing rodents.

Come to think of it, it could very well be rotting animals he was smelling. It was that kind of stink. And if it was, they'd been gutted and wrapped in their own intestines.

He tried breathing through his mouth, but the taste was as bad as the smell. He mixed it up, breathing alternately through his nose and his mouth and just about managed to stave off his gag reflex. Get through ten minutes and he knew he'd adjust.

Meanwhile, he should concentrate on more important matters. Like trying to figure out where he was.

Didn't have much in the way of clues. Couldn't see. Couldn't smell anything other than the rotting stench. But his ears were okay. Maybe he could get some sense of his whereabouts from the odd telltale noise. Although he wasn't entirely sure what kind of noise he'd expect to hear in this kind of situation: traffic, conversation, the sound of a TV in another room, a couple shagging. There was nothing. Not even the occasional gurgle of noisy plumbing.

Shouldn't have thought of plumbing. Big mistake. That damn smell hit him full force again. He swallowed.

Don't think. Listen.

But it was as quiet as it was dark. The kind of silence and darkness you rarely encounter. The kind that seemed artificial.

The only noise was his breathing. It was fast. Too fast. He could hear his heart beating in his temples. He felt himself spinning, even though he was lying down. At least, he thought he was lying down. He breathed through his nose again – Jesus – willing himself to calm down. Panicking wasn't going to do any good. The fuck was wrong with him?

He needed to calm right the fuck down.

Come on. Get a grip.

Work this out.

How long had he been here? Could be night. Could be day. No way to tell.

If it was still daytime, surely a room with windows would have let in some light, even with the curtains drawn. Unless the windows were boarded up. He raised his head as far as he could, ignoring the increased throbbing at the top of his skull, and let his eyes drift from side to side on the off chance that somehow he'd missed a trickle of light. Under a door, maybe. But he couldn't move his head high enough to see that far down. Or, at least, he didn't think so. In the blackness, it was impossible to tell.

Could be Wallace's basement.

Or maybe it was night.

Or maybe Wallace had slung him in his Range Rover and taken him to an abandoned warehouse.

Unlikely, though. Wallace wouldn't have risked the neighbours seeing him bundling an unconscious man into his car.

Maybe, maybe, maybe. Fuck maybe. Maybe wouldn't get him out of here.

And he had to get out of here. The stink was going to make him puke. And if he puked, he risked drowning in it, cause he wasn't even sure which way was up.

Where the fuck was he? Weigh up the odds and the silence would suggest that he was in a windowless room. The basement, then, like he'd thought. Not so good. But at least he'd worked that out.

All alone in Wallace's basement, strapped to something. A bed. Well, there seemed to be a mattress underneath him. It was yielding, at any rate.

Could be worse. Wallace could have killed him. At least this way Pearce was alive. Although he didn't know for how long. There was no way of guessing what Wallace's plans were. Maybe he was intending leaving him here to starve to death. Ah, well, no, that wouldn't work. Pearce would get hungry all right, but he'd die of thirst, wouldn't he? Maybe that was the plan. Pretty shit way to go, dying of thirst.

Jesus, he'd done it again. That was very fucking clever, putting that thought in his head. Somebody should shut him off. Now all he could think of was how much he wanted a drink of water. Pictured the chilled bottle of Highland Spring in his fridge. Ran his tongue over his lips. His mouth had dried completely. Felt like he was licking a cement path.

And the more he thought about it the more it seemed possible that a drink would get rid of the fucking appalling smell. No, it wasn't logical. Having a drink wouldn't mask the smell, he knew that.

Fuck, it was dark.

Wallace wasn't really going to kill him, was he? Not like this, for fuck's sake. This was pathetic.

Pearce cried out, 'Fuck you.' His voice walloped off something and bounced back at him. He guessed he was in a small room. So yelling hadn't been a complete waste of his anger. He just wished he could use it to break out of his restraints. Could he? He gave it his best shot. Straining his muscles till they burned. Getting nowhere. Making a fucking racket. And maybe all he'd succeeded in doing was alerting Wallace to the fact that his captive was awake. Which wasn't what Pearce wanted. Not yet. Not until he'd figured out what was going on, where he was, and discovered the source of that fucking smell.

But who was he kidding? He knew what was in store for him.

This was his future. Right here. He'd piss himself after a while. Eventually he'd shite himself. And he'd have to lie in his own mess and breathe in a fresh stink until he couldn't breathe any more.

That's what Wallace wanted. What a cunt.

'Who's there?' a voice called out of the darkness, causing Pearce's stomach to shoot into his throat.

A YOUNG-SOUNDING male voice and it wasn't Wallace's. Yet until just now, Pearce had been sure he was alone. He'd listened and heard nothing. Apart from his breathing. Maybe it wasn't his breathing he'd heard. Maybe it was this other guy's.

It occurred to Pearce that maybe he'd died. Fuck, yeah, this could be Hell. And if it was, Pearce was going to be pissed off. Nothing worse than dying and finding out that you were fucked cause you couldn't play a tambourine or didn't know all the words to the Lord's Prayer.

The voice spoke again: 'Who is it?'

This guy was clearly in the same room, maybe fifteen feet away. Why had he remained silent for so long? Pearce had been awake for ages before the fucker had opened his mouth. Oh, yeah. He wouldn't have known that Pearce was awake.

'Who are *you*?' Pearce asked.

'A lost soul.'

For fuck's sake. 'How long you been here?' Pearce said.

'Longer than I care to remember.'

Pearce tried again. 'What's your name?'

'You wouldn't believe me.'

'Try me.' Pearce wondered again if he was dead. Was that so impossible? He'd been struck on the head with a heavy object. He'd woken up in complete darkness. Unable to move. In a place that stank like the arsehole of Hell. Now he was hearing voices.

The voice said, 'Jesus.'

Holy fuck. Pearce didn't believe in life after death, but this was fucking freaky. There was no raging fire and no screaming tormented souls. So it wasn't Hell. Maybe he'd gone to Heaven. Although it wasn't the sort of Heaven you got told about at Sunday School. But, fuck it, you didn't get thirsty when you were dead. And he was parched. 'Don't suppose you can untie me, Jesus?' he asked.

Laughter.

'That'll be a no, then,' Pearce said. 'Do you know Wallace?'

'In a sense,' Jesus said. 'In as much as knowledge is —'

'Do you know where we are?'

'In a world of chaos.'

God give him strength. 'I meant more specifically,' Pearce said. 'Is this his basement we're in?'

'It's a place for poor souls. Are you real?'

Was he real? This guy was a fuckwit. 'Yeah,' Pearce said. 'How about you?'

'I don't know,' Jesus said. 'My head's so screwed up I think I'm probably talking to myself.'

'You're not,' Pearce said. 'You're talking to Pearce. Have you been here long?'

'Forever.'

'Where are we?'

'Wallace's.'

'Basement?'

'Yeah.'

Confirmation at last. 'You strapped to a bed, too?'

'I'm in my cage.' Jesus rattled something that could have been bars and started yelling.

Pearce had been right first time. This was definitely Hell.

No, Hell was when the light came on seconds later. A blinding pain flashed behind Pearce's eyes and Jesus rattled his bars harder.

Wallace said, 'You shut up, you dirty fuck, or I'll do it today.' Instant silence. Then Wallace loomed over Pearce and said, 'Why he persists, God alone knows. The window's bricked up and soundproofed. He knows nobody's going to hear him.'

Pearce said, 'Fuck you.'

Wallace asked, 'You want to make a noise, too?' and yanked Pearce's little finger back until he screamed. 'You don't like that? I'll do it again, then,' Wallace said. 'How's your head, by the way?'

THE CAT & DOG Home was down the road a bit, heading east, just beyond Seafield Road's glut of car showrooms. Pearce didn't know of any buses that went down that way. The 12, maybe? There had to be something, but he'd walk. It was a hot dry day and the exercise would do him good.

He'd been to the pet shop in Portobello High Street earlier. Stood a while observing the gerbils. A white male and a fawn female in separate cages. Little bastards could jump. Quick hop-two-three and they were on top of their water bottles. Inquisitive, too. Came up to the bars, started pounding on them with their front paws. Kangaroo boxing to match their kangaroo legs.

In an adjacent cage, a solitary brown-and-white hamster sat cleaning itself in the corner next to its food bowl. It had rocked back on its haunches, its balls thrust forward. Christ, they were massive. Make a couple of nice pillows for a lady hamster. Wee guy was getting a bit carried away now, with all his cleaning. His little pink member was sticking out through his fur. And he was licking away at it with something approaching a frenzy. He stopped just as a tiny parcel of thick white cum appeared. It stuck there, like toothpaste freshly squeezed from a tiny toothpaste tube. Without any preamble, he grabbed the lump of jizz in his teeth and chucked it across the cage.

Pearce was tempted to take this wee guy home. Maybe invite Jodie Foster for dinner. She could walk past the hamster's cage while he chucked jizz at her even if he couldn't tell her he could smell her cunt. But Pearce wasn't here for the rodents. No, he was here for a dog bowl, a collar and an extendable lead.

No sooner said than done.

He left the shop with a spring in his step. Kind of like the gerbils, but not so pronounced. In any case, his water bottle was at home in the fridge.

There was a lot less spring in his step by the time he reached the Cat & Dog Home. But, Christ, much as he hated to admit it to himself, he hadn't been this excited in years. Fortunately, he had a little more self-control than your average hamster.

Pearce woke with a start, mouth as dry as if he'd been sucking a breeze-block, head pounding like it'd been used to wedge a lift door open all night. Last thing he remembered was some guy who thought he was Jesus rattling the bars of his cage, then Wallace making an appearance, bending Pearce's finger back until his whole hand throbbed with pain. Then he'd asked about Pearce's head, how was it after the pistol-whipping. He'd told Wallace to fuck off. Wallace had punched Pearce in the face and head until he lost consciousness.

Jesus in a cage. Did Pearce dream that?

Light seeped through Pearce's eyelids, bright as fuck. As if someone was directing a torch into his eyes from just a few inches away. When he raised his eyelids, it felt like somebody'd stabbed his eyeballs with their fingers. His eyelids lowered. He hadn't been able to make out a fucking thing. He'd try again in a second.

'Too bright for you?' Wallace's voice.

Pearce was at Wallace's mercy once again and from what he'd already experienced, Wallace wasn't big on mercy. This situation was in danger of becoming tedious if Wallace kept up the torture treatment for any length of time. But Wallace was in a perfect position to do what he liked and Pearce couldn't do a fucking thing about it. Or could he?

He'd seen a movie once where a quadriplegic had bitten his assailant to death. Possible re-enactment? Get Wallace close enough, then sink his teeth into his neck. How would he do that? Tell him he wanted to give him a kiss? Problem with that scenario was that having bitten Wallace to death, Pearce would still be strapped to the fucking bed.

Did he want to gamble his life on being able to free himself? Cause he didn't expect anyone else from the outside had access to this home-made prison. And Jesus couldn't help if he was in a cage. Maybe biting Wallace to death wasn't a good idea.

Anyway, Pearce's face hurt too much to consider biting anybody.

Problem was, he had no idea what Wallace was planning. He thought about asking. Maybe Wallace would enjoy telling him. Sadists were like that. On the other hand, Wallace might consider it more sadistic to let Pearce's imagination play out the possibilities.

Which Pearce did. They were all bad.

He opened his eyes again, blinked several times. Eventually he managed to focus. In the light, the stink somehow didn't seem so bad. First thing he noticed was that Wallace had his glasses on. Maybe he was trying to hide some of his facial bruising. Ordinarily the glasses would have made him look young and harmless. But in this instance they made him look psychotic. As Pearce's eyes started to focus properly he saw that Wallace's lips were swollen, like he'd had an allergic reaction to collagen. His nose was a gaudy combination of dark-red and purple. The frames of his glasses only partly hid the big black shadows under his eyes.

Good.

Pearce reckoned his own face must look even worse. Certainly felt it.

Anyway, Wallace held a water bottle in his right hand. Oh, yeah. It was 'are you thirsty' time? Psychological torture now. The fucker was going to enjoy standing there drinking in front of Pearce. Although the water was yellowy brown. Not water at all. Looked more like dark piss, or liquid shit.

Bastard. Pearce would have preferred getting beaten up

again. He'd never been this thirsty. He tried to forget about his thirst and seize the opportunity to take in what he could of the rest of the room. Not being able to lift his head more than a couple of inches (and that hurt), he couldn't see too much. Low ceiling with a totally inappropriate four-tier chandelier dangling from it. Hard to judge the distance precisely, but it looked as if he might bang his head on it if he sat up (if he was able to). Last thing he wanted was to bang his head. The thought alone made his cranium sting and a knot of pain formed in the middle of his head. The wall behind Wallace was made of egg cartons. At least, that's what they looked like. Box on box, all the way to the ceiling. Somebody'd eaten a lot of eggs. And in front of the egg cartons, a cage. Jesus's cage. Tall enough for a man to sit upright in and long enough for him to lie down in. Jesus fuck. There he was. A filthy kid, no more than eighteen, with a bumfluff beard, wearing nothing but a piece of cloth round his waist.

Pearce squinted at Wallace and said, 'Who's he?'

'Didn't he tell you?'

'Told me some shite.'

'Who does he look like?'

'Looks like who he says he is.'

'Then that's who he is.'

'You're a pair of fucking lunatics. Who is he?'

'Jesus.'

Biting Wallace to death suddenly seemed like a good idea again. 'Give us a clue.'

Wallace ignored him, said, 'You don't look too good.'

'You should see the other guy, shithead.' Pearce braced himself.

No blow came, though. Wallace said, 'I thought you might be thirsty. Brought you a drink.' He held the water bottle aloft.

This was worse than getting another kicking. Thirsty wasn't

the fucking word. Pearce realised he was licking his lips and stopped.

Wallace had noticed, though. He was smiling. 'I'm going to undo the strap from around your chest,' he said, after a second. 'You'll be able to sit up. Have a nice long drink.'

'My hands, too.'

'Do I look like a prick?' Wallace said. 'What's your name?'

Fuck, this was playing dirty. Payback for the Jesus thing. 'You know.'

'Would I ask if I knew?'

'I'll tell you if you tell me who you've got caged.'

'Cards in your wallet claim you're called Pearce. Gordon Pearce.'

Pearce hated mind games. He always lost. 'You've been in my pockets?'

'How could I resist?'

'Can I have some?' Jesus said.

Wallace said, 'I didn't invite you to speak.'

Pearce said, 'He's welcome to it.'

'You don't like tea, Pearce?'

Tea? Was it? Could be. But why go to the trouble of making tea? What was wrong with water? Tea. The thought made Pearce salivate, just when he'd thought he'd never salivate again. And he didn't even like tea.

Wallace untied the strap and said, 'Sit up.'

Pearce managed to raise his head a foot or so. Enough not to choke when he swallowed.

Wallace placed one hand behind his head to support him. Put the water bottle in front of his mouth.

Pearce sniffed, trying to determine what kind of liquid was in there. See if Wallace really was playing games with him. Hoping against hope that, fuck, it was tea.

Couldn't tell. Too much of the other stink was still getting through.

Wallace said, 'You've got five seconds. You don't want it, I'll give it to Jesus.'

Jesus. Right. 'Why's he here?'

'Mmm. Jesus was a bad boy.'

'What did he do?'

'You don't want the tea?'

'I'll have a sip. What did he do?'

'Tell Pearce, Jesus.'

Jesus started to sob. 'I'm sorry.'

'I know you are. But tell Pearce what you did.'

Jesus's sobbing grew louder. 'I can't.'

'Oh, but you can. You must.'

Through thick sobs, Jesus forced out the words: 'I slept with May.'

Ah, the boyfriend. The fool who'd got May pregnant. Jesus was dead meat, then. Pearce said to Wallace, 'What are you going to do to him?'

Wallace sighed. 'What am I going to do to you, Jesus?'

Jesus broke down, wailed.

'Not much of a hard man, now.' Wallace strode over to his cage and kicked it. Jesus shut up. Well, he carried on keening, but quietly. 'Used to fancy himself, this one, Pearce,' Wallace continued. 'Take on all-comers, as long as he had a knife and his opponent didn't. But when May told me he wrote poetry, I knew what kind of a wimp he was. Fucking poetry.' He kicked the cage again and Jesus stopped keening. 'Answer the question,' Wallace said. 'Tell Pearce what I'm going to do to you.'

After a second, Jesus said, 'When the time comes, Wallace is going to crucify me.'

Fuck's sake. 'When's the time?' Pearce said.

'Very soon,' Wallace told him. 'Got all the wood. Got my

tools. Bringing it all down later, going to do a spot of carpentry, make a beautiful cross and place it on that wall there so you can get a grandstand view from your bench.'

So Pearce was lying on a bench, not a bed. Pearce was momentarily pleased Wallace had let something slip, until he realised that it didn't make the tiniest bit of difference.

'Now,' Wallace said, 'you want this tea or am I going to have to pour it all down that stinking, bearded fuck's throat?'

Fuck it. Pearce's thirst was too great. He had to try it. He put his lips round the nozzle and sucked. Just allowed a trickle into his mouth. Lukewarm. Waited a second until his tastebuds registered. Wondering if he'd just taken a mouthful of shit. But, no, it was tea. Possibly the vilest tea Pearce had ever tasted, but it was recognisably tea. He took another sip. Then another. If Wallace had pissed in it, Pearce didn't want to know.

'Good boy,' Wallace said, pulling the nozzle away. 'You don't want too much of that, believe me.' He strapped Pearce back up, pulling the restraints tight. 'Now, Jesus has to have the rest. Today, he will see a slice of Heaven.'

Pearce had no idea what Wallace was talking about. But he didn't like the sound of it. The only slice he wanted was a slice of cake. Fuck, he was starving. That's what having a couple of sips of tea did for you. He didn't want to ask, but couldn't stop himself. 'Any chance of something to eat?' he said.

'Do I look like a cook?' Wallace walked towards the cage and Pearce had to lift his head to keep him in sight.

'You eat enough fucking eggs,' Pearce said.

Wallace looked at the floor-to-ceiling egg cartons. 'That's soundproofing, you fucking fool.'

'I might be a fucking fool,' Pearce said, 'but at least I'm not a prick whose wife would rather fuck that poor bastard over there than have me within twenty feet of her.'

'You want to go first?' Wallace said. 'Just keep it up.'

Pearce didn't want to think about what Wallace meant. But he knew, anyway. Wallace was going to crucify the pair of them. How was Pearce going to get out of this sorry situation?

He heard Jesus sucking manically at the bottle of tea. 'What's Jesus's real name?' he asked Wallace.

The sucking sound stopped. Pearce tilted his head and saw Wallace had pulled the bottle away. 'What's your real name?' Wallace asked Jesus.

'Jesus,' Jesus said.

'Good boy,' Wallace said and put the bottle back to Jesus's lips. Just as if he was feeding a baby.

Jesus polished off the dregs and Pearce let his head fall back onto the mattress. He was fucked.

But there were some things he had to find out first. He heard the sound of footsteps receding, looked up and Wallace was nearly at the door. Pearce didn't want to talk to the bastard, but he didn't have any choice if he wanted information. Engaging the fucker in conversation couldn't hurt. They might bond. People did that, bonded with their kidnappers. That's how some of them survived. Happened all the time. Yeah, bond with the fucker. Fucking right. But, supposing you wanted to, how did you do that? Ask him a question. Which is what Pearce was going to do anyway. *So get on with it, pillock, before it's too late.*

Pearce said, 'Why did you kill my dog?'

'What're you talking about?' Wallace said, his hand on the light switch. 'Everybody's obsessed with dead dogs. I like dogs, Pearce. I've never harmed a dog in my life. Why does everybody think I killed their dogs? Don't I have better things to do with my time?'

'You killed him. You killed Hilda.'

'Your dog's called Hilda?'

'What if he is?'

'And it's a "he"?'

'Fuck you,' Pearce said. Yeah, fuck the rapport. Fuck bonding. There was only so much crap a man could take. 'I suppose you don't know who shot up your brother-in-law, either?'

'You think I'd waste my time on poor old Rog? I wouldn't shite on him if he was a giant fly and it was his birthday.'

Weird that Wallace didn't want to take responsibility. 'So who shot him, if it wasn't you?' Pearce asked.

'What makes you think I'd know? I'm the last person anyone talks to.' Wallace's hand carved an arc through the air at his side. 'Family gossip goes sweeping right past me.'

So Wallace was denying everything. That was good. Pearce would ask about the Baxters' dog, expect a denial, then he'd know Wallace was serious and the Baxter family wasn't as mad as Pearce had first thought. 'What about Louis?'

'What *about* Louis?'

'You know. May's dog.'

'Course I know who the dog is.'

'Was. Past tense. The dog's dead.'

'She'll be upset.'

'You saying you weren't responsible?'

'You're obsessed with the idea of me killing dogs. Give it a rest.'

The fucker was enjoying this. 'Well, you planning on . . . you know . . .' Pearce had a question but somehow between his head and his mouth it had gone missing. Odd, and a bit worrying. Try as he might, he couldn't remember what he was going to say. Shit, no. Couldn't remember what the fuck he'd been talking about. Something was a bit wrong with his head. Taken a blow too many, maybe. That was the last thing he needed. A brain that didn't fucking work.

Wallace said, 'I ought to smack the fuck out of you, Pearce,' turned out the lights and spoke into the darkness. 'I'll be back in a few minutes.'

JESUS WAS SHAKING.

Wallace had come back, as promised, and he was now stuck behind Pearce's bench. Jesus couldn't see what he was doing, but he could hear the scrape of saw on wood and knew he'd soon hear the thunk of nails slamming home. Wallace was prepared. No hammer for him. Jesus had seen him carry in a nail gun. Black and yellow stripes. A giant wasp-like thing with a fuck-off sting in its tail. Jesus thought he'd long since accepted his fate, but he felt a brief burning sensation in his penis and a trickle of warm liquid on his thigh and realised he hadn't. A fucking nail gun.

The sawing must have been going on for about fifteen minutes now, which seemed a ridiculously long time. But Jesus wasn't sure about that. Might have been just a couple of minutes or half an hour. It was hard to tell.

The noise stopped and Wallace's head popped over Pearce's bench. Jesus was about to get another lecture, he knew, cause Wallace moved his dust mask to the side. Wallace liked the sound of his own voice, alright, and he liked nothing better than to dish out advice to Jesus. He'd been doing it for a while now. And Jesus was something of a captive audience.

'We're all needy, Jesus,' Wallace said. 'That right, Pearce? We all need approbation. It's what being human is all about. I mean, think about this.' He paused before continuing: 'A man with a big cock who is never told by a lady that he has a big cock, might as well have a small cock. You see what I mean?'

Jesus wondered what he was on about. Now seemed an

inappropriate time for bullshit philosophy and it wasn't Jesus's fault Wallace had a small knob. It was, however, Jesus's fault he'd slept with May. He was very sorry about that and he'd told Wallace countless times. He'd tell him again, but his tongue didn't seem to be working.

'You see what I mean, Pearce?'

Pearce said, 'I wouldn't know.'

'Is that modesty, I wonder?' Wallace smiled at Jesus. 'Sad thing is, I like you, Jesus. Even if you do write poetry and you got my wife pregnant. What I'm about to do here, well, it really jiggles my heartstrings. Shouldn't be long now. Fuck, yes. As my mother used to say, "This is going to hurt me more than it's going to hurt you." I know, you're thinking what a crock of shit, eh? But it's true. I'd much rather I didn't have to witness it.' He paused. 'Ah, fuck, no. I'm lying. I'm going to enjoy it. Hey, want to know a secret?'

Jesus said nothing.

'Well? Do you? I'll tell you anyway. You know that tea you drank?'

Tea. The tea. Disgusting but refreshing. It seemed like a lifetime ago that Jesus had drunk the tea. Yeah, then soon after he'd finished it, Wallace had disappeared. Then Wallace returned with a pile of wood and a saw and that fucking waspy nail gun and put on his dust mask and started making a cross. Yeah, that was it. A nice cup of tea.

'I put something special in it,' Wallace said, and returned to his sawing. No, he didn't. He'd finished that. The first nail slammed home and Jesus winced, imagining it entering his palm.

If he wasn't already feeling sick, that would have done it. But, yeah, already he wasn't feeling too good. Not surprising since he'd been here in this hole for long enough to have lost count of the days, getting fed when Wallace felt like it, watered when Wallace felt like it. Jesus felt queasy, in fact. What had Wallace just said? He'd put something in the tea. Jesus looked over at Pearce, at the chandelier above the bench he was strapped to. The chandelier was moving around like a shiny sea creature. The walls behind it looked grainy. He could see all these little lines and they wiggled. *Motion threads.* Huh?

The thunking sound was like a big ball that Jesus was sure he'd be able to pick up if only his hands were free. But they were free. What was he thinking?

Thunk. Again. Sloop. Right into his hand. Like that.

His hand felt different. Couldn't pinpoint the difference, though. No, yeah, no. Yeah, it felt like he was wearing gloves. He dropped the ball he'd imagined himself catching and it fell silently to the floor.

Quiet once more. Wallace stood up again and wiped his forehead. His glasses looked like they were hovering in front of his face. He bent down again and there was another thunk.

How many nails was good ole jack-in-the-box Wallace putting in this thing?

Jesus heard someone praying and mumbled along with him. No idea what the words were, but he followed the lilt of the sing-song incantation. He wondered if the other guy was praying to God or to himself. Cause he was Jesus now. That was funny but he wasn't laughing cause it wasn't funny after all. Wallace said so.

The realisation sledgehammered into him: he was going to be crucified. He knew it already, but he hadn't accepted it. Somebody was going to rescue him. Wallace would take pity on him and decide not to go ahead.

He felt like giggling. Yet that wasn't how he felt, you know, emotionally. He felt like crying. Did that make any sense? He was wired up all wrong, somehow. Poisoned, right?

Somebody had killed May's dog. Somebody had killed Pearce's dog. Was it Jesus? Did he do it?

Approaching the Cat & Dog Home. One rogue cloud in the sky towards Fife. The heat made the back of his neck prickle. The sound of a dozen dogs barking.

There were cats here too. He couldn't stand cats.

Snap back. NOW.

Wallace was making the cross. That was it, all the wood and the toolbox and the nail gun and all that. Jesus had the vague feeling he'd worked this all out already. Yesterday, maybe. But the cross wasn't here yesterday. Was it? Had it been here that long? But that wasn't very long, was it?

It all sounded familiar, though.

Where was he?

Didn't really matter, did it?

Tiny fluffy toys lined the veins on the back of his hand. They did. He could see them. Not through his skin but in his head. How his hand got in his head he'd no idea but there it was.

Bang. He heard the sound before it happened. Just a split second. Didn't know how he could tell, but he did. Funny thing.

Wallace's head appeared again. No sign of the dust mask. And he'd taken off his glasses too, revealing his ridiculously blue eyes. They were BLUE, like that, capital letters, and they hurt to look at. 'How you feeling now, Jesus?'

Jesus tried to speak, but he couldn't summon up the energy. Tried again, and managed to say, 'Odd.' Sounded like somebody else's voice. Went out his nose and slithered round his chin and entered his left ear.

Pearce said, 'What did you give him?'

Wallace said, 'Heard of psilocybin?'

Pearce said, 'Magic mushrooms?'

'Very good, Pearce. Didn't think you were the type. I brewed up a nice potent batch of mushroom tea, there. And Big J drank it all down like a thirsty baby. I could only give you a couple of sips, Pearce. You should thank me for that. Your world starting to change yet, Jesus?'

Jesus tried to nod but couldn't move his head so he nodded inside his skull and knew that Wallace had seen him do it.

'You had them before?'

Jesus didn't do drugs. Never had. Apart from dope now and then and Es occasionally, but they didn't count. He'd never done acid and nobody did mushrooms these days. Not cause it was illegal, but it just wasn't cool any more to do the hippy flip. He said, 'Nah.'

'For a moderate brew, you'd have around fifty,' Wallace said to Pearce. 'You want to really trip, take a hundred, but I wouldn't recommend it. Certainly not for a first-timer.'

Jesus wasn't entirely sure about the numbers. More or less. Didn't add up. What was a quantity? *I'll have one potato.* Somebody else was in his head. Saw the bastard flying for cover out of the corner of his inner eye. Flying? Yeah, wasn't a person at all. Black and yellow stripes. Had a doubly-bulby face like a wasp.

Somewhere Jesus grabbed hold of the thought that he hadn't been poisoned. Not really. Or had he? Shit.

'You're gone, son, aren't you? Not surprising. Couple of hundred would be enough to make most people psychotic.'

Coupla hundred. *Whee.* Jesus was floating. This wasn't so bad. Bars on the cage were lighter than air. Floated with him. He must have risen a couple of feet, then jolted back down again.

Wallace said, 'I gave you five hundred of the little fuckers, just to make sure.'

A bad thing. Jesus was aware of that. Large quantity like

that. Shit. Lots of drugs were bad, bad. Very bad. Bad. Yeah. One, two, three, four, five hundred. Bad, bad, bad, bad, *bad*. But there wasn't anything he could do. *Is there a problem, officer?* He couldn't tell. Oops. There wasn't anything funny, but he was laughing. Damn, fuck, he had to stop. Five hundred. A lotta mushrooms. Somebody had mentioned that. Was that the other guy in his head? Mr Wasp. *Not a bad price, five hundred, for a bag of mushrooms that size.*

Closed his eyes and saw that he could dream anything he wanted. There she was. May. Thrashing about underneath him. Telling him to do it harder.

Gonna be sick, Lord Jesus. Gonna throw up my spleen, Lord Jesus. Gonna throw up my heart, Lord Jesus.

Scraping.

Wallace had done speaking. Gone back to work.

His heartbeat. Lot of rhythm in this room.

Melody from Jesus.

Nice little number.

Jesus is not my fucking name.

It wasn't but he couldn't remember his name, so Jesus would have to do.

Building a church. A cross. Put it on top. Kill Jesus. Kill me. The dog was dead. Wanted to ask. Where? Why? Who?

The wasp in his head said, 'Don't you think banana is an odd-shaped word?'

Jesus closed his eyes. Mistake.

Heart started jigging around like a pneumatic drill. Bounced off his ribcage. Not too bad, though. His ribcage was made of rubber.

Words flew around in his head like swallows. He reached out, grabbed one. Knew what it was to be crazy. Said hello to the bird and the bird said, 'I'm Robin.'

And it turned cold. Ice cold. Winter cold. He let the bird go, but his whole body was freezing. He shivered. Would have asked Wallace to turn up the temperature, but his tongue was vibrating, and, oh, maybe Wallace wouldn't have obliged anyway. Jesus's ears went numb with the cold and he couldn't hear anything. Wallace was banging away and Pearce was saying something to him and then Jesus couldn't hear anything and his tongue was vibrating and he couldn't take the batteries out.

Felt like a year later when his tongue stopped quivering. Now it was tingling down the left side. Like he'd bitten it and it was healing.

Many months ago. Or a couple of seconds. Couldn't tell.

Ice-cold. He couldn't bite his tongue cause it'd break off. Maybe his ears had fallen off.

Did he have a fever? A cold fever? Could you have one of those?

'Concentrate,' the wasp said. 'You can't just stop breathing like that. If you do, you'll die.'

He'd stopped breathing? He was going to die?

Like fucking shite, he was.

He had to get a grip. Had to stop his thoughts moving so quickly. Kept running ahead of him. Needed brakes. Needed thought brakes. Did they exist? Nope. Patent them and make a fortune. What a fucking brilliant idea! Hang on. What the hell was that anyway? *Exist*. A made-up word if ever he'd heard one. But weren't all words made up?

Shit. He was losing it fast. Wrenched his mind back. Damn thing was like an elastic band. Could play tunes on it. Bing, boing. Would you listen to that!

A memory. Grab it, catch it, hold onto it. Nope. Couldn't find one.

Whoa. Wallace was hovering next to the cage, about a foot in the air. Neat trick. Jesus held his breath. Wallace bent down, unlocked the cage door.

Shhh.

Jesus felt the silence in his belly. Caused a strange reaction. Made him thirsty again. Thought of the tea. Thought of the mushrooms in his stomach. Mushrooms like bullets slamming into his gut, one after the other with no respite. Felt sick, sick, sick. Man, that was a dirty word.

A memory. A fucking memory. Just one. Bunch of kids. Most of them thirteen, fourteen years old. Tooled-up. Jesus in the thick of the scrum, even though he wasn't called Jesus. A hammer in his hand. Useless. Couldn't swing it. Bodies too densely packed. Wearing T-shirts. The New Bar Ox team wearing these tartan jumpers they got specially from a shop in Glasgow. Jesus saying, 'Bastards. Ya fucking bastards.' No affiliation, see. Jesus in the middle taking on everybody. Somebody holding his hand. His mum. Saying, 'You're all bashed up again.' Jesus grinning, saying, 'Aye, I showed them.'

Another memory.

The girl said, 'He'll kill you if he finds out.'

'You . . .' the boy said, '. . . you are worth dying for.'

'You smarmy lying toe rag.'

The boy grinned. 'I'll take my chances.'

'Is this love?'

'Aye.'

'Oh, that's nice. Keep doing that. You got rubbers?'

'I won't come, eh? Trust me. Just. Come on. That's it.'

And there in front of him now was May's dog, he supposed. No, it wasn't. Well, it might have been but it turned into that fucking wasp and said, 'You fucked the girl. You got her pregnant. You fucking deserve everything you get, you fucking idiot.'

'Are you paying attention?'

The voice. What was his name? Brain like soup. Brain like glue. Brain like sizzling bacon. *Szzzzzz.* Like a buzzing wasp. *Szzzzzz.* Dropped in water.

Floobadoob.

I'm Popeye, the sailor man.

Jings, crivens, help ma boab.

'Are you paying attention?'

Nuuuuuuh. Okay.

Sweep to the right. Nothing. Sweep to the left.

Cross, yep. Jesus, yep. That other guy.

God. No, devil. Whoa, yeah. The skin on Wallace's face was shifting up and down like it needed stitching onto the bone underneath.

Pain under Jesus's arms as Wallace lifted him onto something unyielding and tied him down. Tried to resist but his muscles were weak and his body unresponsive.

Sudden clarity. Adrenaline rush. Cancelled the effect of the mushrooms long enough to think: 'Leave me alone, Wallace, you big fucking donkey fucker,' but he couldn't say it. Power of speech denied.

Caught Pearce's eyes. Man looked sad. Gonna be okay, big man. Gonna be okay.

Sound of a man crying. Oh, Pearce, you big poof. But Pearce wasn't crying. It was himself. He was the poof.

Not in pain. Not yet. *In mournful acceptance of your doom?* Thank you, Mr Wasp. That about hit the nail on the head.

Jesus knew what was going on. Just had to fight through the fireworks in his head, focus.

Memory.

No, nothing.

'You with us, Jesus?'

The guy – Wallace, that was it – face in his face.

And there he was, tied down on two planks of wood. He knew that. Felt okay so far. What was all the fuss about?

The end. This was. For him.

B-bam, b-bam, b-bam. Heartbeat, or was he on a train?

B-bam, b-bam, b-bam.

Heartbeat. No train.

More crying. Louder. Wailing, that was the word. And then, 'No.'

Then: whack.

Took a moment to register and then the pain shot through him. Came from the centre of his palm. An intense ache like a giant wasp had stung him. And the heat. His hand was burning.

Whack.

Gonna lose it, gonna fade out. The drugs wouldn't let him.

Whack.

And it *huuuuuurt* like a fucking bitch.

He yelled.

Wallace said, 'That's one hand.'

Whack.

No time to get used to it. The other hand, yeah, done. He looked up, saw the nailhead embedded in his palm and spewed.

'You dirty fucker. Got some of that over my shoes.'

Jesus roared, as much in rage as in pain.

'You got nothing else to say?'

Whack.

Gasps, 'Ah, ah, ah,' didn't help but they were necessary.

Whack.

When pain gets this bad it's almost funny.

Whack, whack.

He screamed.

'Oh, shut up, Jesus. That's the easy part. Now here's where we might have a bit of a struggle. Got to reload the fucker with some big fuck-off nails. Look at the size of these beauties.'

Jesus didn't want to look, but somehow his head turned to face Wallace.

The nail gun was black and yellow, wasp black, wasp

yellow. Wallace was fiddling with the nail magazine, which slotted at an angle underneath. Jesus caught a glimpse of one of the nails and it was fucking massive. He yelled again at the pain in his hands. Struggled, but stopped cause it hurt too much. And then he yelled at the thought of the pain he was yet to experience.

Wallace said, 'Nail's got to be big enough to get through both your feet.'

Jesus yelled again, didn't stop, his mouth wide open, so that when Wallace finished loading the gun he had to shout to be heard. 'Take a deep breath, you dirty little prick,' Wallace said. '*This* is gonna hurt.'

PEARCE TRIED NOT to watch, tried not to listen. Seeing Jesus being murdered destroyed any credibility Wallace's claim that he hadn't killed Hilda might otherwise have had. Of course Wallace had killed Hilda. He was clearly a sadistic fucker. And, anyway, if Wallace hadn't killed him, then who the fuck had?

Pearce had to back off. He was getting emotional about this. He had to detach himself, had to keep thinking straight for as long as he could. Detach. Come on.

Jesus meant nothing to him. Okay, Pearce didn't particularly like to see another human being crucified, but that was ultimately between Wallace and the law. But Wallace had made Pearce sip some drugged tea and Pearce hated drugs. And Wallace had killed Pearce's dog. And that's the main reason Pearce was raging.

But this too. He couldn't deny it. He didn't want to hear it. There it was again. Another nail thumping into Jesus's foot. And that fucking infernal screaming.

De-fucking-tach.

Cat & Dog Home.

'Kind of breed is it?'

'A terrier. Dandie Dinmont. You don't see too many of them about.'

'Why's that?'

'Dunno. They're expensive.'

'Yeah?'

'Show dogs.'

'You'd have thought people would have been scrabbling to get their hands on a little runt like this.'

'He'd have gone in a flash if it wasn't for the . . . leg.'

Yeah, so he had a missing leg. So fucking what? 'He can get around okay, though? He's not in pain?'

'The leg was amputated a long time ago. An old war wound. He arrived here like that. Seems to be perfectly at home on just the three.'

Pearce reached down, stroked the little bastard's head. The dog was predominantly white with brown patches running down his spine. Had a barrel-shaped chest like a dachshund. A feisty-looking little fucker.

'I think he likes you,' the girl said.

'You think so?'

There was something going on now. Wallace was heaving the cross off the floor, lifting it onto his shoulder, dragging it towards the wall. Jesus was yelling louder.

'You'll be okay for a while yet,' Wallace shouted. 'I did my homework. I'm going to lean the cross against the wall. That way your chest won't cave in, and you won't die of suffocation. Cause that would be a shame. I want this to be as prolonged as possible.'

He swung the cross back against the wall and it hit with a dull thwack against the egg cartons, which must have absorbed some of the jarring at least. Wallace straightened it up, looked at Pearce. 'I'll leave the light on,' he said, 'so you can watch. I'm away to fetch someone else who needs to see this. I'm sure you could use a bit of company, right? She might even fuck you if you ask nicely.'

The door squeaked open. Slammed shut. Then Pearce heard the scrape of a bolt being drawn on the other side.

Wallace was off to fetch May. Made sense now. Pearce's bench, the mattress, the restraints, they were here already. Pearce hadn't stopped to think about that. Wallace had been right, Pearce *was* a fucking fool. It had all been planned. But not for Pearce. If Pearce hadn't shown up, May would have been lying here instead. Maybe the one thing he'd done was buy her some time.

Pearce looked towards Jesus and wished Wallace had turned the lights off. The only good thing was that maybe the adrenaline caused by Jesus's fear and pain might be stopping his head from being scrambled by the mushrooms. But that was probably wishful thinking. He looked pretty fucking scrambled.

CRASH

'YOU THINK I need this?' May said, eyeing her brother. She could totally do without all this crap right now. She fell out with her best friend, Joanne, last week. Fat tart always thought she was in the right. Reckoned May should own up, tell the truth. No chance of that, not now, especially after what Flash had just told her. So this would have been crap, anyway, with everything that had happened. But it was May's bad week on top of everything else and she just wanted to lie down with a hot-water bottle over her belly and cry. Well, she was part of the way there. She was lying down. But she couldn't use a hot-water bottle for obvious reasons. And she wasn't going to cry in front of her brother. Anyway, it was all a genuine mistake.

Flash sat down on the bed next to her, sliding the knife back in its leather sheath. Cutey-pie growled at him and when May told Cutey-pie to behave he laid his head back down across her lap.

'Better to be safe than sorry,' Flash said.

'What's going on, Flash? You all think I'm stupid or something but I know there's some serious shit going down. Tell me the truth.'

Flash said, 'Just a precaution. First there was Louis, then Rog.' He shrugged. 'So who knows?'

'What do you mean, Louis?'

Flash couldn't hold her gaze. He said, 'Oh, well. You know.'

'I don't fucking know. Stop trying to cover up and tell me. What's going on? Why wouldn't you let me see Louis? It wasn't cause he'd been run over, was it? And you know who shot Rog, don't you?'

Flash told her the truth.

She wasn't surprised. Wallace was a mean bastard, even

though he'd always been pretty good to her. He'd got a bit frightening sometimes, right enough. Told her she couldn't leave him cause he didn't know what he'd do. Well, that was part of the reason she hadn't left him, wasn't it? She didn't leave him. He threw her out. But it wasn't a shock to find out he was still angry. She'd been entirely to blame. She knew that. 'You *think* it was Wallace?' she said.

'Well, everything points to him.'

'I fucking *know* it was him.' She took the knife from Flash, slipped it in her handbag. 'Why haven't you done anything?'

'What do you mean?'

'You know what I mean. Why haven't you gone round to Wallace's and killed the fucker?'

'Well, he has a gun, doesn't he?'

May said, 'He never used to. When we were together he was more than happy with just his fists.'

Flash told her about Rog's visit to Wallace's. Explained exactly what Rog had intended. That it hadn't gone according to plan.

'Rog was going to do that for me?'

Flash nodded. After a minute he said, 'You okay?'

'Leave me alone,' she said.

'I'm sorry about all this, May. It'll be fine.'

'I said, leave me the fuck alone.' She paused. 'Please, Flash.'

Flash got off the bed, shuffled towards the door, shoulders slumped.

May really wished Brian hadn't done a runner. The very night she told him Wallace had found out about them shagging, that was him. Offski. Didn't even say goodbye. Claimed he was a hard man, but when push came to shove, he had no bottle at all. She could have used the cowardly poetry-writing bastard's help right now. That'd teach her to let a Jambo shag her. You couldn't trust Hearts fans.

She opened her handbag, took out the knife Flash had just given her. Removed the sheath. The thin blade gleamed. The black plastic handle had a price sticker attached. Scottish Dirk, it said. Stainless-steel blade. £39.99. Fuck, that was a lot of money. And Flash had gone out and bought it specially for her. That was nice. She had a pair of brothers to die for, really. It had been a while since she'd had a present even if he'd no doubt bought it from a souvenir shop on the Royal Mile. She made a stabbing motion into the space in front of her. Felt good.

'Hello, Dirk,' she said to the knife.

Brian. Shit. She missed him, especially now that Joanne wasnae speaking to her. She'd love to have shown him Dirk. She opened her handbag and took out the poem he had written for her when she told him she was pregnant. She'd found out that he'd written lots of poems, but this was the first one he'd ever shown anyone. She read it for the hundredth time. He may have done a runner like a total wanker once Wallace found out about them, but he was good at spelling and could make things rhyme. And it was sweet that he was so sure she was going to have a boy. She wondered where Brian had pissed off to. She was mad at him, of course, but she couldn't help hoping he was happy, wherever he was. The fucker.

WALLACE RAN HIS fingers over his chest, then peeled back the corner of the final wax strip. Quickly. *Aaaah*.

Inevitably, most people would view him as a head case. Wallace knew that and he didn't care. In fact, he liked it. Lots of hard cases were also head cases. Always helped your rep if people thought you were a psycho. He wore glasses, and hard men didn't wear glasses, so he had to work twice as hard to maintain his rep. Anyway, rep aside, he had reasons for what he did. Reasons which lay outside the grasp of the ordinary intellect. Okay, that was unfair. The ordinary intellect may well grasp the reasons, but it took a special sort of person to understand and an even more special one to sympathise. He'd thought May had understood. He thought they'd clicked. Soulmates. All that shite.

Anyway, it was all May's fault, all this. Shagging that wee fuck he'd just crucified. And then getting fucking pregnant with that arsehole's kid. For Christ's sake. Wallace didn't want to dwell on that, cause it just made him angry and he didn't want to get so angry he killed her before she'd had a chance to see what he'd done to her boyfriend. And Pearce. What was Wallace going to do with him? Not much choice but to dispose of him as well. Couldn't very well let him go now. So that was May's fault too, in a roundabout way. He hoped the bitch was proud of herself.

Wallace dumped the wax strip in the bin, confident he was looking good. Well, sure, he looked beaten-up, Pearce having got in a couple of lucky blows, but the bruising made him more attractive, if anything. He wondered if he should call May. Just to find out where she was. But he knew she'd be at home. That crazy-arsed family of hers wouldn't let her out of their sight.

Wallace started to button up his shirt. Stopped. Stared at the wedge-shaped white patch on his stomach. So big it had to be a birthmark. But it wasn't. That, folks, was a scar. And mighty proud he was of it, too. Proving a point to a friend of his.

Held a scalding-hot steam iron there for thirty seconds without flinching.

Only downside, these days hair didn't grow there, so he had to wax the surrounding area and he always did his chest too. Right. Splash on some aftershave and then off to get May.

JACOB RETURNED FROM the toilet. When he stepped over the kitchen threshold, he saw a vivid image of Rog screaming in agony. No, it wasn't so much a picture. It had been dark that night when he heard the scream and his visual memory had thrown him the outline of a blurred figure, but that's not how it was. He didn't so much see Rog as hear him. The scream. Deafening. Stunning. Even from the bedroom. But maybe it was the sound of the gunshots. Whatever it was, it was painfully loud. The combination. He could hear it now. Or was that the sound of blood rushing into his eardrums? Jacob felt as if someone was scrubbing his eardrums with a tiny cheese grater. He felt faint.

He must have looked it too, cause Norrie asked him, 'You okay, boss?'

Cold sweat down his back now. Clammy forehead. The stale smell of scones from yesterday suddenly turning sickly. Felt like he'd eaten a dozen and he was faced with the prospect of having to eat the same again. Or what? Eh? What was he asking himself – what was – the sound of each shot blocking out Rog's screams, there, and again, there, and he was waiting to hear the next one to cut off that demonic yelling once and for all, a final shot to the head, and there it came and Rog was silent. Aye, that's how Jacob found him.

Switched on the kitchen light and there was his son, unconscious in a pool of blood. But Jacob could still hear him, that yell gushing out of him.

Of course, that final shot never came.

'Stop it!' Jacob said. 'Stop.'

But Rog wasn't listening. Or maybe he couldn't hear because of the noise he was making.

'Stop.'

No, this wasn't the way it had happened. Rog had lost consciousness. The pain. His screaming. Not much pain. *Liar.* Okay. Lots of pain. Enough to – not for long, then. He'd lost consciousness. He'd lost consciousness. He'd lost. He'd. Lost. Lost. Oh, God.

Norrie said, 'You having a turn, Jake?'

'I'm not,' Jacob said, fighting to get the words out of his mouth, 'having a turn.' Whatever a turn was. 'I'm fine.' Said that easier. And Rog's cries were fainter. 'Just need to sit down a minute.' Aye. Couldn't hear Rog screaming now. He'd gone. Passed out.

Rog was in hospital, for goodness' sake. Safe in hospital. And Flash had just gone to visit him. His boys were safe.

Where was May?

Jacob sat down heavily at the table.

Norrie stared at Jacob and said, 'You sure you're okay?'

Jacob breathed through his nose. Once. Twice. 'Don't worry about me.' Heart attack. Couldn't help but think it. The older you got, the more susceptible you were, and the more aware you were of your susceptibility. And he'd already had a scare. But there was no pain. Not in his chest. Not in his arm. He was okay. He wasn't going to die today.

He was able to observe Norrie frowning, then saying, 'You're really pale. You been this bad before?'

Jacob raised his voice, or at least he tried to, but it didn't come out as loud as he'd intended. 'Stop worrying about me.' A bit of a whisper, in fact. He reached for his fags.

'What did you say?'

Jacob tried to speak again, but the effort was too much. He shook his head instead, lit a cigarette.

'You should lie down. Shouldn't be smoking.'

'I'm alright.' And, come to think of it, he was pretty near okay. A quick draw on his tab and he was even better. Couldn't hear a thing from Rog. Just a roaring in the ears. No gunshots. No screaming. The light-headedness was disappearing. 'Don't need to lie down. Probably just too hot. It's warm in here.' The roaring was fading to a pleasant murmur. He'd just needed a smoke, probably.

Norrie got to his feet and opened the window. 'I'll run a cloth under the cold tap.'

Norrie's mobile phone started to ring. A trendy tune. Norrie liked to keep up with the kids, but it was all lost on Jacob. Norrie's hand dipped into his pocket and he took out his mobile and said, 'Hi, May.'

May? Where was she? She shouldn't be out of their sight. Jacob asked Norrie.

'In her room,' Norrie said.

Jacob couldn't believe kids these days. May was phoning Norrie from her room. Couldn't be bothered to walk to the kitchen.

Norrie said, 'Okay,' and hung up. He looked at Jacob. 'She found out about Wallace. Flash told her.'

That's why Flash had left in such a hurry. Something hard lodged in Jacob's throat. He didn't want May to get involved in this. On the other hand, she might be safer now she knew she was in danger. 'I suppose it was bound to happen,' Jacob said. 'How did she take it?'

'She says Wallace is a dead man.'

They sat in silence for a minute. Then Norrie said, 'So, no word from Pearce?'

Jacob shook his head. 'Flash called him. His phone's off. Tried him at home. Answering machine. Something's happened. Flash called Wallace's work to speak to him. He wasn't there. Tried him at home and he picked up.'

Repeating this really forced it home: one way or another, Wallace had taken Pearce out.

'You think Wallace killed him?' Norrie asked.

'From what I know of Wallace,' Jacob said, 'that's a distinct possibility.'

A SLIGHT BREEZE tickled the back of Wallace's neck as he stood at the Baxters' front door wondering whether he should knock or go right ahead and kick the door in. Did it matter? Bunch of fuckwits inside wouldn't know what had hit them either way.

He didn't know for sure who was inside, but he was prepared for May, her dad (Wallace's father-in-fucking-law), maybe that old retarded arsehole, Norrie, he hung around with, and probably Flash.

Wallace took a deep breath, feeling the gun press against his spine.

Okay, he'd made a decision. He'd knock. Break the door down and maybe a nosey neighbour would call the police. And whoever was inside didn't know he was here. He'd parked in a space a few doors down, which could be to his advantage.

He had a good mind to kick the door in anyway, though. They didn't have a doorbell. And he hated fuckers who didn't have doorbells. How hard was it to get one fitted? Fuck them. He took the gun out of his belt, rapped on the door with the butt.

An age later, the old man's friend, Norrie, answered the door and Wallace grinned at him as he showed him the gun.

Wallace said, 'Step back, Grandad.'

The old guy did as he was told and Wallace followed him inside. Wallace closed the door. Heard a voice from the kitchen saying, 'Who is it?' Sounded like Jacob.

Wallace whispered, 'Tell him it's a pair of Jehovah's Witnesses. And that they're just going.'

Norrie passed on the message.

Wallace continued to whisper, 'Where's May?'

Norrie whispered back, 'In the kitchen.'

Wallace stared at him. 'If you're lying to me, I'll put a hole in your head.' Wallace reached out and pressed the muzzle of the gun between the old guy's eyebrows. 'Right there. Can you feel it?'

Sweat rolled down Norrie's cheek. He whispered, 'She's in her bedroom.'

God, he was pathetic. Wallace had a good mind to blow the old git away right now. Fucking halfwit. Apparently him and Jacob had been pissing about at the factory, seeing who could load a stack of dough-filled trays the highest, and Norrie had slipped on the wet floor, and cracked his head off a giant mixer. Knocked himself out. Never been the same since. Anyway, Wallace would have got rid of him, but whilst there remained the possibility of getting May out of the house without anyone knowing, he wanted to try. It would make life so much easier. He wasn't sure what he was going to do with her old man yet. And he was sure May wouldn't come without a struggle. But this was all part of the fun.

'Who's in the kitchen?' he asked Norrie.

'Just Jacob.'

'Where's Flash?'

'Hospital.' Norrie gave him his version of the evil eye. Wallace almost burst out laughing. Norrie continued, 'Visiting Rog.'

Wallace calmed himself. 'Tell Jacob you're going to the toilet.'

Norrie shouted down the hall. Baxter shouted something in reply.

'Lead the way, Grandad.'

'What if I refuse?'

'I'll kill you.'

'Aren't you going to kill me anyway?'

'Only if you keep asking questions.'

The old nutter shut up and Wallace shepherded him to May's old room.

'What now?' Norrie said as they stood outside the closed door.

'Open it.'

Norrie turned the handle, stopped part way. 'I can't just walk in,' he said. 'She might be indecent.'

Jesus. 'Knock on the door. Tell her you want to speak to her.'

Norrie knocked, said, 'May, can I speak to you?'

Wallace whispered, 'Tell her it's about Wallace.'

'It's about Wallace.'

They heard May scrabbling about inside her room and moments later the door opened.

And that's about when things started going wrong.

PROPPED THE *SLANTED* cross against the *so maybe if he wriggled* egg-carton wall *it'd topple over.* Wasn't *but* wriggling *it would* though *hurt.* Bloodstained palms, bloodstained *he'd not looped* feet *rope round his wrists.*

Eyes *staring down at Pearce anyway* closed.

Pain throbbing through him *drugs throbbing through him* like drugs *like pain.*

Pearce's *side to side* face darting around *where was his crown of thorns? – missed a trick there, cunt.*

Jesus was alive *struggling to get out* inside himself, tearing a *like something out of a horror movie* hole.

He couldn't take any *so he shouted* more of the pain *and Pearce said, 'Shhh. Just try to relax.'*

Jesus raised his *and again* eyelids, but they slammed down. And again. Deafening noise, *relax?* no pain.

Wallace hovered *but he'd gone* beside him. 'Knock yourself out.' *Fuck you.*

Jesus wrapped his tongue *and squeezed* round Wallace's neck.

Wallace shook *'Is it fun in there? Inside your brain?'* his head.

Thought he'd bite his tongue off. Trying to speak. Trying to shout. Not *bastard bastard bastard* knowing who he was speaking to or shouting at or why or what the point was or *fucking fuck* whether he had a handle on his mind cause it wasn't him in there and he couldn't keep his *couldn't keep them shut* eyes open cause there was too *and me* much *on a* information *cross.*

His eyes opened. He knew he was dying.

'No, you're fucking not,' Pearce said. 'Listen to me, Jesus. Just fucking concentrate.'

WHEN MAY OPENED the door, Wallace was taken by surprise. He hadn't seen her in a while, and when he had, it had been from a distance. In the flesh, he was reminded of all that had passed between them. No matter what anyone said about her being young, and people said plenty, none more so than her fucking family, well, she was old enough to decide to get married and that's what she'd done. They'd been happy together. They got on, you know. He did his thing and she did hers and they didn't argue much and when they did it was over pretty quickly. And the sex was great. Wallace couldn't understand why she'd slept with that bearded fuck. He'd asked her about it plenty, but she didn't seem to know either. When he pressed her, she said it was because he had an enormous cock, but Wallace knew she was just winding him up.

Looking at her now, her hair ruffled, face all tired and sad, he wasn't sure he could go through with it, after all. She was his family. He'd wanted to have kids with her. Was he unreasonable to want them to be his own? Fucking bitch. Fucking did this to him, made him behave like this. He hated her but he was fucking close to begging her to come home with him. Figure that out, cause he couldn't.

'You bastard,' she said. 'The fuck you do that to Rog for?'

'I never,' Wallace said, then realised he didn't need to be standing here defending himself.

'And Louis. How in the fuck could you do that to my dog, Wallace?'

'I didn't touch your fucking dog.'

'You fucking did.'

'I fucking didn't.'

'Well, somebody did.'

'Well, it fucking wasn't me.'

'Well, who the fuck was it, then?'

'I don't fucking know.'

'Rog was shot and you have a fucking gun.'

'That's fucking right, you fucking bitch, and I'll fucking use it if you don't shut your fucking gob.'

'You fucking wouldn't dare.'

'Keep your fucking voice down.'

'Fuck off. You think everybody's scared of you. Well, I'm not. I've seen you naked.'

'The fuck's that got to do with anything?'

Wallace shoved the door hard. A dog with a missing leg hopped past him at a fair old pace and crawled under a telephone table in the hallway.

'The fuck was that?'

'Cutey-pie.'

'I've seen you naked, too, May.'

'Well, bully for you.'

'Shut the fuck up.'

'Why, what you gonnae do if I don't?'

Wallace looked at her, hard. She looked back at him, equally hard. He turned to face Norrie and shot him in the chest. Norrie gasped and slumped to the ground. He sat there, bemused, back resting against a utility cupboard door in the hallway.

'Look what you made me do,' Wallace said to May. 'You happy now?'

'I didn't make you do anything,' May said. She started to cry, thank fuck. Took a lot to get through to her sometimes.

The kitchen door burst open. Jacob stood there, armed with a rolling pin and a bread knife. He dropped his weapons when he saw Norrie. Or rather, saw what was in Norrie's hand.

Wallace reeled back as Norrie, bleeding like a burst carton of cranberry juice, pointed a Smith & Wesson .38 at him. Same fucking gun Wallace had in his hand, courtesy of brother-in-law, Rog. Norrie pulled the trigger.

Wallace's left arm snapped backwards. There was no pain. Getting shot wasn't so bad. He swivelled, kicked the gun out of Norrie's hand. It leaped out of the old twat's grasp and bounced off his forehead, landing with a clatter on the floor. Wallace stamped on it, dragged it towards him. He was tempted to fire a couple of slugs into Norrie's brain, but he didn't want to make any more noise. For the sake of the neighbours. There'd been enough noise as it was.

The pain arrived. Oh, yeah, it fucking arrived all right. It was like part of his arm had been torn off. And when he looked down, that's pretty much what had happened. The bullet had got the fleshy part of his forearm, just below the elbow and had torn through the flesh, taking a chunk of it along for the ride, exposing it all the way to the bone. At least, that's what that dark-red-covered white lump probably was. Lucky it wasn't the elbow itself, or that would have hurt like a bastard. And although he was bleeding a fair bit, the blood was oozing rather than spurting, which had to be a good sign. His arm was numbing up, but he wasn't going to die.

May was screaming. A horrible noise. Much worse than the gunshots. And where the neighbours might mistake gunshots for fireworks, a scream was a scream. Wallace was surprised May didn't choke on the gun smoke. It was pretty thick. Getting to his eyes. Stinging.

He pointed his gun at her. 'Shut up,' he said. 'I fucking mean it, May.' And he must have looked like he did, cause she shut up straightaway.

He turned to Jacob. Sized him up. Pathetic old fool with a strapped-up nose, bile-yellow half-moon bruises under his eyes. Wallace almost felt sorry for him. Wallace flexed his fingers. The arm was numb but his fingers were still capable of movement, although he wasn't sure how long that would last. He needed to fix it, keep the bleeding to a minimum. He bent over and picked up Norrie's gun. 'Snap,' he said, showing Jacob both guns. 'A .38, just like mine.'

Jacob looked confused.

'That the weapon used to kneecap Rog?' Wallace laughed. 'It is, isn't it?'

Jacob looked at the pair of guns, staring at them as if they might speak to him, tell him Wallace was lying.

'Why would I lie?' Wallace said. 'If it was me, I'd take the credit for it.'

'But that's not possible,' Jacob said, getting to the truth at last. 'Norrie . . . he's my friend.'

'Some friend,' Wallace said. 'Wise up.'

'No,' Jacob said. 'No.'

'Suit yourself.'

Didn't matter to Wallace if Jacob believed him or not. Anyway, he had to concentrate on what he should do now with this pair of old gits. The pain wasn't helpful in making a decision. Norrie was shot in the chest and was probably going to die. Jacob was pale as a starched sheet and looked like he might keel over any second.

Wallace had no plans to kill Jacob. He'd had no plans to kill Norrie either, come to that, but he'd had to show May he was serious. And Norrie deserved it. Jacob was an old fart, but he wasn't dangerous. Still, if he wasn't going to kill him, Wallace needed somewhere to lock him up until after he'd finished with May.

The cupboard behind Norrie looked inviting.

'What's in there?' Wallace pointed, looking at May. She was doing well, not screaming. She was shaking a bit, though. Hands clutching her handbag, kneading away at it.

'Just a cupboard,' she said.

Norrie moaned. Life in the old fuckhead yet.

'Why's it locked?' Wallace looked at Jacob, then back at May.

'Door doesn't stay closed otherwise,' she said.

'That right?' Wallace asked Jacob.

Jacob tried to say something but he might as well have had a fist stuffed in his mouth for all the sense he was making.

Wallace said, 'Yes or no, Jacob?'

He nodded.

'Move your pal away from the door,' Wallace told him.

Jacob stared at him.

Wallace repeated the command.

Jacob still didn't move.

Wallace pointed his gun at him, and Jacob blinked and

scurried over to Norrie. He grabbed Norrie's left arm and dragged him away from the cupboard. Norrie moaned again, loudly. Jacob ignored him, kept dragging.

'Give him a hand, May,' Wallace said.

May said, 'I'm not —'

'Fucking do it.'

May stepped over to Norrie, doing her best to avoid the blood pooled on the floor, grabbed Norrie's other arm, and father and daughter tugged Norrie clear of the door.

'Now open it,' Wallace said to May.

May turned the key, pulled the door towards her.

Yep, it was just a cupboard. An ample walk-in for storing odds and ends. An ironing board, hoover, stepladder. Wallace couldn't see much more from where he was standing, but it was unlikely there'd be an Uzi on one of the shelves. 'Put him in there,' he said.

Jacob was red-faced and mumbling to himself, but he didn't stop to argue. In fact, Norrie was moaning again and it sounded to Wallace like Jacob was muttering something about him being a cocksucker. Which was the first time Wallace had heard Jacob swear. Fuck, he must be mad. Maybe it was beginning to dawn on him just what his best mate had done, the crazy fucking old fucktard.

Wallace couldn't help wonder why. But it wasn't his place to figure it out. Who knew what had been going on in the old geezer's head?

Anyway, Wallace's arm was still smarting. No, smarting wasn't the word. It felt like a wild dog was gnawing on it. Needed to get it bandaged up soon, but, glancing at it, it didn't seem to be bleeding too badly. He gave it a shake and there wasn't much of a splash. Maybe needed to get it cleaned, though. You never knew where the bullet had been. But first things first.

Norrie was in the cupboard, flat on the ground, wheezing. May and Jacob were looking at him and May kicked him, half-heartedly, then stood still, folded her arms across her chest, and stared at Wallace. She kept glancing at his arm.

Wallace removed the bullets from Norrie's .38. It was tough going, since the fingers of his bad arm were cold. He could sense that both May and Jacob were considering attacking him. Maybe rushing him, thinking he was wounded and so they could take him. He said, 'I wouldn't try it.' They kept their distance.

Once he'd got all the bullets out, dropping them in his pocket, he threw the gun into the cupboard. He had an idea.

'Get in there with your friend,' he said to Jacob.

'I can't leave May.'

'Get in.'

'I'm sorry. I can't.'

'Then I'll shoot you, Jacob.'

'But I can't leave her.'

'I'll be okay, Dad. Just do what he says.'

'Listen to your daughter, Dad.'

'But I can't. Don't you understand?'

'Please, Dad. Just get in the cupboard. He's not going to kill you.'

'It's not me I'm worried about, May.'

'I'm running out of patience, Jacob.'

'Sorry, Dad.' May walked behind him and shoved him in the back. He stumbled towards the doorway. She shoved him again and he lurched inside.

Jacob turned. 'Oh, May. It's me who's sorry.'

'Jacob?' Wallace said.

The old guy looked at him, eyes misty.

'Present.' Wallace's hand dipped into his pocket. He took

out a bullet and threw it into the cupboard. Then he slammed the door closed and locked it.

'What now?' May said to Wallace.

'Fix my arm.'

May stared at him. 'Why would I do that?'

''Cause I'll shoot you if you don't.'

'I'm not a nurse.'

Wallace switched his gun to his other hand, ripped his shirtsleeve in a sudden painful jerk. Handed the torn blood-stained fabric to her. 'Wrap that tight around the wound.'

She took the shirtsleeve and he returned the gun to his good hand. She did as she was told. Tied it in a knot on top. 'Now what?' she said.

'We go for a drive. I want to show you something.'

'And then?'

'Patience. Wait and see.'

Wallace opened the front door, half expecting to see a row of squad cars lined up outside, but it appeared that no one had reported hearing anything. Just like when Rog had come for Wallace. Edinburgh was wonderful. You heard gunshots and decided it was something else. Nobody fired guns in Edinburgh. That only happened in Glasgow.

Something brushed against his leg and May cried out as the three-legged dog bounded down the garden path, yelping, and out into the road.

The scared little fuck didn't last long. Busy road, you know.

JACOB HEARD THE outside door closing. May was gone. He'd screwed up. Wallace had got to her after all their pre-cautions, after all their failed attempts to keep her safe, to enlist Pearce's help. Pearce must be dead. And May was as good as.

He wanted to sink to his knees and cry. Pathetic old fool that he was.

He should have protected her somehow. But how could he have done that without being shot? Not that he would have minded being shot. No, what he meant was that he couldn't have protected her. Any attempt to do so, he'd have been shot like Norrie, no question. And then he'd have had no chance of protecting her at all. This way, there might be something he could do. Something, aye.

Although, right now, he wasn't sure what it was.

He reached behind him, fingers fumbling for the torch. Found it, switched it on.

Jacob shone the light on Norrie. He was gurgling, clutching his stomach with both hands as blood poured between his fingers in little spurts. Blood trickled out of his mouth as he tried to speak.

Jacob picked up the discarded gun, swept the torch around looking for the bullet. Very good of Wallace to have given it to him. Of course, Jacob knew why. The sadistic son of a bitch wanted him to put Norrie out of his misery. Although Jacob couldn't help wondering if Wallace had considered that Jacob might use the gun on himself.

Cause really, when your best friend does something like this, you don't particularly want to live. Your trust is broken and you have to question everything. Nothing's what it seems any more.

There it was. He dug the bullet out from the back of the cupboard, swung out the cylinder of the revolver and slotted the bullet in one of the chambers. Fire a slug into Norrie's skull, or fire one into his own? He pointed the gun at Norrie.

Norrie's eyes widened. He spat a mouthful of blood, which sprayed over his chin. He opened his mouth, teeth stained red, and choked when he tried to speak.

Jacob said, 'You denying you shot Rog?'

Norrie tried to speak again. Finally managed to say, 'No, boss.'

'You're not denying it?'

'Yeah.'

Jacob was confused. Not that it mattered. Norrie had clearly shot Rog. The only question was why. Jacob asked him.

Norrie gasped, squeezed his eyes shut, then opened them again. He was no doubt in terrible pain, but Jacob didn't feel sorry for him. Quite the opposite, in fact. Jacob was pleased his old friend was feeling pain. Jacob had to restrain himself from leaning down and stabbing a finger in Norrie's wound and pressing down hard.

Jacob said, 'You killed Louis, too?'

Norrie's eyes lost focus, then he nodded.

Jacob shook his head. He didn't understand and Norrie wasn't going to last long enough to explain. Unless Jacob got him to a hospital. Thing was, Jacob really wanted to know. He didn't want Norrie to die. Was it the accident that had made Norrie behave like this? People said Norrie wasn't quite right in the head but Jacob had never believed that. Norrie was always perfectly fine when Jacob was around. Lord save him, but although Jacob didn't want Norrie to die, he didn't want Norrie to live either.

So first things first.

Jacob placed the gun on the floor at his feet. Then he stuck his hand in Norrie's pocket. Bingo. Wallace should have looked for it, although he probably didn't care too much what happened now. Jacob took out Norrie's mobile phone, hoping to Christ he had Flash's number on it. Jacob had to find out how to work the stinking thing first, though.

He wished he'd paid more attention.

Step one was turning it on. For the life of him, he couldn't see an on/off switch. What on earth were you supposed to do? He asked Norrie.

Norrie choked, dribbled blood over his chin.

Jacob shook his head.

Norrie held out his hand and Jacob gave him the phone. Norrie pressed a tiny little button with his thumbnail and pressed some other keys and handed the phone back to Jacob.

What now? Dial the number, Jacob supposed. Could he remember Flash's number? It was in the address book by the telephone in the hall. No, Jacob couldn't remember it. 'You have Flash's number on here?' he asked Norrie.

But Norrie had closed his eyes and was making sporadic spluttering sounds that were painful to hear.

Jacob put down the mobile phone and picked up the gun again. He had one bullet. He could finish off Norrie, or he could put an end to his own misery. Or . . .

DOOR OPENED AND off he scooted and a screech of brakes later, Cutey-pie was on his side in the middle of the road. And May was thinking, couldnae be. Nah. A dream or something like Joanne kept having where it was dead vivid like as if she was there and all and it was really happening. Cause Wallace shooting Norrie was totally freaky and totally impossible to believe. Course Joanne was away in her head. A real mentalist. Fat tart. And May was sane. Which meant all this *had* happened.

Look at it again. Still can't take it in. Play it back.

She'd been too busy wondering how she was going to escape from Wallace. Look at him, cocky or what, with his fucking gun? She was glad he'd been shot in the arm. Looked nasty, too.

Screech. Smack.

The driver got out of the car, neck scrunched into his shoulders, arms robot-stiff, palms forwards, the way Italian footballers react when they've fouled an opponent. Dipshit was dressed in a shirt and tie, smart trousers.

And that was enough for May to get really angry. 'Bastard!' May yelled at him. 'Fucking fannyarse!' she said.

He got more stiff-armed and his neck started to disappear like his shirt was floating towards his head. Looked like he was thinking about running away. Scared of the wee lass, was he? Should be.

Or maybe he was scared of Wallace, cause he still had the gun in his hand and was waving it about and shouting, his torn shirtsleeve stained red already where some blood had soaked through.

May joined Wallace. 'Fuck you!' she said to the driver. 'You fucker!'

But she realised that Wallace was shouting at her.

Anyway, the driver swivelled round and got back in his car.

May could have thrown some more insults (and she had some bad ones, she just couldn't think of them) at him, but, oh well, what was the point? More important, what was she going to say to Flash? She couldn't just tell him straight out that Cutey-pie had been run over.

Tyres screeched as the driver screamed off out of there.

Good. Glad to see the back of the bastard. Maybe everything was going to be okay, though. Cutey-pie's eyes were open. His top lip was curled up, baring his teeth. Looked for all the world like he was grinning.

May bent over him.

Wallace said, 'Watch he doesn't bite.'

'He won't bite.'

'Hurt dogs are dangerous.'

'Can't blame them, can you?' Arsehole. How was an injured dog supposed to know you were trying to help? All they knew was that it was sore and they didn't want any more pain. 'That cock jockey' – see? – 'was going too fast.' The rage had seized hold of her again. She wanted to kick that poncey twat of a driver in the balls.

'Bloody dog ran out in front of the car,' Wallace said. 'Nothing the driver could do.'

Nah, kicking his balls wasn't enough. Cut them off. 'Ten miles an hour slower, he'd be okay. I've seen the adverts.'

'Don't think so.'

'Thoughtless bastard.' Cook them and smother them in tomato sauce and feed them to Cutey-pie. 'He'd be fucking okay. Anyway, you opened the door. It's your fault.'

Wallace was quiet for a second, let her stroke Cutey-pie's cheek. Wee fella's eyes flickered towards her, looked away again. And he sighed as if he was bored of all this and just wanted to get on with whatever was going to happen next. Cool dog, or what?

May said, 'We need to get him to the vet's.' She gave Wallace her best stare. If he argued, she'd bloody well do him. He had a gun, but she didn't give a shit. He only had one good arm. She had some nasty thoughts swirling around in her head right now. And she had Flash's present in her handbag. Good old Dirk. Wallace could do his worst but she wasn't going to let Cutey-pie lie on the road and bleed to death.

She told Wallace how she felt.

'All fucking right,' he said. 'Just calm down.' He put his hand on her shoulder and she got a lungful of aftershave. Or more like a throatful, cause it didn't go all the way down before she coughed it back out. Same kind of fuddy-duddy stinky old-guy crap Sue's dad wore. Stink City. Sort of smellies Dad got for Flash at Christmas and he thanked Dad for and never used but he couldnae bring himself to chuck in the bin.

The toes of Wallace's shoes were totally gleaming. May patted her skirt down, just in case he was thinking of using those gleamers to sneak a peek of her pants.

Cutey-pie's tongue flicked out and disappeared again almost immediately. 'You thirsty, darlin'?' she asked him. Looked at Wallace and said, 'You wait with him while I get some water.'

Wallace grabbed her. 'Take me seriously,' he said. 'Or I'll shoot the fucking dog.' He pulled a face like he was constipated.

May said, 'You wouldn't.'

He pulled back the hammer and placed the gun against Cutey-pie's head.

'Okay, okay,' May said. She was forgetting that it was Wallace. Most times when they were together when she said he wouldn't do something, he'd gone ahead and done it. He was a loophead. She should be scared of him but she was still too angry. Why was she so fucking angry? She didn't know. The rage had started simmering when Flash gave her the knife and she realised they'd all been scheming behind her back. All of them. There wasn't a single fucking one of them she could trust. Since then, she'd got gradually angrier. Wallace barging into the house and shooting Norrie and threatening Dad hadn't helped. And now Cutey-pie had been run over.

Cutey-pie needed to get to the vet's as quickly as possible. His eyes weren't looking too bright. Probably a wee bowl of water was neither here nor there. So, okay. Judging by the way he was flopped out, he'd be hard pushed to do much more than look at it, poor soul. She slipped her fingers under his back and lifted him as gently as she could, making shushing noises all the while. 'Where's your car?' she asked Wallace.

'Up the street a bit,' he said. Then he shook his head. 'You're not taking the fucking dog.'

She tried hard to keep her voice calm. 'Please. Just let me drop him off at the vet's. Then you can still show me whatever it is you want to show me.'

'No.'

'Come on, Wallace. What's it to you?'

'I just fucking shot somebody. And, in case you hadn't noticed, I got shot too.'

'Get in the car, then. Stop standing in the middle of the road, bleeding.'

'Lay the dog down.'

'Consider *this* your good deed for the day.'

'I'll fucking shoot you, May. Swear I will.'

She turned her head, spotted the Range Rover, and headed towards it. 'He's just a wee thing but he's getting heavy. Get the door for me.'

Behind her, Wallace roared something.

She felt her back itch. A calculated risk. But she knew how to play him.

He charged after her, overtook her, his face red. 'Why won't you fucking do what you're told?' he said.

Her armpits prickled with sweat. 'Would you get the door, please?'

He grunted, slammed the gun down on the roof of the car and dented it. Stupid bastard. Then he moved like a pit-bull was after him. 'Fuck, fuck, fuck,' he said, yanking the door open.

She laid Cutey-pie carefully on the back seat and said to him, 'Hang in there, sweetheart.' She climbed in after him.

Wallace said, 'He's bleeding all over the seat.'

'What about you?' she said. A thin line of dark blood had seeped out from the bandage, trickled down his arm, and was dripping off the end of his little finger.

'It's nothing.' He shook his arm.

'We need to get him to a vet, Wallace.'

Wallace slammed the door closed, bolted round to the driver's seat and sat behind the wheel, staring at her in the mirror. She looked away, stroked Cutey-pie's head. After a second, the engine purred into life. She rested Cutey-pie's head on her lap. It looked uncomfortable, though, cause he didn't have the longest neck in the world, so she lowered his head back onto the seat. God, she hoped he was going to be okay. She'd ask the vet what kind of dog he was, cause she had no idea. A terrier of some kind, yeah, but he was some kind of special breed, she was sure.

She stroked his cheek and he stuck out his tongue and licked her hand. Just once. Seemed to take a whole lot of effort.

There wasn't much blood. Wallace had been making a fuss. Just a bit from the back of Cutey-pie's head and the area just above his missing leg. He was going to be okay. If they got to the vet's in time. She was sure of that. 'Can you go faster?'

'I'm not going anywhere with that dog.'

'Then I'm getting out.' She reached for the handle.

He glanced over his shoulder. 'I'll shoot you.'

'Then you won't get to show me whatever it is you want me to see.'

Wallace stared at her. 'May, I've a good mind to call your bluff.'

She stared back at him. 'I'm stepping out of the car with Cutey-pie in five seconds.' She paused.

She opened her mouth again to start counting, but Wallace cut her off. 'For fuck's sake,' he said. He pulled away from the kerb. The car jumped forward in fits and starts, Wallace having difficulty with the gears. After a bit, he sussed it out, drove one-handed. 'I don't know where I'm going, May.'

'To the vet's.'

'I know *that*. I just don't know where to find one.'

'Well, there's bound to be one around here somewhere. Everybody's got a pit-bull or a Rottweiler or a Doberman. Joanne's brother's got a lizard. I ever tell you that?' She spotted a likely punter heading towards them. 'Pull over and ask this biddy with the poodle.'

'Why would she know?'

May had married a real thick dipshit. A real thick violent dipshit. She explained to him: 'She's taking her dog for a walk. She must live round here. So she's probably taken it to see the vet at some point, yeah?'

Wallace's eyes held hers in the rear-view mirror. 'Anybody ever tell you you're a cheeky little bitch?' he said.

'Yeah,' she said. 'My husband. All the time.'

'Sounds like the kind of guy who knows what he's talking about.'

No, he was a first-rate wanker. Jesus. She pressed her handbag closer to her, popped the clasp. If he didn't shut the fuck up and get to a vet's, she'd introduce his balls to Dirk. See how he liked that.

. . . OR JACOB COULD do this.

He stepped back from the cupboard door and aimed the gun at the lock. Figured that if he shot it, he'd get out, call Flash on the landline, rescue May before Wallace did whatever he was going to do to her.

Please God.

No time to hang around asking Norrie why he'd done what he'd done. Not that Norrie would be able to tell him much.

Jacob dabbed his left eye with the heel of his hand. It came away wet. But he wasn't crying over Norrie's betrayal. No, he was crying because he was going to lose May. He knew it.

He had to hurry.

He pulled the trigger.

Big noise. So loud it made his eye sting. And it was still stinging. He couldn't see out of it. Kept blinking and all it did was make his vision worse. He dabbed it with his hand again and his hand came away red.

Felt himself start to panic. Knew he had to keep calm. Panic and he'd be no good to anybody.

Keep it together, Jacob.

Close the eye. Close it. It was no good anyway.

He tried, but it wouldn't stay shut. Something in it, and the eye wanted rid of it. Blinked some more. And something kept making him try to see out of it. Had to believe that it wasn't as bad as it felt.

He forced it shut and it stayed that way, sort of, the eyelid fluttering, but at least he was able to see out of the other one.

The lock had shattered. Wood and metal had splintered. And that was the problem. He must have got something in his eye.

He dropped the gun. It was useless now. No more bullets.

He pushed open the door, stepped into the hallway. He avoided looking in the mirror. Didn't want to see how bad his injury was. Not yet. Had to make a call first.

Focused with his good eye, hands shaking as he opened the address book and squinted to read Flash's number. He dialled. *For God's sake, answer, Flash.* Then he realised Flash was in a hospital. Probably have his phone turned off.

The phone rang three times and then Flash said, 'What is it?'

God love the boy. 'My eye,' Jacob said, before realising that that wasn't what was important right now. 'Wallace's got May,' he said.

Flash swore. 'Where are they?'

'I don't know. They've gone. He shot Norrie.'

'Jesus. Is he okay?'

'I think he's dead. Or nearly.'

'Shit. I'm sorry, Dad.'

'I'm not.'

'What?'

'Norrie shot Rog. It wasn't Wallace. Norrie thought he was . . . look, I'll tell you later. Go get your sister. Head for Wallace's.'

'Jesus. You okay, Dad?'

'Never better, son.' Jacob hung up. A giant hand squeezed his heart and he keeled over.

CUTEY-PIE'S CHEST was barely moving. May bent her head to listen to his breathing. His tongue flopped out and touched her chin. She sat up, determined not to cry. Her emotions were all over the place. God, she felt like shit today. Couldn't have been a worse time for all this crap to be going down. How many more years of these frigging stomach pains? She couldn't wait for the change of life. After she'd had three kids. Two boys and a girl. That'd be cool. Joanne reckoned May should go on the pill. Safer. But also to make her periods more regular and less heavy, cause when they came, they fucking came. May wasn't sure she could trust Joanne's advice, though. Joanne had two kids already and she was three months younger than May. Anyway, kids was a touchy subject. And so was that fat tart, Joanne.

Wallace gave May that look in the mirror again. Like she was stupid or something. He knew how to make her feel small. Horse tosser.

'You know where we're going, then?' she said. The biddy had given them directions. Nearest vet's was some distance away, apparently. Wallace seemed to know where she meant. May didn't have a baldy.

Wallace said nothing.

May looked away. Didn't want to communicate with him, anyway, the murdering fuckwit. Well, Norrie wasn't dead when she'd left but the chances were that he would be before too long. Wallace really didn't give a shit sometimes. He was like some kind of psycho. Anyway, she wasn't going to talk to him. You didn't step into somebody's home guns blazing. It wasn't right. And he'd kidnapped her, which wasn't right either. And maybe he hadn't done things to Rog or done things to Louis but it didn't bear thinking that she'd let that fucking animal inside her. Christ, she felt fucking filthy, and not in a good way.

She spoke to the dog again. Keeping him relaxed. Daft, right, she knew, telling him not to worry, but what else were you supposed to say? Not as bad as talking to plants, eh? And she'd done that before. Had a spider plant that died very slowly over a couple of years. Probably wouldn't have lasted six months if she hadn't spoken to it. Anyway, she talked to Cutey-pie for a while, hoping her words would have the same life-prolonging effect they'd had on the plant. After a while she felt pressure build up behind her eyes, knew she'd lose it and start to bawl if she let so much as a single tear escape.

Thinking about plants, now. Like a useless fanny. Who was she trying to kid?

There was only so much she could do, wasn't there? She wasn't a bad person. Not really. If she was, it was Wallace who'd made her bad.

She stroked Cutey-pie, watching his eyes narrow, widen, narrow again. She wondered what it was that Wallace wanted her to see. He'd been pretty keen. Keen enough to force her out of the house at gunpoint, keen enough to shoot Norrie to get the fact he was serious across. Had to be something grotesque, then. It'd be something that was getting back at her in his own special way. Well, fuck him. No, she didn't want to think about that. Anyway, it was never like . . .

Fuck, she was crying.

Tony Twelve-Inch. Not that she'd ever slept with him, but Joanne said Tony Twelve-Inch had shown it to her and that it was maybe nine inches but no more than that. May didn't believe her. Joanne liked nothing better than to lie about stuff to her friends. She probably hadn't even seen it at all. Why would Tony show it to her? She said she'd had to show him her tits to get him to unwrap it, but May couldn't imagine Tony wanting to see those walloping great fat puddings. But then, he was a bloke and blokes didn't seem too fussy.

Fuck's sake. Here she was thinking about Tony's tadger and Joanne's boobs and Cutey-pie was at death's door. From plants to Tony Twelve-Inch. What was going on in her stupid head? She was stressed. That's what it was. She'd had a bad fucking time of it recently, what with one thing and another. She apologised to Cutey-pie and bent over to kiss his nose. She talked to him. He liked that.

She was trembling all over. You'd think it was the middle of winter and she wasn't wearing any clothes. Cutey-pie would warm her up. But he was cold, too. His nose was freezing. She kept her head down, whispered in his ear.

When she felt the car start to slow down, she sat up again. The tyres crunched over gravel. She looked up, saw that they were in a churchyard. Place was surrounded by trees. No other cars in the driveway. The church was locked up. Big oak doors sealed tight. She'd never been here before.

Wallace winced as he pulled up on the handbrake. Then he

turned off the engine. Caught her eyes in the mirror again. He looked pissed off.

This was bad. May didn't know why exactly, but she knew. Something was wrong with him. They shouldn't be here. This clearly wasn't the vet's and it wasn't their old house. This was nowhere. A churchyard. Hidden from the road. Could be anywhere.

Had he planned all along to take her here? Was there something here he wanted to show her? There was nothing around but gravestones. Was that it? Had he dug a grave for her?

May's forehead felt as if somebody had slapped a cold cloth on it. Her bravado vanished, like it always did. She could only go so far. She craned her neck, scanning left, right, behind her. Heard the rumble of traffic. Not too far from the road, then, even though she couldn't see anything through the trees. She could run. She'd have to run. Back down the driveway. She tried the door handle. Door was locked.

Caught his eyes in the mirror again. Still he didn't smile. He was watching her.

'This isn't the vet's,' she said. Stupid fucking thing to say. She was itching under her arms. Sweat. She could feel it prickling at her skin like nettle stings. 'Is there something here you want to show me, Wallace?'

'Yeah, but it's an appetiser. The main course comes later,' he said. 'Let's call this foreplay.'

The fuck did that mean? She opened her handbag, fingers shaky.

He turned, faced her. 'May,' he said, 'I'm going to fuck you senseless.'

'No, you're not.'

'Really?'

'Really.' She took out her knife and stabbed him in the neck.

He didn't bleed until she yanked the knife back out, just pulled a surprised face, all totally wide-eyed. But once the blade was out, blood streamed from the wound. He put his hand to his throat and his fingers slowly turned red. He popped the locks, fumbled for the door handle, fell out onto the driveway making choking sounds.

She got her phone out and dropped it, her hands were so shaky. Picked it up. Called Flash.

WHEN HIS DAD called, Flash had been sitting in the car in the hospital car park, windows open, letting out the dog smell, which was very faint now, but you still got an occasional whiff when you weren't expecting it so it was safer to wind down the windows even if it was raining, which it wasn't, not at the moment anyway, although the sky was overcast and it could go either way. Right now, he could use a cigarette. He'd been sitting in the car since he arrived, chalking up a bloody great parking bill, but he couldn't bring himself to go in and see Rog lying there in that state, so he'd sat in the car watching patients and hospital staff weave in and out of the hospital, whilst he tried to summon up the courage or whatever it was to open the door and drag his sorry arse inside.

But he hadn't been able to and he was just about to start the car and drive back home, when Dad called to tell him Wallace had shot Norrie and kidnapped May.

Flash's instinct was to drive over to Wallace's. He wasn't sure what he could do, but he had to get there and even if he didn't expect Wallace to turn up on his doorstep with May in tow, there wasn't a helluva lot else Flash could do.

What had Dad meant by saying he wasn't sorry about Norrie? That Norrie had shot Rog? Sounded like he was raving, maybe banged his head or something. Norrie was his best mate. Of course he was sorry Norrie had been shot.

Flash flirted with the idea of phoning the police, but he knew what they'd say about Wallace: 'Why won't your family leave the poor man alone, Mr Baxter?' But it was different now, wasn't it? There was a corpse back at Dad's. Maybe he should call them, after all. But Dad would have called them if he'd wanted to and maybe Flash should stay out of it, just concentrate on trying to find May, and maybe then, once he'd located her, he should contact the police and let them know where she was.

That was an idea, so with that plan in mind, Flash was halfway to Wallace's when May rang him. She was in a state, yelling at him, saying he had to help, she'd used Dirk, she'd killed Wallace.

Once he'd worked out that Dirk was the knife he'd bought her, Flash's immediate responses were mixed. Somewhere buried underneath the shock was pride that May had finally done what no one else had been able to do – not Rog or himself or Dad or Norrie or Pearce – and killed the bastard, but there was also guilt that he'd provided her with the means to do it. Cause her life would never be the same again. 'Stay where you are,' Flash told her. 'I'll be right there.'

'I don't want to stay here,' May said. Her voice broke. 'I'm scared.'

'Well, I'll meet you somewhere nearby.'

Quietly: 'Okay.'

'Right. So where are you?'

'I don't know, Flash. Never been here before.'

Shit. Flash knew he should call the police right now but he just couldn't bring himself to do it cause he couldn't leave his little sister to the mercy of those fuckers. They'd tear her to pieces. 'What's it look like?'

'What's what look like?'

'Where you are. Describe it.'

'Dunno,' May said. 'Churchyard. With trees and bushes. A driveway. And lots of graves. Both sides.'

Bollocks. There were dozens of churches like that in Edinburgh. That was no good.

May said, 'Maybe we should call an ambulance.'

And Flash found himself saying, 'The medics won't know where you are either, May. It'd be pointless.'

'But maybe they could find me.'

THE LEFT SIDE of Jacob's face was wet. Down the hallway, he heard Norrie cry out. A choked yell. Still some fight in the auld bastard.

Jacob thought about picking himself off the floor and redialling, but he didn't think he could. The pain radiating down his left side was too intense. So intense, he hardly noticed the pain in his eye any longer. If he put any pressure on his left side, he felt like his heart would burst. He was sprawled on the floor, aware that he wasn't breathing too well. A bit shallow. He raised his head, managed that okay. All he wanted to do now was put his hand over his chest. But he couldn't get into position. It was a stupid thing to want to do anyway, but he knew it would make all the difference. The gesture would be a strange kind of comfort.

He breathed through his nose, as best he could through the bandaging. Or at least, that's what he thought he was doing. But in fact he wasn't breathing through his nose. He wasn't breathing through his mouth either. And his vision was going. Not red. Not blood-smeared. No, it was shrinking, black-edged.

He didn't want to go like this, not knowing what was going to happen to May.

But there didn't seem to be much he could do about it.

'IF THE AMBULANCE can find you,' Flash said to May, 'so can I.'

'And then what?'

Good question.

'Flash, I really think I've killed him.'

So now she was suggesting there was some doubt. 'Is he breathing?'

'Hang on.' Pause. Then she screamed.

'May? May? Speak to me. What's going on?'

'He grabbed me.'

Ah, fuck, no. This wasn't happening. The only thing more dangerous than Wallace was a wounded Wallace. 'Get out of there. Run. Go on.'

'It's okay. It's okay. He's let go. I think he's dead now. Properly.'

'May, you have to leave. If he's still alive, he's dangerous. Get out of there now.'

'I can't.'

'Course you can. Just start walking. Find a street sign. Tell me where you are and I'll pick you up.'

'I can't.'

'Come on, May. You don't know he's dead. You have to get out of there. One foot in front of the other. A step at a time. Come on.'

'I can't leave Cutey-pie.'

Pearce's fucking dog. Jesus in a basket. 'What's the fucking dog doing there?'

'Don't swear at me.'

'I'm sorry, May. What's with the dog?'

'This guy, he ran Cutey-pie over.' Her voice was piercingly loud. Flash had to hold his mobile away from his ear. 'Wallace said he'd take the dog to the vet's.'

Why the fuck would Wallace do that? He wasn't known for his kindness, particularly when it came to the Baxters. Flash had to keep calm and he had to keep May calm. 'May, I need you to walk to the nearest street and tell me where you are.'

'I can't.'

'Do it, May. Do what you're told.'

'Flash, please.'

'Don't fucking say you can't. Just do it.' Damn. He was swearing at her again. Stay friggin' poised, *amigo*.

'Flash, I've got blood all over me.'

'Is any of it yours?'

'Some of it's Cutey-pie's. Some of it's Wallace's.'

'May, is any of it yours?'

'No.'

She wasn't injured, thank Christ. He should have asked her that first. Jesus, what kind of brother was he? 'Get out of the car. Walk a few yards until you can tell me where you are. Then you can wait by the car with the dog until I get there.'

'You don't think we should call an ambulance?'

Flash said, 'Find out where you are first. Then we'll decide. Now start moving. And keep talking to me.'

'People will see me all covered in blood. They'll run away screaming. The police'll come. I'll get arrested. I'll be —'

'Slow down, May. It won't be as bad as you think.'

'It is, Flash. I can't let anybody see me like this. They'll freak out. I'll get put away.'

Flash thought for a second or two.

'Flash? You still there? Don't go.'

'Can you wipe the blood off?'

'Where? With what?'

Jesus. Flash closed his eyes and hoped that he'd manage to stay calm cause he was churning up inside. How was he supposed to know where May could clean herself up?

'And I can't leave Cutey-pie,' she said again.

Which gave Flash an idea. 'If you take the dog with you,' he said, 'anybody sees blood, they'll think it's the dog's.'

'I can't move him.'

For fuck's sake. 'May, you have to.'

'Flash, help me.'

Jesus fucking Christ. What was he supposed to do?

KISS, KISS,
BANG, BANG

MAY HAD BEEN hysterical for a while and Flash hadn't been able to get any sense out of her. He still didn't know where she was, so he was just sitting at the wheel, idling along, going nowhere slowly.

Flash squeezed his phone hard, he was so friggin' frustrated, and said, 'Speak to me, May.'

'Gotta get out of here.'

Fantastic. A response. 'Yeah. Just hang on. I'll be with you soon.'

'Gotta get out of here.'

'I know.' Shit, shit, shit. He didn't want to lose her again. She was talking to him now. He had to keep her talking. 'Keep calm, May. Please.' She wanted to get out of there. Good. But would she leave the dog?

'Gotta get out of here.'

Yep, patience. 'One foot in front of the other. Come on, you can do it.'

'Oh, Jesus, Jesus.'

'What is it? May? Speak to me. What's happening?'

'Jesus. He moved again, Flash.'

Oh, Jesus, Jesus. 'Run.'

'I can't.'

'Fuck's sake, May. Do it.'

May said, 'I have to kill him.'

'Don't do that. Please don't do that.'

'He's not dead, Flash.'

'I know, but you can't just go ahead and kill him.'

'But he should be dead.'

'I know he should be but . . .' Shit.

'I already killed him. I can do it again.'

Christ. What the fuck should he tell her? 'Wait for me in the car. Can you do that? Sit in the car. Lock the doors.'

'Dirk.'

'You still have it?'

'It's in his hand.'

'Don't think about that, May. You have to help me find you.'

'I'm sorry,' May said.

'It's okay,' Flash said. 'Keep talking. Please. Give me some idea where you are.'

'I can get Dirk. Wallace has stopped moving again. It was just a jerk.'

'No.'

'I'll get the knife. Kill him.'

He had to distract her. She had to get out of there. Last thing she wanted to do was pick up the knife again. Wallace sounded like he was still alive. Which was good news for May if Flash could get her out of there. 'May, listen to me. *Listen.* You listening? May?'

'Aha.'

'See how the dog is.'

'Huh?'

'Cutey-pie needs your help. He's scared.'

'He is?'

'That's right. Go on. Quickly.' Pause. 'You doing it?'

'What about Dirk?'

'You can get it later.'

'I don't think I want it now, anyway.'

'That's okay, then.'

'Flash, will I go to prison?'

'Don't worry about that.'

'He tried to . . . it wasn't my fault.'

'I know. You won't go to prison. I promise.'

'But they'll find the knife and they'll blame me. Doesn't matter that Norrie shot him.'

'Norrie shot him?'

'In the arm.'

Norrie had been busy. And where had he got a gun? Never mind.

'And it was Norrie who shot Rog.'

Fuck. Maybe Dad wasn't raving.

'But he's dead now. Wallace shot him.'

Flash knew that. This wasn't the greatest topic of conversation. It was clearly upsetting her.

As was the business with the knife. She repeated: 'They'll find Dirk, Flash.'

'They won't know who the knife belongs to.'

'But they'll be able to trace it.'

'Don't worry about it.'

'Fingerprints.'

'May, we'll sort all that out when I get there. Just help me find you. Please. Where's the last place you remember?'

'I dunno.'

'Think. Where did you go when you drove off?'

'Supposed to be going to the vet's.'

'Which vet's?'

'Had to stop and ask someone.'

And would Wallace have headed in that direction, if he never had any intention of reaching his destination? Flash had to hope so. He closed his eyes. 'And where did they suggest?'

'I . . . Slateford, I think.'

Warehouses and old breweries. And, yes, churches. 'Okay, I'll find you.'

'Cutey-pie's still breathing,' May said. 'What should I do now? I don't want to leave him alone in the car.'

God, this was hard. 'Stay in it, then.'

'Okay.'

'Great. Lock the doors.'

'Hang on. Okay.'

'You're doing good.'

'Flash?'

'Yeah?'

'I wet myself.'

'That's okay, darling. It's okay.'

Her teeth chattered. 'Flash?'

'Yeah?'

'Wallace has still got his gun.'

TUNE STARTED PLAYING. Funky drumbeat. Human beatbox shit. Annoying the crap out of Pearce. He said, 'Give it a rest.'

Thank fuck the shouting was over, though. Words had been popping into Jesus's head and coming straight out of his mouth, making no sense at all. Nothing Pearce could do about it. Just had to lie there and listen. Try as he might, he couldn't get the crazy fucker to shut up.

'Pop into my mouth. Come out of my head.' That was the most coherent response to anything Pearce had said in the last while.

Jesus's brain wasn't prepared to play ball. Not yet. Maybe not ever. It was cooked.

Enough of Jesus. Pearce knew that if he stayed here, he was going to die. If he didn't free himself, that was. It was a fucking weird situation, lying here pinned to a bench with Jesus looming over him on a cross. If Pearce didn't keep a grip, there was a panicky edge just dying to creep in and take over. He had to be careful, keep control, not allow that to happen.

It helped having the lights on. In the dark, as he'd been previously, it was as if he'd lost the power to think rationally. There was too much out there, too much of a distraction in the unknown. Of course, he knew there was only Jesus out there, but here he was, not scared of the dark exactly, but finding it harder and harder to see a way out of this situation. Even if Wallace had intended letting him go, Pearce was now a witness to a crucifixion. Wallace couldn't let him go. The only question was how Wallace was going to dispose of him. Another cross, or would Pearce get lucky and take a bullet in the skull?

While Jesus stayed quiet, just moaning occasionally, Pearce thought through his options. They were . . . zero. There was absolutely fucking nothing he could do. Almost everything he thought about was patently, almost painfully, impossible. He'd been there, thought about it, no matter how ridiculous it seemed, and realised it wasn't up to him. He couldn't do anything. The restraints were too powerful. Pulling against them did nothing other than hurt his arms, made the pain in his side flare up.

His fate was out of his control.

He was as good as dead. He could see himself dead. Close his eyes, he was dead. Open them, he was dead. Peer through slitted lids, still dead.

He had to remind himself he wasn't dead. Not yet. It was all in his head. Although he knew now what it was like to be dead. And it didn't seem so bad. Some comfort, at least, as far as Mum was concerned. But it was still a state he'd prefer to avoid if possible. The question was, how?

Come on. He could figure how to get out of here. That's what he had to do. Wallace must have missed something. Left some kind of loophole. Look, if Wallace was some kind of mad genius, he'd have attached Jesus's cross to the wall instead of propping the damn thing against it. Wasn't very safe. Damn thing could keel over any time.

See, now something was brewing. An answer. Came as an image. Or two. Wallace leaning the cross against the wall, stepping back, the Good Lord Jesus leaning forward like an angry, dirty swan, all his weight on his chest. Couldn't have that, cause he'd suffocate in no time at all. Which is why Wallace hadn't done it. He'd leaned him backwards, at a slant. Wallace had propped him up like that for a reason. To draw his death out as long as possible. Fuckhead.

Pearce dug his fingernails into his palms. His broken pinkie swelled with pain. Kept his brain ticking over, though. Use a bit of pain for clarity. Jesus was shouting again. Swearing. 'Shut up,' Pearce said.

Jesus opened his eyes and looked down at Pearce. Jesus was pale. Agony tugged at his cheek muscles now he was awake and experiencing the full horror of his plight. He was a skinny rake of a thing. A healthier, fitter person might have been able to survive this, but being kept in a cage for God knows how long meant that this particular Jesus wasn't likely to last a hell of a lot longer. Barring a miracle. He might once have been hard, but he'd had the shit kicked out of him. Wallace knew what he was doing.

Pearce wished Wallace were here. He'd try luring him over. Maybe call him names or whisper something and then, when he leaned in, nut him. Get a lucky butt in, maybe. Or bite him, like in that movie.

But that wouldn't help him escape. He'd have the satisfaction of getting another blow in, or ripping out a chunk of his neck, but it wasn't a practical solution. He'd still be in the same position he was in now. Strapped to a fucking bench.

WALLACE DROPPED THE knife. Her knife. It clattered to the ground and he mouthed the word 'shit' and clamped his hand to his neck. He staggered towards May, his free hand tugging the gun out of his waistband.

May knew she should have seized his weapons from him when she had the opportunity. She shouldn't have listened to Flash telling her to leave things alone. She should have followed her instinct. A little voice reminded her that it was her instinct that had got her into this nightmare mess in the first place. She told the little voice to fuck off if it couldn't be helpful. She'd had no choice. She'd had to stab him.

'What am I going to do?' she asked Flash. Maybe he'd give her better advice this time.

'Just sit tight.'

Didn't sound great. 'What good's that?'

'He can't get in the car.'

But he could. Course he could. Bleeding like a bastard but it wasn't stopping him from aiming his gun at the windscreen.

She told Flash what was happening.

'You have to get out of the car, May.'

'But you told me I'd be safe here.' She shouted at him: 'You told me.'

And Cutey-pie made a tiny growling sound and May said, 'Sorry, baby.' And into the phone, 'I'm scared, Flash. I don't know what to do.'

'You have to . . . shit, I dunno . . . shit.'

'Flash?' She'd have to decide for herself. Stay where she was and hope the bullet didn't smash the window. Right. Stay where she was and hope that Wallace didn't want to risk killing her. Right. After what she'd just done to him? Maybe

Wallace might drop dead any minute. Right. She'd have to fling open the door and totally sprint like the Devil himself was after her. Which wouldn't be hard. Cause, in a way, he was.

She said, in a whisper, 'I'm going to run,' into her phone.

'Don't hang up,' Flash yelled.

So she didn't.

Wallace fired, and glass smashed everywhere.

HOW *DID* A guy who was strapped to a bench and weak with hunger and thirst and blows to the head and stiff with lack of movement, and another guy who was nailed to a couple of planks of wood and out of his tree on magic mushrooms, get rid of their restraints and break out of a locked room? Tough assignment, right?

Pearce had to focus.

Wallace had gone, but could return any minute. They had to get out of this shithole. Right now. The stench hit Pearce again and he gagged. Or maybe it wasn't the smell but the memory of it.

Same difference. Same result, anyway.

Jesus spoke. Bit of breathlessness in there. 'I'll give it a shot,' he said.

Give what a shot?

Jesus clearly had a plan. Which was fine by Pearce.

Jesus strained. Head and upper body rocking forward. Just a bit. Then he slid back. Cried out. Palms bleeding again. Again. Worse, this time. The strain. The cry.

'Hey,' Pearce said. It was tough to watch. But Pearce knew what the poor bastard was up to.

Shouting now from Jesus as he went for it a third time. The forward movement causing his hands to slide along the nails until they thrust against the nailheads. Then he fell backwards.

'Look,' Pearce said. 'Don't —'

Jesus yelled, tried again. Pearce was impressed. Maybe Jesus was pretty hard after all. Even if he *was* crying. The sound made the bench Pearce was lying on vibrate. He could feel the cry in his thigh bone.

But, no. No fucking way would Jesus be able to yank those nails out. Poor bastard.

Jesus rested, closed his eyes. Tears rolled down his cheeks.

Pearce wished he could reach out and slap him. Stop him feeling so fucking sorry for himself and try again. *Again. Now.* Why, Pearce didn't know. There was no fucking point.

'Rock,' Jesus said. 'Rock.'

And Pearce joined him. 'Rock,' he said.

AND BECAUSE MAY left her phone on, Flash heard what happened.

A sound, like somebody'd dropped a tray of pint glasses, and Flash could almost see the liquid splashing everywhere and the shards and splinters of glass, but of course he knew that's not what it was, however much he wanted it to be, and then in his head he saw the driver's window pulverised and knew that's what had happened and his stomach shrank and went cold.

And then a scream, the likes of which Flash never wanted to hear again, unless it was made by the shitfucker who was doing this to his sister, in which case the cunt could scream fit to rip his throat and that would be okay with Flash.

But at least he knew from the scream that May was alive. The bullet might have hit her, but it hadn't killed her.

Then a thud, and who knew what that was, but the screaming stopped so Flash had to imagine the jizzwad

cocksucking bastard had hit May and yeah, when Flash
replayed the sound in his head, it had that dull smacking
sound that a solid object makes when it connects with bone.

But then May said, 'You bleeding fuck,' and Flash realised
he'd imagined it all wrong, somehow.

'What the fuck's happening, May?'

'I twatted him a beauty,' she said.

'You punched him?'

'Nutted him.'

Fuck's sake, *hermana*. 'Right, well, brilliant. Now leave the
dog. Get out of there. You'll have really pissed Wallace off now.'

'GOOD,' MAY SAID into the phone. Flash shouted at her, so
she put the phone on the passenger seat. She couldn't make
out what he was saying.

The horsetosser had shot at the window, shattered it, stuck
his hand inside, unlocked the door and clambered in.

Thought he was in charge, with his fucking smoking gun in
his hand.

She'd thrown herself forward. Didn't think about it. Last
thing he'd expected. Hit his chin with the top of her head. It
felt swollen already.

Now Wallace was sprawled half-in and half-out, dribbling
blood from his neck wound. He was lying face-down on the
driver's seat, head twisted slightly to the side, and she couldn't
see the gun anywhere.

He wasn't moving. This was her chance to make absolutely
sure she was going to get out of this alive.

She peered down at him, looking for the gun. God knew
what had happened to the knife. There wasn't a weapon of any
kind in his good hand. Couldn't see his other hand, though.

Oh, fuck. She'd been here before and she wasn't taking any chances this time. She'd run. But if she ran, he'd wake up like some baddie from a horror movie and chase her. She'd never make it to safety. The only way to stop him was to put him permanently out of action, wasn't it? Which is what she should have done before.

She got out of the car. Stepped round to the driver's side, ready to sprint if he so much as twitched. His hand was empty. He must have dropped the gun. No sign of it on the ground. It must have slid under the car and she wasn't crawling under there looking for it, cause she'd be trapped if he woke up. Okay. What was she going to do?

Put him out of action. Properly. Right. She didn't want to touch him, but she knew there was no other way of doing this. She forced herself to grab hold of the back of his belt. He was heavy. She had to jerk hard to get him to move at all, but eventually he slid towards her, face dragging on the leather upholstery, until he was almost entirely outside the car, only his forehead resting on the seat.

Good. Everything was nicely lined up. Yep. What she was about to do would put him out of commission for sure.

She yanked back the door and slammed it hard. On his head.

And, fuck, if that didn't wake the bastard up.

He sat bolt upright. Just like he'd been messing around and playtime was over. He looked pretty dazed. And then his eyes narrowed.

She turned, started running. But she hadn't gone more than a few steps when the noise of the engine turned her knees to liquid.

She glanced behind her. He'd crawled back into the car and was sitting in the driver's seat, wiping blood from his eyebrow.

She was in for it now. Unless she could outrun the car.

Like she said, she was in for it now.

PEARCE UTTERED WORDS of encouragement as Jesus rocked back and forward once again, yelling with pain as his palms thrust against the nailheads.

The cross bounced off the wall, slapping against the egg cartons.

Jesus wept, but he was a tough wee fucker.

Pearce tried talking to him again, but his brain was clearly too fried. But fried or not, Pearce was sure Jesus had some inkling of what he was trying to achieve. He was trying to topple the cross over.

Okay. Maybe he wasn't. Hard to tell. Maybe he was just doing what his body felt like. Did he have a plan? Did he know why he was rocking backwards and forwards? Surely he must do, however fucked up his head was. Otherwise, he wouldn't inflict that kind of pain on himself. Or maybe that *was* his purpose, to inflict pain on himself, somehow use the pain to keep himself sane.

Well, regardless of whether Jesus knew what he was doing or why he was doing it, enough momentum and he'd tip over. And that would be something. Pearce wasn't entirely sure what, but he knew they'd both get some sense of achievement out of it.

'Come on, J,' Pearce said. 'Put your back into it.'

Jesus roared as he threw himself forward once more.

That was the spirit. Maybe he couldn't speak, but he knew what Pearce had just said.

To Pearce, it seemed to happen in slow motion. The cross left the wall and hovered there, not knowing whether it was going to fall forwards or backwards. Jesus didn't appear to know either. He leaned forward again, and that was enough, finally, to topple himself and the cross towards Pearce.

Shit. Planned or not, Pearce noticed the big fucking flaw in it right then. As eight or nine stones of admittedly under-nourished Jesus, nailed to a couple of solid planks of wood, tipped towards him, Pearce realised that he had no means of protecting himself. He was going to take a solid hit. He turned his head to the side, braced himself.

Which was just as well. He took a blow to the side of the head. And another where Jesus's chin hit him midway between his stomach and his balls. Could have been worse. Could have been a foot lower. Or smack into his side, where his ribs still nagged at him.

Jesus hadn't got off so lightly. He was screaming into Pearce's shirt, his breath warm and wet.

It sounded as if something had snapped. Maybe bust a bone in his arm, maybe a rib or two. A mattress cushioned the bench Pearce was strapped to, but Pearce was solid and unyielding and Jesus had been in no better position to protect himself than Pearce.

Jesus was making a phenomenal racket. Not good. He had to deal with the pain or this was simply a pointless exercise. Which it might be anyway, but Pearce wanted to find out what was next.

Pearce knew about pain and having to deal with it. The crossbeam was pinning his head to the bench and it was starting to hurt. Really badly. Flashing bright lights, no doubt similar to those Jesus was experiencing, but these weren't caused by drugs. Fuck, no, he was losing consciousness and that was no bloody good at all.

Jesus needed him. As much as he needed Jesus, in fact. A perverse kind of codependency.

THE INSIDE OF the car didn't honk of dog so badly now although that was probably on account of Flash having got used to the smell and his concern over May making him not give a shit what the stink was like cause all he wanted to smell was burning rubber.

He desperately wanted to put his foot down, but he knew if he wanted to find her he'd have to keep it slow.

He'd climbed up Ardmillan Terrace and was turning into Slateford Road. According to May's recollections of where Wallace had been headed, the church ought to be around here somewhere.

'May,' Flash said into the phone. 'This church, does it have a big spire?' Then he'd see it no problem from the road so he could speed up, which is what he really wanted.

'May?' But May didn't answer. Flash thought he might puke and the feeling was so strong he lowered the window just in case.

The car crawled along, Flash saying his sister's name into the phone time after time while he scanned both sides of the road, looking for a church, a spire, a driveway, May, the dog, knowing he needed to take it nice and slow, even though every sinew in his body was screaming at him to get a move on because every second was precious and she wasn't answering even though he kept saying her name over and over and he was telling himself to calm down now so he closed his mouth because that was the only way he could keep from screaming and he was thinking that it didn't help that he didn't know this area particularly well and why hadn't he ever paid attention when he'd been along this way before and he couldn't help himself, no, he shouted into the phone: 'May. You there? May.'

This time someone answered. A man's voice.

Flash felt sick again.

Wallace said, 'May's got something to tell you. Listen up.'

And Flash heard the engine rev and a thump and a scream and he shouted into the phone, swearing at the bastard fucker cunt and was quiet, oh, very fucking quiet, when he saw Wallace's Range Rover about to pull out of a driveway twenty feet ahead.

With a dented fucking bumper.

Wallace was at the wheel. Bloodstained, shirtsleeve ripped and wrapped round his arm, and looking like he was drunk.

Flash glanced to the right. A church spire.

He didn't think about it. Slammed his foot on the accelerator.

'You're a dead man,' he yelled into his phone.

Which was a mistake because Wallace clocked him and pulled out into the road, tyres screaming.

Flash eased his foot off the pedal. He could have followed, and he had considered doing so for a second or two, too long to be proud of the thought, but he couldn't leave May.

His face was hot and sweaty and he gripped the steering wheel like he was squeezing the life out of it. He turned into the driveway and really surprised himself: he started to pray.

'STOP THAT FUCKING racket,' Pearce said out of the side of his mouth, his face flattened into the mattress. Maybe he was being too hard on Jesus. It was probably the racket that was keeping Pearce from blacking out. Ought to be grateful to him, but shit, it was hard to be grateful to someone when they were making such a ridiculous noise. And, Christ, did young Jesus smell bad.

Pearce decided that there were two choices. One: he could sing along with Jesus, cause his yowling was strangely melodic. Two: he could make a concerted effort to get the noisy, stinky bastard from off the top of him. It'd be nice to be able to breathe freely again and relieve this pressure on his head and he never had much of a voice, so the decision wasn't hard.

A man of action acts. He doesn't talk, or think. Doesn't repeat himself. Nope. Just acts. Is what he does. That's how you judge a man. Not by what he says but by what he does.

Yep.

So stop talking to yourself and get the fucker off you.

Okay, sir.

Now he was talking to himself.

Jesus was still yowling.

Pearce pushed with his neck and shoulder against the crossbeam. It hurt, but that hardly mattered. Just another bit of discomfort to add to all the rest. He pushed again, felt it shift. Once again, and it shifted a little further. Progress. He stopped for some air. Took a few gulps, the muscles in his neck smarting. Wondered how the foul air wasn't so foul anymore. Concentrate. One, two, three: another shove. Bingo. The crossbeam slid down onto his torso, which was great, but it dug into his collar bone, which wasn't so great.

A small victory, though.

And Jesus had finally shut up, which was a second small victory. Unless he'd died. There was no victory in that, small or otherwise. Pearce needed the bearded lunatic to help get him out of here. Unless he killed him in the attempt.

OH, YEAH, SHE knew it was going to be bad, but she wasn't prepared for just how bad.

She didn't feel any pain. Not at first. Didn't happen like that. No, a light dazzled her. Weird. And no mistake.

And how weird was it when she realised she was seeing the pain? Not feeling it. Crazy, sure, but yet it made some kind of sense. The pain solidified into a thin bar that buzzed. Like a light sabre.

All in a split second.

She couldn't tell where she'd been hit. Base of the spine, hip. Must have been somewhere round there. But she could tell that she was airborne.

She braced herself for what was to come.

Couldn't feel anything. Maybe that meant her spine had snapped. But, no, she could see the pain still, it just hadn't had time to register yet, most likely.

She totally smacked off the windscreen. Shoulder first, then the side of the face.

Dropped to the ground. Winded.

Wallace drove off. Cutey-pie in the back.

She tried to breathe, but it was as if the car was parked on top of her chest. She was cold with panic. Never been so scared.

Another attempt to breathe.

Nothing.

Dark patches at the corner of her vision.

And then, a gulp of air that was oh so sweet. And another. And another.

Pain shot through her hip.

She tasted blood in her mouth.

A dull throb in her shoulder.

And in a minute, Flash was standing over her, shouting at her and she couldn't work out why he was angry.

She couldn't hear a word he was saying.

WALLACE HARDLY NOTICED any longer that he was sitting on shards of glass. He'd pulled over to the side of the road, tried sweeping the pieces off the seat with the back of his hand, but they'd dug into the fabric, got lost in the little grooves. And he kept dripping blood from his neck directly onto the seat, which was really fucking annoying – almost as annoying as the freaky fucking dog in the back seat opening its eyes and staring at him – so he sat down and got moving again.

He needed medical attention, and not for his scratched arse. But if he went to a hospital, he was fucked. He'd live, but he'd go to prison. Nothing much for it but to struggle on for as long as he could, hope he didn't bleed to death. The bitch had missed his jugular, thank fuck, but there was a lot of blood coming out of the wound, a steady trickle.

Shame she wasn't going to see her boyfriend nailed up. Nothing ever went to plan. Wallace was going to go home, patch himself up, dispose of the bodies in the basement.

Ah, fuck. Who was he trying to kid?

He'd shot the old guy at Jacob's house. He'd run over May. He was fucked. Nothing he could do but finish off what he'd started.

He still had the gun. Grabbed it from behind the front wheel. Could put a bullet in his head right now, or go home first, tidy up, then do it.

If the police weren't waiting for him. For all he knew, somebody had reported gunfire at Baxter's house and Baxter had spilled his guts. And why wouldn't he? In the same situation, so would Wallace. Then again, if nobody had reported shots fired, then Wallace was safe for the time being.

Was there a way out of this?

Nope.

If he was going to go, he was going to take Jesus with him. He didn't mind so much about Pearce, but that little shit who'd slept with May . . . Fuck, no, he didn't even mind leaving him alive, but he did want him to know May was dead. Okay, so maybe she wasn't dead, but Jesus wasn't to know.

Wallace floored the accelerator pedal.

His arm was okay, still bleeding, the shirtsleeve wrapped around it mainly dark red now. But his neck was the main problem. Fucking wife of his had nearly took his fucking head off. His collar was saturated with blood. He needed to take a shower and change his shirt before he did anything else. Some people might want to die dirty, but Wallace wasn't one of them.

FORTUNATELY, JESUS WASN'T dead. Just temporarily passed out with the pain.

'Where does it hurt?' Pearce asked him, trying to get him talking to stay awake now he'd come round again. Pearce hoped that the pain had sobered him up, counteracted the mushrooms a little.

'Leg,' he said. A reply. A bit of dialogue. Excellent. And he wasn't screaming any longer. Pearce guessed he'd gone into shock. Well, deeper into shock, since he'd probably gone into shock the minute Wallace smacked the first nail through his palm. He was doing pretty well, considering.

Although maybe he'd gone into shock before that. In his cage, when he realised he was never going to get out of this room alive.

'Teeth,' Jesus said, and Pearce was totally confused. 'Strong teeth.' Jesus pulled back his lips like some crazed chimpanzee.

Oh, fuck. He'd really lost it now.

FLASH DIDN'T KNOW whether he ought to pick her up, or move her or, or what he was supposed to do, and he stood there like a plonker playing with his car keys and feeling like he was about to cry, but he figured that if he left her there like that on her back with her nose busted and bleeding she'd drown or something and he couldn't stand back and watch that happen, so he told her he was going to move her head.

She smiled at him, which was worrying.

Blood trickled out of her left ear and that was worrying too.

He shouted, but that didn't seem to get through to her either, so he gave up trying to communicate and took off his jacket and rolled it up and bent down. Slowly, he lifted her head and saw her cheek was red and puffing up and there was a bump under her eye that looked hard like maybe it was bone and he said, 'Fuck,' cause this was looking really bad. He turned her head to the side and lowered her gently onto the pillow he'd made of his jacket. The other side of her face looked normal.

She said, 'I'm cold,' and the words came out slurred.

He took off his sweatshirt and draped it over her. Crossed his bare arms. It was cool, hardly T-shirt weather.

She said, 'I can't hear anything. Can you hear me?'

He nodded.

She said, 'I can't feel my legs. Doesn't hurt at all. Isn't that funny?' She shivered.

He looked down and moved the arm of the sweatshirt out of the way but he couldn't see anything without removing her clothes and he wasn't going to do that, so he dialled 999. Let the experts handle this. About time, huh?

And as he sat waiting for the ambulance to arrive, and the

police accompaniment cause they never sent one out without a police escort, he looked at her broken body.

She said, 'Flash.'

He stroked her hand. 'What is it?'

She shook her head ever so slightly to tell him she still couldn't hear him. 'Promise me something.'

He nodded. 'Anything.'

'You'll get Cutey-pie.'

'Okay,' he said.

She shook her head. 'Now.'

He pulled a face. She couldn't expect him to go after the dog. Not when she was all fucked-up like this and needing him.

She squeezed his hand. 'Don't stay with me. There's nothing you can do. That was the ambulance you called? So go now.'

'You want me to go?' Flash couldn't just walk away. She needed him and the police would want to ask him questions and it was too complicated.

She was reading his mind. 'You can speak to the police later. I'll tell them I made you go after my dog.'

She pleaded with her weepy eyes and he said, 'I can't, May. I can't just leave you here like this. Not for a dog.'

'What?'

He mouthed the last sentence again, slowly.

May said, 'Then go kill Wallace for me, Flash. Before the police get him.'

Flash looked at his hand, where the keys were bunched in his fist. 'Okay,' he said, squeezing his fingers tightly around the keys.

'Take mine,' May said.

'Your what, May?' He had to mouth the words for her again.

'Keys,' she said. 'In my handbag. Find it.'

PEARCE HAD FIGURED out that the series of leather belts strapping him down were pulled tight and buckled on the underside of the bench. At least, that's the way it had to be, since he couldn't see any buckles no matter how far across he leaned.

Jesus had been chewing away at the leather strap for ages now, and there wasn't anything Pearce could do to stop him. He had attacked the strap where there was a gap, between Pearce's waist and his right forearm and Pearce's arm was now wet with dribble.

This was the craziest idea Pearce had ever heard. But Jesus had dreamed it up from somewhere in his near-psychotic brain, and there was nothing Pearce could do to stop him. Thing was, Pearce had nothing better to offer.

'Any progress?' Pearce asked.

The weight lifted off him. 'Soft,' Jesus said.

'What's it look like?'

A pause. Jesus said something that sounded like 'Wasp.'

'Okay,' Pearce said. 'That's good.' What was the poor bastard thinking? Something about chewing a wasp? His gums were bleeding, and no doubt his jaw had to be aching. He should take a breather.

'No,' Jesus said, shook his head hard.

'Okay,' Pearce said. 'It's not good.'

Jesus calmed down again, looked like he was about to get stuck in once more.

'Hang on,' Pearce said. 'Maybe I can rip those fuckers out of the bench now. Let me have a go.'

Jesus seemed to understand. He lifted his head out of the way.

Pearce waited a second, psyched himself up, then shoved against the wrist restraint. It tightened, but didn't give.

He yanked again, till the pain in his side made him stop. No good.

And the effort had exhausted him.

'Chew,' Jesus said. 'No.'

Poor bastard realised he wasn't doing any good. Wallace would come back, kill them both.

Jesus said, 'Floor.'

Floor? What now?

FLASH DROVE OFF, leaving May behind. He'd go to Wallace's right now and kill the fucker with his bare hands.

What Flash really wanted was to talk to Rog, just pass a bit of *español* between them, a bit of banter. Rog would understand and give him just the right amount of sympathy without being over the top, cause he needed sympathy right now the mess May was in. Not every day your sister was run over and if he wasn't mistaken, fair enough, he wasn't a doctor, but it looked like she might be paralysed and that didn't bear thinking about.

But he couldn't talk to Rog. Rog wasn't fit enough to take this on board and in any case Flash didn't have the time. Sure, if Rog was well he'd be right here in the car sitting by Flash's side, but although Rog was much better he was still very far from well.

Wallace. The cunt. Flash wished Pearce had fucked Wallace up big time. Course, he couldn't help thinking that if Wallace had beaten Pearce, there really wasn't much hope for him, but Wallace was fucked-up, wasn't he? Shot and stabbed and weakened from all the blood loss and anyway, Flash didn't give a shit. Maybe it was true that even in his current injured state, Wallace would chew him up and spit him out. Maybe it was true that he was a psycho and psychos had the strength of ten normal men. Everybody knew that. But, fuck it, Flash was going to give it his best shot. He owed it to May.

PAIN LEG IN his. Just to add to the other pains hands and feet. Levelled had off the drugs. The pain helped. Mushrooms. Could think now, just, in bits together that made sense. Speak was hard. Couldn't much. Hear the chirping? Birds. Are they Greek? How'd they get in here? Open window. Handy. No open windows. Weird.

Twist.

Mum used to do the twist. Only dance step she knew. Every bloody song. The twist. Danced to.

Not good dancing. Why did Pearce? Three bobs short of a bob-bob-bob-bob.

Twist, yes, right, Jesus understood. He was the one doing the twist. Not Pearce. Twisting round. Positioning himself. That kind of twist, too, not the other one. Nobody was dancing. Not Mum, not him, not Pearce. He yelled, something digging into him. Couldn't quite locate the pain. Seemed to be shifting. Animal burrowing inside him. Could feel claws. In his thigh. Yuck. Bird feet.

Not birds. Not down here. No.

And he understood what Pearce was asking him. How'd he do that?

The bird noise was Pearce speaking.

That's what it was.

Not birds.

Not down here.

No.

Birds were outside.

Not in here.

'You can you do it,' the wasp said.

Jesus panted. Tried to speak. His jaw hurt. His teeth hurt. His gums hurt. His lips hurt. Do what? 'Do what?'

'What you're doing.'

What he was doing.

Yeah. 'Yeah.'

Muttered: 'Didn't think I was getting through there.'

Jesus paused, then said, in his head, 'Not sure you are.'

'Fuck, that was almost a conversation. Go on. You can do it.'

'What?'

'What you're fucking doing.'

And the room tipped upside down.

Jolt of pain. Intense. On the floor, though. Bolt of fire down his hip and along his ribcage. Heat, heat, heat. He couldn't see Pearce any longer, but he could certainly hear him, willing him on, telling him he could do it. Or was it the wasp?

No more birdsong, which was a relief.

So what was he doing down here on the floor? No leather straps to chew. Did he have to catch the birds and see if he could speak Greek? Was that it?

Just lying on his back, staring at the pretty lights. In pain. Staring at the

Chan

del

ier

above the bench.

Spectacular. Thing of beauty. Could get lost in it forever. Forget about the pain. Lose himself. Startling textures. It had remained intact. Cross toppled, missed. Higher up than it looked. He let his mind fall into the damn thing, let it swallow him up and not let go. Yep. He was sinking, falling deeper into the shimmer. Inside it, and there was another chandelier, and he sank into it, too. And then he pulled himself out with a jerk, like a man who's almost nodded off to sleep at the wheel. But he was one chandelier short, so he jerked himself out of that one too.

Afraid, now, that if he fell into it, he'd never get out. Sink deeper and deeper and the surface would be a distant memory of something no longer obtainable. And the chandelier, absorbing. A story the wasp wanted to read to him. *The Enchanted Chandelier.*

He closed his eyes to avoid looking at the light. Heard the wasp's rasping voice. He'd been quiet for a while, but he was back, telling Jesus a story.

Once upon a time there was a young boy called Brian.

He smiled. So long since anyone had used his first name.

And Brian was a bad boy.

No! Never!

And he was taken into the dungeon by a bad man called Wallace.

The wasp had to shout to be heard over Jesus's screams. But he managed, powerful pair of lungs on him.

Wallace didn't like bad boys. In fact, Wallace used to take all the bad young boys of the village down into his dungeon and strap them to benches and leave them there to rot in their own stink.

Like Pearce. Not like Jesus. Jesus had a cage. What about that, Mr Wasp, think you're so smart?

Sometimes he'd come down and talk to them. Sometimes he'd give them tea to drink. But the tea was poisoned and made them see things that weren't there.

Sometimes the boys would think there was a giant wasp in the dungeon with them, but that was the poison playing tricks on their senses.

And sometimes the boys would hear screaming and yelling and when they asked who was there, Jesus would reply and tell them he was helping them escape, but he was nailed to a cross so it was a slow, painful process and they'd have to bear with him.

'Thanks,' Jesus said. 'I think that's enough of that story.'

The wasp hovered, silent, then flew away, zigzagging out of sight. No voice in Jesus's head now, but lights flashed bounced spun around inside his skull, vivid colours dancing and words swelling into cushioned shapes that softly kissed the surface of his brain.

He was getting lost again and he heard someone shout.

Jesus screamed again and the word, 'Jesus', appeared in his head, yellow, the fat 'J' tinged orange at its base. It was a beautiful thing to behold. 'Come, ye, and see the word "Jesus" in all its glory.'

Other words popped into his head: 'shark', 'custard', 'Heathrow'. 'Custard' was a good-looking word. The other two were thin, stark, cold, blue. Like Wallace's eyes.

'Jesus.'

It was the wasp again. The fuck did he want?

'The nail gun.'

The fucking nail gun. Nail gun. Big fat stripy waspy nail gun. He raised his head. In the corner, there it was, was it? Was that a nail gun?

But he couldn't get over there. He'd have to crawl. Drag this cross with him.

No fucking chance.

Somebody started screaming and after a while the screaming got to be rhythmic and it didn't sound like screaming any longer.

He was a nice guy. Look, he was going to all this effort for Pearce, wasn't he? Fucking hurt.

Or was he doing it for the wasp? Where was the fat, ugly, stingy thing? Couldn't see it any more.

Fuck the screaming. It was making the nails vibrate, which made his palms tingle, which made his feet tingle, which made his forearms tingle, which made his shins tingle, which was something.

He tried to move.

A screech.

More pain.

A gentle sobbing, panting, and a groan.

He closed his eyes. Saw the chandelier in his head, swimming, like it was made of liquid. Above it, the grains in the ceiling wriggled. Opened his eyes. Turned his head. Saw the floor, slivers of worms.

Caught his breath on the edge of his larynx.

What was he doing? Where was he? Who was he? What was all this pain?

'Nail gun,' the wasp said.

FLASH STARED OUT the window, cars blurring past on one side, the odd pedestrian on the other, nobody giving anybody a glance, nobody caring what anybody else was up to, nobody caring what happened to anybody else, nobody caring what became of May, nobody, but, yeah, Rog would care if he knew, and Dad, sure, yeah, God, if May died and that, Godfuckingdamnit, that wasn't unlikely, you know, Rog would be fucked and it would end Dad and —

Fuck. The baby. May might survive, but there was no way the baby was going to.

If May lost the baby it'd definitely end Dad.

Gotta speak to him. Tell him.

Flash groped for his phone. Dialled. No reply.

Which didn't seem right. Dad ought to be there, and when he was on the phone earlier he'd sounded out of breath, and Flash remembered him having chest pains before.

Flash had to make a detour. 'Sorry, May,' he muttered, swinging a left. Wallace would have to wait.

GETTING HARD TO see. Wallace kept blinking but his vision stayed blurry. The neck wound wasn't getting any better. He hated to use the word, but, well, it was gushing. Like someone was pouring warm water down his Adam's apple. Wasn't so good. And, yeah, he did feel a bit woozy.

Wasn't just his collar that was soaked. Shirt front was drenched. Definitely have to change it now.

Tried to press his foot down but it wouldn't respond. Like his hand on the wheel. Not moving. Just sitting there clutching the grip, not turning, not doing what he was telling it to. His foot felt light. Feather light. Little feathers at the ends of his legs. Feathers at the ends of his arms.

Fuck. He was hard. Prison hard. Anybody called him a pussy, he'd show them. Beaten by a wee girl? By his fucking wife?

Fuck was he on about feathers for?

Jesus fucking Christ.

No way he was going to make it home in this state. There was only one thing for it.

He slammed both his feet down. This time they responded. The car came to a halt.

He took a breath and turned the car round, headed back to the churchyard. If he was quick enough, he'd still catch her before the ambulance whisked her away.

He'd die dirty. So be it.

ALL JESUS WANTED to do was close his eyes and drift away on the waves of pure tangerine that were coursing through his veins. He was in too much pain to be caring about anything any more, no matter what he was being told. The wasp wanted him to fetch something, but the wasp could go fuck itself. He hurt all over. Really badly. His hip was fucked up. And it felt like his palms were about to slide right through the nails. Thought for a minute that the right one had and that his arm was hanging loose and free. Tried to wave to the guy on the bench. And pain flooded through his hand anew.

Turned his head to the side. Very nice. As he thought. His right hand was pushed forward, the nail head disappearing somewhere within intricate folds of flesh in his palm. His hand was halfway out.

The throbbing pain was excruciating.

A lucid thought. Zapped into his head by the wasp. *You're going to die in a psychedelic haze if you don't get on with it.*

With what?

Get to the fucking nail gun.

Imagined he was halfway there and he hadn't even tried. Just the constant weight of him, hanging. The thrusting forward, the rocking, the dragging of the fucking thing on his back across the floor. Somehow.

A good hard tug. Was that all it would take? If only he could get some traction.

He closed his eyes, saw fireworks, opened them again. Still saw fireworks.

I'm not crazy I'm not crazy I'm not crazy.

But he probably was. Couldn't be here, could he? Not

possible. The cage against the far wall, that guy whose name he couldn't remember up there on his bench, the cross. All these fucking egg cartons glued to the wall. A giant wasp.

Nah, but he knew what was going on. He knew he was Jesus, knew he'd been crucified. Not much doubt about it.

And he hadn't been able to think straight for a long time, but he was thinking straight now and what he was thinking was that if he was Jesus he could perform miracles, right? Just cause his hand had a nail driven through it didn't mean it could stop him. Not God's son. He could pull his hand out of that. Easy.

His breath was shallow and he really wished he could wipe off the sweat that was dripping down his forehead.

So he'd do that, then. Pull his hand out of the cross.

Psyche himself up. Get ready for it.

And go.

Tug.

It hurt. It shouldn't have.

Aaargh. He was Jesus. He could do this.

If he really fucking tugged.

Fucking fuck fuck.

It burned and burned and burned and burned and burned and burned like a

F U C K E R

No ripping sound. But his hand came free. He stared at it, a hole through the centre, and started to cry.

FLASH PULLED INTO the side of the road. He needed to take a minute to calm himself.

Naturally he was worried about May, and even more worried about her baby, but the more he thought about it, the more scared he became of what he might find at home. He went over what his dad had said the last time they spoke. About Norrie. About him being shot and Dad not caring. About Norrie shooting Rog. Flash still couldn't believe it, even though May had said so, too. It wasn't right. Nothing about this was right and Dad wasn't answering the phone. He might have gone out, but Flash didn't think so.

Not like he had a mobile.

But maybe he'd called an ambulance for Norrie. Maybe that's all it was, and he'd gone off with him.

Norrie was his fucking friend.

Well, Flash would find out the truth soon enough cause he wasn't far away from Dad's now.

He pulled back out into the traffic.

JESUS WAS SOBBING his heart out and saying, 'Look,' but Pearce couldn't see anything, couldn't get his head high enough.

Pearce was fed up of saying, 'What? What am I supposed to see?' He felt like crying himself. His physical state didn't help, either. Lying here for so long, it had begun to feel as if he was packed in sand. His limbs were so heavy from lack of use that the very air around them seemed to press down on them. The various straps across him were weighty as lead. But inside, he was lighter than air.

Very strange. He didn't like it at all.

Jesus started to move.

Pearce couldn't see him, but he could hear the wood of the crucifix scraping against the floor.

'Can't get more out,' he said.

Can't get more out. More what?

But he was moving quickly. And then, suddenly, he was on

the floor below Pearce, looking up, holding a hand out to Pearce.

'Look,' he said.

And there was a hand, free of the nail, ugly hole in the palm.

'Jesus, you're a hard bastard all right,' Pearce said. Respect where respect was due. 'Can you reach underneath here and unbuckle me?'

It was hard for the poor bastard to manoeuvre, since he still had three limbs attached to the cross. Must have been even more of a struggle with his fried brain. But he managed. Maybe it was because he was so shot full of adrenaline. Something had to be countering the mushrooms. Otherwise, he'd have been nothing more than a slobbering wreck. Mind you, this guy wanted to live. No doubt being crucified helped minimise the effects of the drugs, kept you sober, to a degree.

'This a good thing?' Jesus asked.

Pearce didn't know what he meant, but he said, 'Yes.' The leather shifted on his forearm. Not like it had when Jesus was tearing at it with his teeth. This was a gentler motion, a tugging motion. Had to be hurting the poor fuck, after what his hand had been through, but he wasn't uttering a word of complaint.

A bolt of nausea hit Pearce hard. He thought he might be sick. Which is something he didn't want to do, lying here on his back, so close to being released. At least, released from this fucking bench. He held it back, saliva flooding his mouth. God, no, he wasn't going to get panicky again. Fuck that. Of all the times in the world to get panicky, now would be incredibly ill-timed. He was about to escape, for fuck's sake.

He balled his fists as hard as he could, but they weren't responding. He couldn't feel anything other than a numb ache in his little finger. If it weren't for the slight pain, he wouldn't have known if his hands were still attached to his arms. And even then, there were such things as phantom pains, weren't there? Good fucking Christ. Nobody had cut his hands off, they'd just gone numb from lack of circulation. Fuck's sake, he had to concentrate on what was real. He hadn't swallowed a bucketload of magic mushrooms. Didn't bear thinking about what he'd be imagining if he had. He'd have no idea what was real and what wasn't.

Pearce felt the strap round his chest loosen.

WALLACE PULLED INTO the church driveway. Wasn't going to get much further. There were two police cars, various uniformed cops running around, and behind them, an ambulance. No sign of May, so presumably they'd already taken her inside. Patched her up. Set those broken bones.

He was weak, limbs felt leaden.

Fingers were numb, but not numb enough to lose grip of the gun.

He got the car door open. Stepped outside. Glass fragments dropped from his trousers to the ground when he stepped forward.

Somebody screamed. Somebody else shouted, 'He's got a gun.' Bodies darted to and fro, ducked down behind the car.

Poor little policemen. Not allowed to carry. Couldn't very well take him on, armed with just their batons. Not that he minded if they tried.

Silence.

He was cold. Very fucking cold. And the gun was very fucking heavy. Had to keep a firm grasp. Didn't want to drop it.

Took another look around, saw a head poke over one of the police cars. Raised his ridiculously heavy arm, pointed the gun and the head disappeared.

Heard the crackle of radio static. Calling for backup. Armed Response Unit. That lot would be bringing guns.

Good. Let them. This wasn't going to take long.

He looked up. The ambulance driver was frozen in his seat, shiting himself.

Wallace nodded to him as he staggered past. Headed round to the back of the ambulance. The door was closed.

May was inside.

All Wallace had to do was open the door and shoot her.

OF COURSE, NOW that he was here at Dad's, Flash would have done anything to be able to avoid going inside, you know, Norrie having been shot and Dad not answering the phone, and whatever that signified, but he got out of the car and headed up the path to the door and turned the handle, his voice cracking as he said, 'Dad?'

But Dad didn't answer, even as the door swung open and Flash called for him again.

The hall cupboard was busted open, looked like somebody'd exploded a tiny bomb in the lock. A chunk of the woodwork was missing.

The door was ajar and a pair of boots stuck out from inside, looking horribly lonely for some reason, maybe because Flash recognised them as Norrie's and knew the man wearing the boots had been shot and maybe he'd deserved it, which was an even worse thought.

Flash would have explored the cupboard further, but on turning his head to the side he saw Dad sprawled out in the hallway beside the phone, and rushed over to him. As Flash drew closer, he saw the pool of blood on the floor, not much, just a trickle, but it was coming from Dad's head, which wasn't good, fuck, no, Christ, shit. And it was worse than he thought, cause he bent down and raised Dad's head and saw the eye fucked-up good and proper, something sticking in it, something thick and pointed and wooden, and knew that Dad wasn't going to reply to him no matter how many times he said his name, cause that's what he was doing, just repeating it over and over, 'Dad, dad, dad,' like that, and Dad was saying nothing and he'd never say anything again, cause that thing in his eye, fuck, that thing in his eye, was only something to blind him, not something to kill him, but his heart wasn't what it used to be, as if they all didn't fucking know, and that's why he wasn't breathing. Chest still. No breath from his bandaged nose or his blue lips. Cause Flash checked, as best he could, even though he knew that Dad was dead. You don't lie with your mouth open and your eyes open and say nothing, not try to speak, not try to breathe, if you're alive.

The thing in his eye, making him cry blood: a chunk of jagged wedge-shaped wood. Just a big splinter, that's all. Not something fatal, a splinter. Not possible he could die from a fucking splinter. No fucking way. He couldn't be dead. Couldn't be. Wasn't. No. *Fuck off.*

It was not fucking fair.

Flash lowered his dad's head to the floor, trying to keep it out of the pool of blood, which seemed important somehow, like it was the least he could do. Got to his feet, walked over to the cupboard and peeked inside. Yep, it was Norrie and not just somebody wearing Norrie's boots. And he was just as dead as Dad.

Had Norrie shot Rog? Dad had said yes. May had said yes. They'd been here, heard something or seen something that had convinced them. Why did Flash find it so hard to believe?

He spotted a gun lying nearby, but when he picked it up and

checked the chamber, he found it was empty. He placed it back where he'd found it, and as an afterthought, wiped his prints off it.

He was calm. Calm as a cunting cucumber.

PEARCE BREATHED, FELT his chest rise, felt the strap yield. Jesus tugged, and the strap fell away.

'Get my wrist,' Pearce said.

'Wallace?'

'No, wrist.'

'I love May.'

'That's lovely. Can you undo the strap on my wrist?'

Jesus's fingers touched Pearce's hand. Pearce wasn't sure if Jesus had much of an idea of what was going on. But Jesus cried in pain as he pressed on his wounded hand, and Pearce felt the buckle loosen. For the first time, he began to have some real hope that they'd make it out of here.

Pearce's hand popped free. His good hand. At least, it was the one that didn't have a broken finger. Be nice to say being freed was bliss, but his hand was numb and it hurt like it'd been frozen and was now thawing out. That old expression about being all fingers and thumbs was ridiculous, cause Pearce was definitely all thumbs and no fingers.

Pearce slapped his hand against his chest in an effort to get the circulation going and after a minute started fumbling at the strap securing his other hand.

Jesus moaned. Pearce spoke to him, but didn't get any form of coherent reply.

Pearce undid the strap and tried to sit up. His right hand was numb, and his left was at the pins and needles stage. He flexed his fingers – those that would respond – curled them into a fist, straightened them again.

He needed a drink.

Jesus needed a drink. Jesus needed something else, too, cause his brain was fried. Pearce wasn't sure what, if anything, would help. Quite likely it was too late.

He was starting to feel his fingers again. Thousands of tiny pinpricks stabbing at him. And one big pain in his pinkie. A few more minutes and he'd be able to drag himself out of here.

His hands had enough sensation in them to get to work on the strap securing his legs. He undid it and stared at his legs, willing them to move. But they refused. Wouldn't budge. He couldn't feel them.

He should rub them. Get the blood-flow going again. He balled his fist and gave his legs a good pounding.

Twisted over, ignoring a spasm in his side, let his legs dangle over the bench, careful not to kick Jesus on the head. But Jesus was out of reach, prostrate on the floor, weeping silently, or maybe laughing to himself. Hard to tell. Pearce's circulation was improving by the second. Give it a bit longer, swinging his legs back and forwards here, and then try to stand. Hell, it'd be like learning to walk again. Not that Pearce remembered what it was like learning to walk first time, but . . . no, forget it. It was bound to have been much harder the first time.

He licked his lips. His mouth tasted weird. All this time, it'd been musty and stale in here and no doubt his breath was deadly.

Pins and needles were shooting through his feet now. Which was a good sign. He wanted to stand up and stamp them out. Was he ready? Yeah, fuck it, why not?

Easy.

Lowering himself down to the floor, keeping his elbows bent, hands clutching the bench. Be embarrassing if he fell on his arse. But here he was, standing up again. Yeah, his legs felt a bit weak, like he'd had them in a cast and the cast had just come off, and the pins and needles were worse, but he'd taken one hand off the bench and the other was going . . . now.

Piece of piss. Standing was fucking easy. There was a stabbing pain in his side where Wallace had caused some damage, but he ignored it. At the moment, it was a minor irritation.

Stepping over Jesus, now, that might be a bit of an ordeal.

But he could do this. He took a step forward. Wasn't just his legs. He was stiff all over. It was like the second day of the school holidays. First day, he'd go tattie picking. Day after, he'd swear to God he'd never pick another tattie ever again, he was so fucking sore. But he'd wait a couple of days until his muscles didn't ache so much, then go back. And second time was never so bad. But the day after the first time, like now, every movement was fucking agony. The second step, Pearce knew, wouldn't be so bad. He lifted his foot off the ground and slammed it down.

Jesus said something that Pearce didn't quite catch. Pearce's head felt fuggy, like he'd been walloped with a blunt instrument. But maybe that was because he'd been walloped with the butt of Wallace's gun, which was indeed a blunt instrument.

One foot after the other. One step at a time. Easier with each step. Until he got a rhythm going. Walked over to the nail gun, picked it up. Maybe that's what Jesus had been trying to reach. Then he turned, walked back again.

'How's it going, Jesus?' he said.

Got back a weak smile in a tear-streaked face. 'Wallace.'

'No, I'm not Wallace. Wallace isn't here.'

'Wallace.'

'Don't worry about Wallace.'

Jesus shook his head. 'Don't kill me, Mr Wasp.'

Jesus Christ.

Jesus said, 'Stuck.'

And he was. Still nailed to the cross. Pearce looked at the nail gun. If Wallace had a nail gun, then he ought to have a hammer around the house somewhere. But no doubt it was on the other side of the locked door. Fair enough. Pearce would have a look around, see if he could find anything. Be nice if he spotted some spare wood, too. Make a little splint for his finger.

BUT KILLING MAY wasn't as straightforward as Wallace had imagined. The ambulance door was locked. Bastards.

Wallace reeled forwards into the door, banging his head hard. The collision wrenched his neck, which was a problem cause he was now leaking blood at an alarming rate. He wouldn't try that again in a hurry.

He slammed the door with the butt of his gun. 'Open this fucking thing, or I'll kill the bitch like I should have done first time.'

Nothing happened. Nobody moved inside. Nobody replied.

Shit. He could do without this.

A voice cried out to him from behind the nearest police car: 'Put down your weapon.'

'Oh, shut up,' he said, and fired the gun at the car. He missed, and the bullet made that *pee-ow* sound you heard in old Western movies. He adjusted his aim and fired again. This time, he hit the rear hubcap of the nearest cop car. That'd do. Keep them cowering for a while.

He used the fleshy part of his fist to ram against the door, and said, 'If you don't open the fucking door, I'll shoot a fucking hole in it.' He turned the gun round, burned his fucking fingers on the muzzle, dropped it, picked it up again and held it the right way round.

Come on.

Something clicked on the other side of the door, and the door swung open, slowly.

A medic was perched inside, young guy, all in green, looking terrified. And on a trolley along the wall, a small body lay covered by a white sheet.

Covered. Head to toe.

'May?' Wallace said. 'May?' He stepped into the ambulance, turned to the medic. 'Why's that sheet over her face?'

The medic looked away.

'I'm talking to you. Why the fuck is her face covered?'

He gave an apologetic shrug. 'She didn't make it.'

'Oh, yeah?' Wallace said. He didn't believe it. He hadn't killed her. He couldn't have. He'd just bumped into her, a gentle little smack, sent her tumbling. Couple of broken bones, maybe, but she couldn't be dead. He couldn't be cheated like this.

'Get out,' he told the medic, who didn't need to be told twice. Wallace closed the door after him.

Alone with May, Wallace stooped over the shroud. Pulled back the sheet. Her eyes were closed and she didn't look to be breathing. He leaned forward, kissed her forehead.

It was warm.

Her eyes opened. A smile flickered. She whispered, 'I always loved you, you know.'

She was alive. That fucking medic was a fucking liar. Cheap trick, pulling the sheet over her head. You'd think the little smart-arse would have thought of something more inventive than that.

'Kiss me,' she said. 'I don't want to die alone.'

He pressed his lips to hers. Didn't have to think about it. He loved her too. That's why he had to kill her. But he could kiss her goodbye first.

He was thinking how unresponsive her cold, dry lips were, when he felt something sharp slam into the back of his neck.

THE STINK NEAR Jesus's cage was putrid. How the poor bastard had managed to live in there, Pearce didn't know. Suppose he didn't have any choice. But, still. A shit bucket lay inside the cage's open door, and despite needing a piss really bad, Pearce couldn't bring himself to do anything. At the thought of staring into that bucket, his stomach started to rebel. So he gave up on the idea. Held it in. Wasn't so bad, since he'd had practically nothing to drink since he'd arrived here.

No sign of a hammer anywhere. And the DIY splint for his broken finger would have to wait till he got to a hospital.

Pearce walked away from the bucket, limping slightly on account of the pain in his ribs, and waited by the door, nail gun in his good hand. He couldn't work out whether to turn off the lights or leave them on. Seemed like he'd have more of a chance of nailing Wallace if it was dark. That way, the light would be behind Wallace, and Pearce would be under cover of darkness. Had to be an advantage. But then he reckoned that when Wallace returned, even if he breezed through the door, he'd register straight away that the lights were off, which was not how he'd left them. But, still, it would take a moment for him to register the fact, because he wouldn't be expecting it. First thought he'd have would be that something was wrong. And Pearce could nail him before he realised exactly what it was. Pearce just had to be careful he didn't get May by mistake.

'What do you think?' Pearce asked Jesus. 'Lights on or off?'

But it was a good fifteen minutes now, since Jesus had said anything coherent. He was babbling to himself almost constantly, only stopping to take a breath now and then. He didn't even look towards Pearce, concentrated instead on slapping himself on his head with his free hand, muttering Wallace's name and jabbering on about big teeth and poetry.

Pearce hit the light switch and the room went dark. All he could do now was wait.

WALLACE'S CAR WASN'T parked outside, so Flash deduced that Wallace wasn't at home yet, but he couldn't think of what to do other than wait for him. Which was fine. He could wait as long as it took.

No indication that there was a burglar alarm, so Flash'd just have to chance it. If he'd been intending burgling the house, he'd have scouted the place properly but there wasn't time. He didn't like this, cause he was cautious by nature, but he had to set his nature aside and get on with it. There were greater things at stake here.

Flash took the keys May had given him out of his pocket, not convinced they'd work even though May had claimed there was no way Wallace would have changed the locks cause he'd never have expected her to go back. Flash tried them and they worked.

No alarm, unless it was a silent one and, well, he was fucked if it was, but there was no point living your life worrying about what-ifs and maybes, not when a psycho had run over your sister and been responsible for killing your dad. Didn't matter now who'd shot Rog. Chances were there was no alarm, cause Wallace wasn't the type who'd concern himself over security, not when you considered that he reckoned he could police his own world all by himself.

Flash stepped into the hall. Stair led to the basement, the sitting room-cum-kitchen was straight ahead.

He opened the door, stepped inside. The sitting room was nice, white leather settee, big white rug, pile of blankets and a pillow in the corner, like maybe Wallace had been sleeping in here. Kitchen, not bad. Nice shiny hob, pristine worktops, big fuck-off fridge with a pile of fridge magnets and some photos stuck on it and the photos were mainly of May. In fact, they were all of May. Maybe Wallace was camera-shy or maybe he'd taken all the pictures.

Flash slid a knife from the rack. Nice big fat blade. He'd have a look around, secure the area. Yep, soldiers and burglars weren't all that different, although Flash wasn't sure which he was today.

WHATEVER IT WAS, it slowed Wallace right down. Fucking medics knew their damn drugs, and that fucker who couldn't get out of the ambulance quick enough must have loaded May's syringe with some knockout shite while Wallace was outside banging on the door. Smart fucker.

Wallace's bitch of a wife had stuck the needle in him and plunged it before Wallace could react fast enough to get away from her. He felt sluggish as fuck, and it was worsening by the second. The needle was still sticking out of his neck. His neck was a fucking mess, no two ways about it. Holes all over the place now. And he could hardly keep hold of the gun, weakened as he was by the blood streaming out of him, and the drugs pumping through him. But he had to try. Had to move it over May's head, aim between her eyes.

And then squeeze the trigger.

Wallace tried to lift his hand, but it was reluctant to move. He felt like he'd been awake for a week. The other arm was completely dead, no chance of getting it to respond at all. The shirtsleeve dressing on his forearm looked like the kind of disgusting bleeding mess where, if this was a TV soap, he'd lose his arm. Well, Wallace had another arm. Problem was, it wasn't responding either.

His head was sinking towards May. Having problems keeping it upright, like his neck muscles had turned to soft rubber.

His gun hand fell on top of May. Panic in her eyes as she fumbled for it, but he held on tightly. He thought it strange that she didn't kick her legs. Anyway, he had to do it now, or he'd never be able to. Knew he could do it. Knew it. Fucking knew it.

He squeezed the trigger.

May bucked underneath his hand before he collapsed, bounced off the trolley and smacked onto the floor. Landed on his back. Stared at the ceiling and then it went out of focus. Then grey. Then nothing.

THE BEDROOM WAS on the left at the bottom of the stairs and Flash wondered what was inside that warranted a heavy-duty bolt as thick as two of his fingers. Had to be a reason that room was bolted.

He slid back the bolt, pushed the door away from him. It was dark inside and there was an overpowering stench. He turned his head to the side, just as something black and yellow flashed out towards him.

PEARCE'S MUSCLES TENSED as he heard the bolt being pulled back. Here it was, finally, his chance to escape. He braced himself, squeezed the grip of the nail gun. Would Wallace remember he'd left the light on? Shit, now Pearce wished he hadn't touched it. He stepped forward as the gap in the doorway widened, thrust his arm out, aiming for Wallace's head.

'Fuck, *amigo*,' a familiar voice said. 'Easy, there.'

Pearce licked his dry lips, tried to place the voice. Got it. It was the Baxter kid, the dickhead, not the fat one who'd been shot but the other one, the skinny one with the bad fashion sense. What the fuck was his name? Whatever, the dickhead deserved to be shot with a nail gun for talking Spanish, but since he'd just opened the door for Pearce, Pearce'd let him off for now. He let out a long breath. Lowered the nail gun. Snapped the light on.

'Pearce?'

No fucking flies on this one.

'Fucking hell,' the boy said. 'The fuck happened to you?'

Pearce assumed he was talking about the state of his face. The least of Pearce's problems, but it felt tender, and probably looked worse. 'Been having a party down here,' he said. 'Glad you could make it.'

The boy gazed at the nail gun, now hanging by Pearce's side, loosely grasped, and decided it was okay to step inside. He did a double-take when he looked across at Jesus's cage. Then he – the fuck was his name? – cupped his hand over his nose, glanced at Pearce again.

Pearce shrugged.

The boy stepped passed him. 'Fuck,' he said, catching sight of Jesus, who'd gone quiet. Probably passed out.

Pearce closed his eyes, which was a mistake. He was immediately battered by images. A quick-cut montage. Flick, flick, flick. And he was losing himself inside his head, like he'd been the one taking the drugs, until he latched onto a particular image. A book. A hardback. Big heavy leather thing, stinking of pigskin. Enough to make you heave.

The book was on a shelf, inside a bookcase, inside a row of bookcases, inside a roomful of bookcases.

A library, that's what it was. A familiar library. Portobello library.

Untying Hilda outside. Looking up. Across the road, there was Baxter's son, the dickhead, shoelaces undone, clocking him. Legging it. Pearce wondering how come he didn't trip, fall flat on his face.

Pearce opened his eyes, which was easier said than done. They didn't want to open. No, they were happy to be closed and stay closed. The lids weighed a ton, like a pair of elephants were sitting on them.

His body telling him it was all over. But his mind knew differently.

The dickhead, Pearce had seen him at the library, hanging outside. Streak? Lightning? Flash, that was his name. Pearce had known it was something stupid.

Well, he'd forgive him his daft name. He needed to get something to drink. He opened his eyes. He thought for a minute that Flash must have sneaked past him and run away. How fucked up would that be? Your rescuer arrives, then decides he can't be arsed to rescue you. Pisses off, bolts the door after him. No fun at all. But, no, Flash was bent over, muttering something to Jesus. No doubt never seen a crucifixion before.

Flash stood up, his hand still shielding his nose. 'Hardly recognised him,' Flash said. 'With the beard and all.'

Of course. Flash would know Jesus if Jesus had been friends – intimate friends – with his sister. Made sense.

Flash continued, 'He's in a bad way.'

Pearce said, 'I don't imagine too many people who get crucified are in a good way.'

Flash repeated his earlier question: 'The fuck happened to you pair?'

Pearce told him, quick as he could.

Flash said, 'What kind of drugs?'

Drugs. Fuck, every time Pearce heard that word his stomach shrank to a cube of ice. It was bad at the moment. This little ordeal had made him extra-sensitive or something. His sister had died a long time ago, but the rage was still there like it had happened yesterday. Pearce had killed her dealer, and there was some therapeutic value in that. But, thing was, she'd been gang-raped afterwards, and the sick fucks responsible had never been found.

'Magic mushrooms,' Pearce said.

'You know how many?'

Pearce told him.

'Holy fucking Jesus.'

Holy fucking Jesus indeed.

FLASH RANSACKED THE kitchen, opening drawer after drawer, found a glass, which was handy, but wasn't what he was looking for. Finally got it, on the worktop in a container marked SUGAR. He pulled out what he thought was the cutlery drawer, but it was stuffed full of envelopes and receipts and instructions for white goods. Drawer next to it was the one with spoons in it, so he lifted a tablespoon out of it, filled the glass with water and took all his bits and pieces back down to the basement.

No, he hadn't forgotten he'd said he'd try to get the fucking dog back for May, but the best way to find the dog was to wait here for Wallace to return, cause he'd also said he'd kill Wallace, and meanwhile Brian was dying and Flash was gasping for a cigarette but he didn't have any on him and Wallace didn't have any lying around cause he didn't believe in putting toxins in his body, not even tea or coffee according to May, and there was no way Pearce or Brian would have any fags, so he'd just have to suffer for a little bit longer.

Saw that cage again, wondered what went on in some people's heads. Wallace was a serious fucking nutcase, just as they all knew he was and if anyone doubted it, thought the family had overreacted or something, well, the fucking loony had run over May and shot Norrie and been responsible for Dad having a heart attack and here was even more proof that he was a screwed-up, dangerous, twisted fuck who should be put out of his fucking misery. What sane person keeps another human being in a cage? And then crucifies him?

PEARCE GULPED DOWN the glass of water, felt much better, asked Flash what he was doing with the jar of sugar. Flash explained that the sugar would bring Brian down. Hopefully.

Brian. Hmmm. 'He's already down,' Pearce said. 'Managed it all by himself.'

'It'll stop him tripping.'

'That right?' Anyway, Pearce didn't think Jesus looked like a Brian.

Flash walked over to where Jesus was slumped on the floor, took the lid off the sugar container. Stuck the spoon inside. Brought it out, heaped. 'Open up,' he said.

Jesus was awake. He groaned.

'Medicine,' Flash said. 'It'll help.'

Jesus opened his mouth as the spoon approached. Spoon

slipped inside. He clamped his mouth round it and recoiled. Pearce sympathised. That had to be seriously sweet.

'Swallow it,' Flash said. 'Go on. It's for your own good.'

But Jesus spat it out.

Flash dug the spoon into the jar again, brought out another heaped spoonful.

Jesus batted him away with his free hand, moaning as he made contact.

'Leave him,' Pearce said.

'He needs to take this,' Flash said.

'He's way beyond the help of a fucking spoonful of sugar.'

'Let me try once more.'

Pearce watched Flash pop another spoonful into Jesus's mouth. Same result as last time. Jesus opened his mouth wide afterwards, made a gagging sound.

Flash said, 'One more.'

Jesus said, 'Fuck off, Wallace.'

'Brian, it's me. Flash. I'm not Wallace. Take this. You'll be right as rain in minutes.'

But Jesus wasn't having any of it. Good for him.

'We need to get an ambulance,' Flash said, giving up, dropping the spoon.

Pearce said, 'Help me take him upstairs.'

'Best to leave him where he is.'

'Jesus is going upstairs.'

'"Jesus"? That's sick.'

'So spew.' Flash was good at that, Pearce seemed to remember.

'Look, he won't fit through the door, not attached to that . . . thing.'

'We'll unattach him.'

'Why can't we just leave him where he is?'

'He's been in here too long. It's time he got out.'

Flash said, 'Wallace might be back any minute.'

'We'll need to hurry, then.' Pearce took a quick look round. 'Think you could find me a hammer?'

BY THE TIME Flash came back with the hammer, Pearce was over by Jesus. Pearce's legs were fine now. Maybe he couldn't have performed a river dance, but the feeling was back in them sufficiently for Pearce to give Wallace a good kicking if he came back unexpectedly. First things first, though.

As Pearce yanked out the nails, Jesus made almost as much noise as he'd made when Wallace was hammering them in. Pearce had considered the slow and gentle approach, but decided he should just go for it, pull them out quickly, like ripping off a plaster. As it was, unfortunately, he was forced to take it slowly on account of his broken finger. He'd given it a shot left-handed, but couldn't get a proper grip.

And Flash wouldn't help. He wouldn't even watch.

Pearce was disappointed in Jesus, though. He was being a wuss. After everything he'd been through, you wouldn't think he'd be a cry-baby about this.

You'd think Pearce was pulling teeth.

Jesus passed out again while Pearce was removing the nails from his feet. These nails were a bitch to get out, right enough. Really fucking big bastards.

PEARCE AND FLASH grabbed an end each, Pearce trying to keep his little finger out of the way and failing for the most part, but they staggered and stumbled and got Jesus out of the basement, up the stairs and dumped him on Wallace's sofa. Each step helped loosen up Pearce's limbs, but it aggravated the pain in his side. Probably a cracked rib or two. Jesus wasn't bleeding much, but he had a fair amount of blood on him already. Shame about Wallace's nice white leather sofa.

Pearce studied Flash for a minute. The boy was surprising him. Ought to be shitting himself, worried sick that Wallace was about to arrive home, cage him up along with Pearce and Jesus.

But he seemed very composed. Not like the first time Pearce had seen him. Green-faced and calling for his dad.

Pearce was in a much better condition now, too, and tooled up, which no doubt helped the lad compose himself. Pearce saw him sneak a look at the hammer he'd stuck in one of his belt-loops. Pearce handed it over and said, 'I'll go get the nail gun. You get Jesus some water.'

Back in the basement, Pearce felt incredibly grateful to Flash. Wanted to give him a hug, or something. Which was peculiar. Because other than his mother and his sister, Pearce had never felt like hugging anyone.

He came back, dumped the nail gun on the settee next to Jesus, resisted hugging Flash.

God, it was good to breathe clean air.

Hammer tucked under his arm, Flash was giving Jesus some water, and he was gulping it down. He would survive. He was a tough fucker. But they should definitely call an ambulance for him.

Pearce walked over to the window, parted the curtains, peeked outside. Nothing moving. He turned, eyed Flash. Had a sudden image of him again as he was loitering around outside the library the day Wallace killed Hilda. Which Wallace had denied. After previously admitting to it. Or at least, that's what Flash had claimed. Shit, no. Pearce saw how he'd been played. Fuck, the only question was how far this shithead had taken the game. 'Did you drown my dog?' Pearce said.

Flash pulled a face, let go of Jesus, stood up. He took the hammer out from under his arm, weighed it in his hand, bent down and laid it on the ground. Then he shuffled his feet in his unlaced trainers and said, yes, he'd stolen Hilda. Not that he knew Hilda's name. He'd said, 'Your dog.' And in fact he hadn't said 'stolen' either. The actual word the skinny little fucker had used was 'dognapped'.

Pearce said, 'Say that again.'

Flash's face paled. 'We wanted you to kill Wallace.' Behind him, Jesus looked like he was listening, but Pearce doubted the poor bastard understood anything anyone was saying any more. 'I never intended hurting the dog.'

Pearce was having difficulty understanding this himself. 'Wallace didn't have anything to do with it?'

Flash shook his head. 'Nah. Nobody else. It was me.'

Pearce said, 'So all this shit was avoidable.'

Flash looked away. 'S'pose. But if I hadn't snatched . . . your dog . . .'

'Hilda,' Pearce said.

'. . . Hilda, then you wouldn't have been able to save . . . Jesus.'

Pearce let his head slump. He should lamp the little fucker, maybe retrieve the hammer off the rug and pound the bones of each and every last one of Flash's fingers and toes. Or pick the nail gun up off the settee and fire a couple of projectiles into his crotch. But Pearce was exhausted. He just wanted Hilda back. He said, 'At least Hilda's safe.'

Flash didn't look at him. Stared at his trainers. Gave the hammer a tap with his toe.

Pearce said, 'Hilda's safe, right?'

'Well.'

Pearce had the little fucker dragged across the room and pinned to the wall before he had time to look up. One hand round his throat, pinkie throbbing, but who gave a shit? 'What did you do to my dog?'

Flash was shaking.

'Huh? The fuck did you do?'

'It was an accident, *amigo* —'

'I'm not your fucking *amigo*. What did you do?'

'Nothing, I swear, don't hit me. An accident. The dog got out. Wallace let the dog out. Got hit by a car. Wasn't my fault. Wallace's fault.'

Flash moved his arm, so Pearce squeezed his throat tighter. Raised his other fist. 'Tell me everything.'

Flash pawed at Pearce's wrist. Pearce gave another sharp squeeze, jerk of his fist, and Flash's eyes widened.

'Quickly,' Pearce said.

Flash tried to speak but couldn't do much more than choke unintelligibly, so Pearce loosened his grip. No question now that the feeling in his fingers was back. His little finger was fucking agony, though. Last thing he wanted was to have to wallop Flash, but if he had to, he'd hit him hard enough to break another finger if that's what the little fucker deserved.

Flash blurted out the story about Hilda getting run over. About his sister trying to persuade Wallace to take the dog to the vet's. About Wallace knocking her down. About Hilda still being in the back seat of Wallace's car. And more stuff. Rambling about Norrie, a pal of his dad's, maybe being the guy who'd shot Rog in the legs, that Wallace had shot the old guy but maybe not Rog, and his dad had had a fatal heart attack. But Pearce didn't care about any of that right now.

'Is Hilda alive?' Pearce asked.

'No idea,' Flash said. 'But he was still breathing last May saw him.'

'Where's Wallace?'

'I don't know. I thought he'd be here.'

'And none of this would have happened,' Pearce said, controlling his temper as best he could, 'if it wasn't for you.'

'I came for the dog. I came to rescue your fucking dog from the back seat of Wallace's car.'

'Why the fuck would you do that?'

'May asked me to.'

'My fucking dog,' Pearce said.

'I know.'

'And you stole him. Let him get run over.'

'It's Wallace's fault,' Flash shouted. 'I wasn't even there.'

Adrenaline crashed through Pearce's bloodstream, running riot like those mushrooms in Jesus's veins. Pearce imagined picking up the hammer. Turning it so the claw-side was facing Flash. Saw himself club the skinny little fucker, yank the hammer back out of his head, sink it back in again.

'Don't,' said Flash, as if he too could see what Pearce was seeing.

Who the fuck did he think he was, telling Pearce what to do?

'I came to help,' the skinny little toerag said.

Pearce saw the hammer swing again, saw Flash drop to his knees, stunned expression on his face. Fuck, no. He couldn't. Pearce loosened his grip on Flash's throat.

'Thanks,' Flash said.

'What are you thanking me for?' Pearce asked him. Without waiting for a reply, Pearce drew back his good fist and sent it smashing into Flash's nose.

Flash bounced off the wall, straight back into a second blow. The stunned expression Pearce had imagined seconds earlier now appeared for real.

Pearce took a step towards him, grabbed him by the hair, spun him round. The little shite would never know how close he'd come to a sudden violent end. But he wasn't going to get off scot-free.

Pearce nutted him. He reeled backwards, dropped to the ground. Wasn't enough to put his lights out. Slithered about on the floor, groaning, blood dripping from his nose. Raised himself onto his hands and knees. Pearce stamped on his hand, kicked him under the chin. Flash keeled over, tucked his hand under his armpit, curled into a ball.

Flash said, 'Wallace's fault. Wallace.'

And Jesus said, 'Wallace,' as he sprang off the settee and landed on top of Flash. Flash screamed, flapped his hands uselessly, and twisted onto his back. Jesus pressed the nail gun against Flash's chest, said, '*Bzzz*,' and pulled the trigger. Jesus yelped, his hands presumably smarting as the nail shot out, but he didn't let go. The gun must have had a bump trigger: before Pearce managed to wrestle him off Flash's body, he'd fired three more times.

Flash didn't look too good.

THE POLICE ARRIVED just after the ambulance. They asked Pearce questions, lots of questions, checked out the basement, took his statement, took it again. They whisked Jesus away, took their time over Flash before bundling him into a second ambulance. By then he was dead and lots of detectives had arrived, along with the forensics team in their white overalls.

Pearce spent three hours in hospital, had his face looked at, was told he had a cracked rib, and his finger was put in a splint. Then he spent four hours in custody before they told him they'd found a three-legged dog in Wallace's car. They gave him the phone number of the vet Hilda had been taken to. Wouldn't say if Hilda was dead or alive.

After another couple of hours Pearce was released without charge. For once, they believed him.

PEARCE KNOCKED ON the door. Private room, had to be a bad sign. No reply, so he shifted the flowers into his other hand and turned the handle. Checked the number again. This was definitely the right room.

Opened the door slowly.

A young girl was asleep in bed. Pearce took a couple of quiet steps into the room. Hard to tell from a distance, but close up, you could see it was May, face swollen and bruised, but recognisable.

The visitor was sitting at the far side of the bed in a wheelchair. He looked different without the dark-blue suit, and was a lot fatter in the face than last time Pearce had seen him. Still had powerful-looking arms, though, which his faded 'Spain Is Different' T-shirt showed off to good effect. An XXL, and yet it was tight round the biceps.

'The fuck you doing here?' Rog Baxter said, looking like he'd just taken a mouthful of grapefruit when he'd been expecting an orange. He had a little scar above his top lip.

Pearce ignored him, looked for somewhere to lay the flowers. There were flowers everywhere, none of which he recognised, apart from some bright yellow tulips. He wasn't good at identifying flowers. Anyway, there was no space for his carnations (these he knew), so he settled on placing them on the floor. 'Maybe get one of the nurses to put these in a vase,' he said to Rog. Paused. 'How is she?'

'How does she fucking look?'

Pearce nodded. 'What about the . . .' he said, '. . . the baby?'

Rog said, 'Fuck you, Pearce. Get the fuck out of here. Haven't you done enough damage to my family?'

Pearce looked at his hands, ran his thumb up the side of his cheek. 'Flash was an accident.'

'You better hope I'm never able to walk again.'

'You going to come after me, Rog?'

'Too fucking right I am. The police might think it's okay for you to go around letting crazy people slam nails into my brother, but I hold you accountable.'

'If you come after me,' Pearce said, 'I'll kill you.' That shut the bastard up. 'I'd rather not, but if you're going to be an arsehole, I won't have any choice.'

'You as good as killed him.' Rog's face was tight, his fists clenched. Perched on his wheelchair, he looked like someone seriously constipated.

'I'm sorry about what happened,' Pearce said. 'Believe me.'

'You're sorry? Fuck good's that to me?'

'I don't know. What do you want me to say?'

Rog's hands went to his knees. He shook his head. 'I don't know either.'

'I'm going,' Pearce said. 'I didn't come to see you, anyway.' He turned. 'I hope she makes it. And I hope the baby's okay.'

He was at the door when Rog said, 'There's no baby.'

'Shit,' Pearce said. 'I'm —'

'No,' Rog said. 'You don't understand. There's no baby. Never was.'

Pearce looked at him, wondering if he understood what Rog was telling him. There was never a baby. There. Was. Never. A. Baby. How hard was that to understand? 'She got rid of it?'

Rog ran a hand through his hair. Shook his head. 'She was

never pregnant. The doctors checked and ... well ...' He shrugged.

This family was too fucked up for Pearce. She wasn't pregnant. Yet she'd told everybody she was. All this shit had stemmed from that. 'Why the pretence?'

'She didn't fucking pretend. She was mistaken. Missed a couple of periods. Assumed the worst.'

'She didn't take a test? Or go see her doctor?'

'You criticising my sister?'

'Just curious.'

'I'll show you something curious.' Rog uncurled his fist, showed Pearce a scrunched-up piece of paper, words in a metre written on lined paper in block capitals. 'This was in her handbag,' he said. 'Your friend wrote it.'

Pearce took the paper. It read:

HARD MAN
A Poem by Brian Trotter

where's my madness?
anger's gone, now only joy
and love spilling out in the darkness,
my lovely little boy

safe, all sweet and warm
no more a wanting inside me
a thing of beauty, her sleeping form
lies curled beside me

fatherhood is daunting,
milky scalp, his baby smell
his tiny body, haunting,
her nipple will bring him Heaven, he will bring down Hell

but this is what it is to be father,
not husband, not son
I do not have a brother
it hurts to love this much, little one

floating again, no drugs,
oh, no, no need of that shit
not now, not ever, not mugs or thugs
we're just us, we're our own hit

'he's mine, arsehole,' the hard man says,
dancing in circles on his own.
My son, watching me, those eyes, my eyes,
not the hard man's eyes, our eyes in tears will drown

where do we go from here?
only the narrow-minded fail to appreciate sacrifice
the beauty of it, killing what you fear
when what you fear and love, you despise
that's what the hard man says,
it's all lies, all lies,
I hope the fucker dies

'What do you make of it?' Rog asked.

'It's shit,' Pearce said.

As Pearce handed Jesus's poem back, his fingers brushed against Rog's and Rog grabbed his hand. The poem dropped to the floor.

'I've lost my father,' Rog said, 'and his friend, Norrie. Wallace shot him.'

Norrie. The name rang a bell. Flash had mentioned him. He was possibly responsible for crippling Rog, if Pearce remembered correctly. Pearce let it go. Better for everybody that Rog still thought his assailant was Wallace rather than some old dead friend of his father's.

'And my sister's fucked up,' Rog continued. 'And as if that's not bad enough, you let that fucking crazy bastard kill my brother. You expect me to talk to you like nothing happened?'

'Jes — Brian didn't know what he was doing.'

'But you knew what he was doing. And he's locked up in a loony bin. While you're free.'

'So what you going to do?' Pearce said. 'Squeeze my hand until I beg for mercy?'

'I'm going to make you suffer.' Rog let go of his hand. 'Once I'm well again.'

'You're angry.' Pearce nodded. 'If I were you,' he said, 'maybe I'd want to make me suffer too.' He paused, took a last glance at May. 'But if I were you, I'd know I'd lose.'

'You know who loses?' Rog said. 'Mugs who play fair.'

'And that means?'

'Watch your back, Pearce.'

'You got it,' Pearce said.

'Hey,' Rog said, looking at the piece of paper on the floor, 'think you could put that piece of shit in the bin?'

Pearce stared at him. Then walked over to his wheelchair. Grabbed the side of it with both hands, and heaved. Tricky with his sore finger. He raised the wheel off the ground but Rog was a big heavy fucker, even heavier since he'd been shot and wasn't getting any exercise. Pearce heaved again, and Rog's flailing arm grabbing at Pearce's T-shirt didn't stop him from tipping out onto the floor.

'Put it in the bin yourself,' Pearce said, as Rog moaned and swore. 'And, Rog, if you're going to be angry, for fuck's sake be angry at the right person.'

Pearce looked across at the bed. May was awake, her eyes gummy. She smiled at Pearce and called him Cutey-pie.

He left the room without a word.

WALLACE WAS NEATLY wrapped. Neck braced to keep his head steady, head and arm bandaged. Soft restraints held his wrists by his side. His eyes were closed, and his face had the bloated look of a drowned body. Various tubes spidered across the bed, connected to drips and machines, taped down across his smooth-shaven chest. There was a huge wedge-shaped scar on his stomach, but it looked like an old one.

A big clear breathing tube was stuck between his parted lips. All Pearce had to do was pull it out or unplug the ventilator. Didn't even need to pinch Wallace's nostrils and cup his hand over his mouth afterwards. And he'd probably get away with it.

But did he want to? It appeared that Wallace, despite his violence towards almost everyone else, hadn't harmed Hilda. Pearce took that on board. See, Pearce had been wrong about Wallace. It had never been personal. At least, not until Pearce, like the dumb fuck he was, made it so.

Pearce turned away. Yeah, wasn't his business. He'd leave Wallace for Rog. The big guy might have lost the use of his legs, but as far as Pearce knew, he still had a working pair of balls. And if he didn't, Pearce was pretty sure May did.

PEARCE SAT FOR ten minutes at the vet's before they let him into a room at the back.

'There's the wee fella,' the vet said. 'Proper little hard man.'

Hilda was in a large cage. Shaved, stitched, wearing a cone round his neck, groggy, trying his hardest to wag his tail.

Pearce spoke to him. Told him he was a fucking rascal.

Hilda wagged his tail all the harder.

They'd warned Pearce that Hilda wasn't completely in the clear yet, and they'd need to keep him in for a few days before he could go home, but the signs were good that he'd make a full recovery.

'I'll leave you two alone for a few minutes,' the vet said. 'But don't excite him too much.'

SINCE GETTING OUT of Wallace's basement, Pearce had found it hard to sleep. And when he did fall asleep, he'd wake up after seeing visions of Jesus on a cross, and that fucking awful stench getting right up his nose. He spoke to his mum about it, but she wasn't much help. Told him to get a grip, it was all in his head.

He'd spent another restless night last night, lying on in the morning hoping to nod off again, but with no success. He ate lunch, thought about going to the library, swap those books he'd never opened for another couple he'd probably never open, but decided to go for a walk instead. Get back in practice for when Hilda came home.

It was cooler along the promenade and only a few people were about. Mainly dog-walkers, mothers with their kids, old men with the shakes. One or two of the folk he passed gave him odd looks. Understandable. His face was at the purple stage of bruising, looked like he had a massive port-wine-stain birthmark with dirty yellow trimming.

A couple of toddlers were walking along the beach wall, looking like they were going to topple off any minute. They hadn't spotted Pearce, which was probably a good thing cause their mother had and she couldn't stop staring.

Pearce was so busy staring her down as he walked by that he bumped into someone walking the other way. He turned. A tall guy, around fifty, familiar. Pearce was about to apologise, but the guy was grinning. Something wasn't right here.

The tall guy looked *really* familiar. The look in his eyes, like he was amped. And he was right in Pearce's face.

Pearce caught a whiff of his cheap aftershave and remembered immediately who he was: Happy Harry, the old junkie Pearce had barged into once before in this same spot, the junkie Pearce had called a paedophile.

Happy Harry's recall clearly wasn't as efficient as Pearce's. The old junkie stepped back, said, 'Do I know you?'

Pearce held out his good hand. 'Pearce,' he said. 'You okay?'

Happy Harry took Pearce's hand, shook. 'Never been better,' he said, and skipped off.

Pearce sat down, leaned against the wall. God, he was tired. He was glad Harry hadn't kicked off. Too much violence takes it out of you.

One of the toddlers, a wee boy with a chocolate mouth and tear-streaked cheeks, looked Pearce in the eye and pointed towards Happy Harry's back. 'Bad man,' he said.

His mother said, 'Come on, Davey. Your brother needs the toilet.'

'It's okay, Davey,' Pearce said to the kid. 'The bad man's gone.' He closed his eyes. He was a liar. The bad men were never gone.